DARKNESS DROPS AGAIN

Melissa E. Manning

To Finnegan, Lourdes, and Sabine -
remember it's never too late to start over

Chapter 1

I throw open the door of the upscale Mexican restaurant, running at least ten minutes late. Handing Declan and Seamus off to our sitter turned out to be trickier than expected. The boys are always so clingy on Friday nights after a long week at daycare. I hate leaving them, but Patrick and I desperately need a night out. To say we've begun the sad slide from lovers to roommates would be kind. Once inside, I consult the large entrance windows to smooth down my frizzy mouse-brown hair, reapply my go-to matte lipstick, and dab the sweat off my brow. Feeling moderately more pulled together, I approach the adorable millennial hostess.

"Welcome to Mercadito. How can I help you?" the petite brunette named Anna, according to her badge, says with a toothy grin.

"I have a reservation for four people at seven o'clock. It's under Shaw."

Anna nods knowingly. "Oh, yes, I just received a call about this reservation. Someone named Patrick said he was running about thirty minutes late. He wanted reassurance we wouldn't release the table. Now, normally, we release tables after fifteen minutes," she says to me conspiratorially, "but he promised to leave a disproportionately large tip if I worked a bit of magic. So I did. Your reservation has been pushed to seven forty-five."

I feebly return Anna's smile and offer my thanks, all while willing myself not to be disappointed. So Patrick is running late for a dinner I've spent a month planning. So what? I won't let this slight snafu ruin our night. I scan the trendy restaurant and my gaze lands on the sprawling bar running along the back wall of the adjoining room. A fruity drink should do the trick and raise my spirits. I belly up and order my favorite, a Paloma Diablo. As the first sip of grapefruit and habanero hits my taste buds, I reach into my purse to retrieve my cell.

Me: *Apparently Patrick is running thirty minutes late. What's your and Ethan's excuse?*

As usual, it only takes a few seconds for my bestie since college to return my text.

Zara: *Oh, shoot. I wanted to give you and Patrick some alone time before crashing your dinner, so I invited Ethan for a drink near my office. He just arrived.*

Me: *Dammit! The whole point of inviting you two was to take the pressure off this dinner. I need my wing people to make this less awkward.*

Zara: *Girl, it's just a drink with your husband. Calm down.*

Irritated, I drop the phone back into my purse and return to nursing my drink. As I scan my surroundings, I'm reminded that Mercadito was supposedly a frequent haunt of none other than Kristin Cavallari when she was in the city during football season. The lighting throughout the restaurant is dim and the decor is heavy on dark wood and large Mexican-inspired paintings. The servers wear cheeky T-shirts that say things like "The Taco That Changed My Life" and "The Shrimp Tacos Made Me Weep."

After a few more generous sips of my drink, my attention is drawn to the other patrons. The crowd is younger, probably late twenties or early thirties, and fashionably dressed. I immediately feel self-conscious in my maroon skinny jeans and figure-hugging black long-sleeve blouse. It was the cutest thing I could find in my closet that would: a) keep me warm on this surprisingly cold March night in Chicago, and b) minimize the potential for muffin top. Granted I've lost all of the pregnancy weight from Seamus, but I haven't gotten back into working out like I used to before kids. My core could definitely use some toning, as could my rear end from sitting all day at the office. A repressed memory chooses this moment to resurface. It was the last time I tried to initiate intimacy with Patrick. He was lying on his back in bed when I'd finished washing my face in the bathroom. The covers were pulled down a bit revealing his bare, strong chest. I crawled under the covers and cozied up next to him, resting my head on my hand so I could lean down for an exploratory kiss. Returning the affectionate gesture, Patrick ran his hand under my tank top and along my waist. He then stopped and gave my small love handle a little squeeze before removing his hand and rolling to the other side. Even months later, my face blushes scarlet at the memory.

I'm saved from further contemplation, by the brush of a quick peck against my cheek. I'm so startled I actually spill the last few drops of my drink.

"Oh, sorry about that. I didn't mean to scare you."

While dabbing the bar with a drink napkin, I look up and see Patrick's apologetic grin. I'm struck anew by Patrick's good looks. Handsome and fit as when we met in grad school with nary a strand of gray in his brown hair. I've always felt I'd married up.

Looking around, Patrick queries, "I thought Zara and Ethan were joining us."

I can tell he's as disappointed by their absence as I am. I rush to diffuse the awkwardness. "Oh, you know those two. They're always late." After a beat, an idea pops into my head. "Want to place a friendly wager on how long they make us wait?"

Patrick grins and his dark brown eyes light up. "I'm always up for making things interesting, Maeve. A crisp Hamilton says they make us wait for at least another half hour."

My mood immediately lifts. I can't count how many wagers we've made over the last fifteen years. Everything from how long it will take our food to arrive to whether an inexperienced skier will bite it getting off the ski lift. "You're on, sucker. I'll take the under on that action."

A waiter appears at Patrick's side to show us to our table. We are seated at the middle of six tables pushed up against a long cushioned bench with barely enough space between ours and our neighbors' tables to squeeze through to our seats. I'm reminded once again that I'm now too old and impatient for hip haunts. Once our drink and appetizer order is taken, Patrick and I fall into uncomfortable silence. I find myself becoming absorbed in the drama unfolding at the adjoining table. What started as sniping between two roommates over bills and chores is quickly escalating into an all-out argument.

"So…how were the boys?"

My head and attention snap back to Patrick. "Oh, you know. Fridays are tough. They're tired and clingy. They were both in tears when I left, but I'm sure MacKenzie got it under control within minutes of my departure." MacKenzie is a twenty-year-old blond currently in her junior year at Loyola and yet to pick a major. While I'm sure that is a significant source of tension with her parents, I selfishly hope she never graduates. My boys adore her. Seamus insists on being picked up as soon as she gets her coat off so he can nuzzle into her ample cleavage and stay there until bedtime. I guess he's bitter his mom has a bit more of an athletic build on top.

While raising his craft beer to his lips, Patrick can't help but point out, "I told you a Friday night dinner was a bad idea."

My blood pressure instantly spikes. "Do you seriously want to go through this again? It was the only night the four of us could agree on before May!"

Sitting his drink on the coaster, Patrick doubles down. "I still don't understand why you insisted on rushing this. The Saturday in May sounded perfect. At least by then it would have been warm. I froze my ass off getting here. And I had to cut short a call with my boss."

Unbe-freaking-lievable. I take a long sip of my second Paloma before sarcastically adding, "Well, excuse me for thinking maybe we should get out of the house and go on a date more than once a quarter."

Patrick darkly scoffs, "I'm not really sure I'd call this a date."

Just as I'm about to say something I'll regret, I feel the hand of my best friend since freshman year at DePaul University rest on my shoulder. Sensing the tension, she sheepishly apologizes, "I'm sorry we're so late. You two are probably hangry."

I look up and flash an appreciative smile. Zara Patel always looks cute, but tonight she looks stunning. Clad in a short black faux leather skirt and oversized black and white sweater. Zara never wears much makeup, as she is blessed with flawless light brown skin from her gorgeous mom, a minor Bollywood actor. She draws attention to her delicate features by keeping her black hair in a cute pixie cut. "Where's Ethan?" I inquire.

Just then Ethan Colopy strolls up to shake Patrick's hand and give him a slap on the back. "Sorry, just needed to make a quick stop at the loo. Good to see you, man." Although exercise-phobic, Ethan has a trim figure and sharp cheekbones. He's also a bit of a snob. Hence the random British colloquialisms.

"You two are ridiculously late and I should be furious, but you just won me a crisp ten-dollar bill from this guy," I say nodding in Patrick's general direction, "so I'll let you off the hook."

Zara shakes her head. "You two aren't still betting on every little thing, are you? I thought you'd grow up a bit after having kids."

"Never!" I promise as I smile triumphantly. Patrick good-humoredly rolls his eyes at Ethan. It seems Patrick is following my lead and letting go of our earlier tiff for the sake of the evening.

After the waiter takes Zara and Ethan's drink order, I give an appropriately short update on the boys. Early on in my pregnancy with Declan, I swore to Ethan and Zara I'd never turn into one of those moms who waxes on interminably about her offspring. "Seamus is a chubby, happy little guy and Declan and I are working on reading. He'll start kindergarten in the fall."

Zara gasps. "You're going to have a kindergartener! That's so crazy."

"I know!" I agree. "Weren't we stumbling along Fullerton Avenue trying to find our way back to dorms like a minute ago and now I'm touring elementary schools for my son."

Ethan groans loudly. "Please, don't be like all those other moms at our firm who act like choosing the right kindergarten is a life or death decision. Just pick a school and be done with it. The kid will be fine."

Now, it's my turn to roll my eyes. "Who are *all* these other moms at Mulvaney Stewart? There are like three of us. The rest got laid off." Ethan and I are fellow twelfth-year associates at a large AmLaw100 law firm, a distinction given to the one hundred biggest law firms in America. To say women lawyers are underrepresented would be a major understatement.

"Well, speaking of knocked-up lawyers," Ethan obtusely continues, "there will be one less roaming the halls for the next several months. Nicole was put on bed rest for the remainder of her pregnancy."

"What!" I'm shocked. Nicole is an overachieving junior partner who just announced her pregnancy a few weeks ago. She can't be more than fourteen or fifteen weeks along. I've never heard of anyone going into labor that early.

"You need to get out of your office occasionally, Maeve. You do know Nicole is pregnant, right?"

"Yes, Ethan," I say emphatically as I reach across the table and lightly slap his arm, "but she is only just starting her second trimester."

"Well, someone must have forgotten to tell the baby because Nicole went into labor on Thursday. The doctor was able to stop it, but she's on bed rest until she delivers."

I shake my head as the waiter appears and attempts to create enough space at the minuscule table to accommodate our order. "That's so scary."

"Yeah," Ethan continues. "The crazy thing is she was in the office when the contractions started. That overbearing English client she has makes her re-review *all* of the discovery the associates mark for production before it goes out. There are literally *hundreds of thousands* of pages to turn over because it's a big unfair trade practices case." Ethan loads up a tortilla chip with mango guacamole and devours it in one bite before continuing. "Well, Nicole was at her desk around midnight clicking through documents when she started having contractions. She said it just felt like tightness in her stomach on and off. She knew she'd have to go into the ER and get it checked out, but she wanted to put in another hour before going."

"That definitely sounds like Nicole," I interrupt.

"Yeah, well by the time she got to the hospital, she was having regular contractions. They thought she was going to lose the baby. They were able to stop everything, but she is not to even look at her work email for the next twenty weeks."

"There's no way Nicole will be able to stay away from her client emails. But I hope she proves me wrong and takes it easy. This isn't the type of thing to take lightly."

"Anyway, let's get the focus back on me," Ethan characteristically remarks. You don't have dozens of women, and a fair share of men, regularly comment on your dark hair and blue eyes without letting a bit of it go to your head.

"Now my murder trial team is down a member. Maeve, you need to jump in and help us out. You'd be doing me a solid and it could be really good experience for you. Maybe even look good on your proposal for partnership."

My stomach immediately clenches. "Out of the question." I shoot Ethan a look of warning while attempting a subtle side glance. Patrick seems to be enjoying his salad oblivious to the abrupt change in the conversation's tone. "You know I don't do criminal work," I snap. Ethan realizes he has stepped into sensitive territory and nods slightly while averting his eyes. Confident I made my point, I add, "Well then, as I said, it is out of the question. I am more than satisfied with my caseload of defending student loan companies against consumer protection violations." Feeling my stomach begin to unclench, I take a large sip of my third Paloma.

"*Alleged* violations, counselor," Ethan chides.

Having polished off his plate, Patrick rejoins the conversation. "Murder trial, eh? I love that stuff. Couldn't get enough of the *Serial* podcast. Ethan, fill me in on all the gruesome details."

Like a happy puppy who's been thrown a bone, Ethan leaps at the suggestion. "Oh, it's pretty sordid stuff actually. Our client has been rotting in prison for two years awaiting trial for the murder of her only daughter. This case has it all: drugs, sex, beauty pageants, and strangulation. The prosecution even sought the death penalty before it was abolished in Illinois."

Patrick's jaw drops. "Wow, that sounds intense." After a pause, he adds, "Maeve, this should be right up your alley. Wasn't your father a criminal lawyer?"

I feel my pulse quicken and my breathing become ragged. Fixing my gaze firmly on the table and striving for nonchalant, I respond, "Oh, he never tried a murder case. Didn't have the stomach for the stuff." Raising my gaze to Ethan, I say pointedly, "And neither do I."

***

I lie down in bed immediately after paying MacKenzie. As I struggled to calculate the amount to Venmo, I realized those three Palomas went down a bit too easily. That inkling was confirmed as I staggered up the two flights of stairs in our Lincoln Park townhouse to reach our master suite. I will definitely have a headache in the morning. The days when Patrick and I could close a bar down and still get up and run five miles along the Lakefront Trail are long gone. I raise my head cautiously and see Patrick brushing his teeth in the bathroom across the hall. Just then his phone lights up on the bedside table. Uncharacteristically, I grab it and hide it under the covers. I'm shocked at my own behavior. I've never been the type to snoop. And yet, here I am ducking down to read his latest text. It is one line.

Macy: *I want you. Send pics.*

My throat clenches and it feels as if the whole room is shaking. I throw Patrick's phone back on the side table, dart to the bathroom, and barely reach the toilet before my cheese enchiladas make a reappearance.

Patrick makes a startled noise before letting go with a little chuckle. "I knew that third Paloma was a bad idea."

He kneels beside me and starts to pull back my hair, but I shake him off. I attempt to regain some composure while wiping my mouth with Cottonelle and flushing the toilet.

"I'm fine," I snap and proceed to the sink to brush my teeth for the second time tonight.

Patrick looks a bit confused, before ultimately shaking his head and going to bed. I keep brushing until I hear snoring. Then I head downstairs to Declan's room and curl up in a fetal position on his bottom bunk. It still feels as if the floor is shaking underneath me. Little tremors warning me that my whole world is about to collapse.

Chapter 2

I sit criss-cross applesauce on the wood floor of my mother's sewing room playing with my Barbies. The room is dusty as I can't remember the last time Mom has sewed anything. In the back of the room is my grandma's large, wood dining room table on which now sits my Mom's black Singer sewing machine and piles of fabric in various prints. On the shelves along the wall are extra bobbins and spools of thread as well as knickknacks from my grandma's estate that never found a permanent home after the funeral. My brunette doll, Stephanie, is looking for a boyfriend, but, thanks to my strict father, I don't have any Ken dolls to play the part. I search the room for a stand-in and my eyes land on the fourteen-inch Jesus statue that used to sit on my grandmother's bedside table. Even at seven years old, this feels wrong, but I'm desperate. I jump up and take the statue off the shelf and return to Stephanie who is drinking an Orange Julius at the mall. She's mildly interested as she sees a tall man in a red robe and a halo overhead scoping her out from inside the Radio Shack.

As I hear the doorknob turning behind me, I push the statue away and hold my breath. Someone takes a step into the room and stops. From just that one step, I know it is my father. His steps are heavy and even, unlike my mother whose walk is a bit wobbly lately. He sighs before taking a step back and closing the door. I wonder how I disappointed him this time.

I resume Stephanie and JC's flirting at the mall scene until I hear what sounds like angry whispering coming from my parents' bedroom. I quietly lay down the dolls and stand, tiptoeing from the sewing room to the living room couch. I mouth a silent thank you to the new poop brown shag carpet that muffles my steps.

Kneeling on the couch cushions, I put my ear against the wall next to my parents' bedroom. They are definitely arguing, but it's hard to make out the words. I jump as a loud thud hits the wall like something was thrown against it.

"Goddammit, Joanna! You've got to get your shit together," my father yells.

"I'm just taking a nap, Michael. Go back to work," my mother mumbles.

"How much have you had to drink today? Do you even know where your daughter is? What kind of a fucking mother are you."

"She's fine, Michael. She's at school," my Mom reassures.

Another thud hits the wall by my ear. "It's seven o'clock for Christ sake! Do you even know what day it is anymore? Has she had dinner?"

My heart pounds in my chest as I slowly back away. Have things with Mom really gotten this bad? She's always tired and distracted lately, but does she really not know what day it is? I tiptoe down the hall to my room, noiselessly shut the door, and crawl into bed. As I curl into a fetal position, I feel my bed begin to shake.

Chapter 3

I wake gasping for air, curled in the same fetal position I was just in during my dream. My throat constricts. My mind races. It's Sunday night. Patrick has already left for Boston. Then my anxiety goes into overdrive.

What am I going to do? Will Patrick leave me? I'm almost forty with two young kids. No one will ever love me again. Will my kids have a stepmom? Is she prettier than me? This is my fault. I lost focus and let it all fall apart.

My brain then helpfully creates a porn short of Patrick and a tight, thin, young blond kneeling together on our bed. Patrick grabbing her breasts from behind and kissing her neck while she rolls her head back on his shoulder in ecstasy.

I have to pull it together. I grab my cell from the side table and call Zara. After three rings, she answers.

"What's wrong?" she says sleepy, but alert.

"I…can't…breathe," I gasp. Tears rolling down my face.

Zara immediately defaults to our long-established routine. Her voice soft and reassuring.

"Shhh now. Listen to my voice and concentrate on breathing. You're okay. I'm here."

I use the breathing techniques that have seen me through countless panic attacks. Long slow breaths in through my nose and filling up my lungs. Then slow exhales through my mouth.

Zara continues with her calming mantra, "You're okay. I'm here." She breathes along with me for several minutes before moving on to our next step.

"Now count with me to fifty. Slowly. One…two…three…four…five…"

I clear my mind and count with Zara. I concentrate on nothing but the number I'm on. I picture it in my head, breathe, and move to the next. I can feel my throat begin to open. I take deeper breaths as the tightness in my chest starts to lessen. When I'm back in some semblance of control, I pull the phone away from my ear to check the time and see it's after three. I need to pull it together so I can care for the boys when they wake in just a few hours. Zara interrupts my thoughts.

"Are you ready to talk about what happened?"

I honestly can't think where to begin. Then the text message pops back into my head. "I want you. Send pics." I start to sob. Once I start I can't stop. I'm howling as tears pour down my face punctuated every few seconds with large gasps of air. I hear Zara's breath through the phone, but she says nothing. Letting me expunge all the pain. The only difference between this and all the episodes in college was in our dorm she would lay my head in her lap and gently stroke my hair while I cried myself to sleep. Now she just silently waits until I physically can't produce any more tears and I lie quietly in our marital bed. Exhausted.

Zara then delicately asks, "It's Patrick, isn't it?"

I'm too tired to wonder how she guessed. I answer simply, "Yes. He's cheating. I found a text."

Never one to beat around the bush, Zara inquires, "Will you leave him?"

My heart skips a beat. That idea has never occurred to me. Not once over the weekend as I floated through our family obligations as if suspended in a dream. I watched Patrick cheer Dec on at his Little Kickers scrimmage and spot Seamus as he toddled all over the equipment at his play and learn class at Gymboree as if observing our family from above. Patrick seeming to chalk my disassociation up to a good old-fashioned hangover. But now Zara has put the question out there.

"Building this family has been everything to me. Leaving isn't an option."

Zara exhales. Whether she'd been holding her breath hoping for this response or dreading it, I can't tell. I choose not to ask. A plan forms quickly in my head.

"Patrick was just lonely. All of my focus has been on the kids and work. I've given nothing to him for months. And on top of that, I let myself go. When Patrick and I met, I was a size six."

"You were anorexic and have been since high school," Zara exclaims.

"I was on a diet!" I retort. "And I was in shape. Patrick and I used to run together four days a week. I couldn't run a mile now without having to walk and catch my breath. That's all going to change. Starting today, I'm back on the program. I'll work out every day. I'll eat better. He'll see the effort I'm putting in and find me sexy again," I declare triumphantly, my face flushing with enthusiasm for my new "save my marriage challenge."

Seconds tick by and still Zara does not respond. After thirty more, I cave and ask.

"What do you think?"

I can tell Zara is choosing her words carefully. "I think I love you, Maeve." Zara inhales and exhales deeply before continuing. "And I'm here for you." Zara pauses for another minute before adding, "But I wish you'd learn that not everything is your fault."

I refuse to let her temper my gusto. Instead I thank her for talking me through my "episode" and end the call.

As I continue to lie in bed, my mind wanders back to Patrick's departure just a few hours earlier. As a Senior Manager in the Transaction Tax practice group at Ernst & Young, Patrick is at a client site almost every week. So his Sunday night goodbyes have become routine. Yet, I couldn't help but sense this time that Patrick desperately wanted to confide in me and couldn't quite find the words. After giving tickles and bear hugs to the boys, he pulled me in for our usual hug and chaste kiss by the front door. But this time, when he started to release his embrace, he stopped. He held me by my shoulders and looked deep into my eyes. His own eyes clouded with sadness. "Maeve," he said weightily. But before he could continue, Seamus started crying and pulling on the leg of my sweats. The mood was lost. Now, I can't help but wonder what he wanted to impart. Was he going to confess his affair and beg for forgiveness? Or leap straight to divorce? All I know is I have to win him back before he gets up the courage to broach that topic again.

Since going back to sleep is not a realistic possibility at this point, I put on my wine-colored Lululemon yoga pants, sports bra, and a white tank and head down to the basement to begin my challenge. I OnDemand Jillian Michael's *Yoga Meltdown* and "get ready to get ripped" as Jillian promises. Thirty minutes later I'm sweaty, but less stressed.

While waiting for the shower to warm up to the near scalding temperature I prefer, I take stock of my current physical state in the mirror behind our double vanity. Overall not bad for thirty-nine, but not great either. No rolls or obvious cellulite. Still, my thighs are uncomfortably large and tree-trunkesque. My boobs showing evidence of the havoc nursing two babies can wreak. Not to mention the telltale six-inch ledge along the top of my pubis from my C-section with Seamus. This reminds me of a Heidi Klum quote I once read; I guess pregnant women would come up to her after she had her first or second child and ask if they would look like her after giving birth. She said something like—well, did you look like a model before you got pregnant? That story still annoys me. Not all of us are blessed with tall, tight bodies. And, sure, maybe some of us indulge in cookies and wine a bit too much. But can't you throw us a bone and feed our delusions that after childbirth we will magically transform into German supermodels? Well, I can't do much about the childbirth indicators, but I can take off some inches from my waist, thighs, and butt. Operation "Bring Sexy Back" has officially begun.

Chapter 4

After walking the block to drop the boys off at daycare, I begin my mile trek to catch the El. This walk to the train always reconfirms my belief that I live in the perfect neighborhood. The lovely tree-lined residential streets interrupted by small parks every few blocks give way to the DePaul college campus, the first place to ever feel like home. Arriving twenty minutes later at the massive downtown skyscraper that houses the law firm where I have been employed for the last twelve years brings a different mixture of emotions. Pride in the fact that I am still working at an AmLaw100 firm. Not many women from my law school class can say the same. Many have moved to inhouse positions that promise, often falsely, a better work-life balance. Some followed more noble pursuits with various advocacy and legal aid groups. And increasingly many of them have chosen to check out of the legal field entirely and stay home with their children. A luxury I'm only a tad bit jealous of. Really, just a tad. Yet, while I feel pride in the abstract of having stayed in the game for this long, the other emotion I have as I walk in the forty-eight-story steel and glass structure is dread of actually having to work another day in a field I feel increasingly disillusioned with.

In law school, you study only the most important legal decisions handed down by the highest court in the land. *Marbury vs. Madison* holding that Congress cannot pass laws in conflict with the constitution. *Brown v. Board of Education* striking down the Southern rationale of separate but equal. *Gideon v. Wainwright* guaranteeing the right to counsel in criminal proceedings. *Roe v. Wade* protecting a woman's right to choose. What they don't tell you is the vast majority of law school graduates are going to be working on far less earth-shattering or noble cases. Most involve using your legal talents to defend large corporations in suits brought by the consumers they routinely screw over.

Oh, and if that isn't disillusioning enough, you will work for predominantly older white male assholes who consistently under appreciate your efforts and berate you for not cranking out the kind of billable hours they did when they were at your level. What goes unsaid, of course, is that they all had stay-at-home wives who raised their kids, cooked their meals and cleaned their homes. Leaving them time to work all night and even a little extra for the occasional tryst with the assistant that men of a certain age and economic status feel entitled to.

But even as I've gotten more disillusioned with the work and with my "superiors," I've never seriously considered quitting. Never even returned a recruiter's call. When I walked through the doors of Thorne Hall on the first day of orientation at Northwestern Law, it was with one goal in mind—to shatter the glass ceiling and make partner at a big law firm. At the time, of course, I saw myself representing the biggest clients in headline-grabbing lawsuits. I pictured myself with a cushy corner office handing out document review and research assignments to a half dozen associates, all of whom were honored to be working for a legal legend in the making. Maeve Johnson, now Maeve Shaw, the picture of self-sufficiency and independence. Even as my vision has drastically scaled back over the years, my goal has remained the same—to make partner.

Getting off the elevator, I stop at the forty-fourth floor "cafe" to make myself another cup of coffee. Selecting a dark roast container, I slot it into the Keurig and wait for it to work its magic. Two French vanilla Coffee-Mates later and I'm ready to tackle the day. My assistant Jeanine, a petite lady of around sixty, sits in a cubicle directly across from my office door. Jeanine sports the white-haired perm common with women of her age and her cubicle is adorned with photos of her grandson and granddaughter. While technically she is my assistant, we both know her three partner assignments get the vast majority of her attention. The most she is willing to do for a twelfth-year senior associate is submit my occasional travel expenses for reimbursement. Still, she is very sweet and always asks how the boys are doing.

"Good morning, Maeve. Running a little late again, are we?"

Oh right, I forgot to add she also never forgets to point out my tardiness. Maybe Jeanine isn't so sweet after all, actually.

"Yes, Jeanine. But I'm here now and don't plan to take a lunch."

As my laptop powers on, without even intending to, I find myself pulling up the Ernst & Young website. I locate the search tab and type "Macy." Holding my breath, I hit enter. No search results. It strikes me for the first time that Macy is an odd name. I've never met anyone named Macy. Maybe Patrick, his head clouded with hormones, made a typo. After all, Mary is a much more common name. The search for "Mary" turns up four results. But as I scroll through the hits, none of the Marys work in tax or are based out of the Chicago office. I can't imagine where Patrick would come across a Mary in the Global Fraud & Corruption group based out of D.C. or a Mary in the Healthcare Data & Analytics Group from Virginia. Maybe I'm going about this wrong. Patrick would have fixed a typo. It is more likely he misspelled her name on purpose in case I ever came across a text. Macey? No hits. Marcy? No hits. What about Marcie? And there she is. Marcie Spellman. In the Transaction Tax practice like Patrick, but based out of the New York office. Still, since client teams are made up of managers from multiple offices, it wouldn't be hard for them to meet. I was right about her being blond and pretty, but she doesn't appear to be much younger than me. Her picture though exudes a confidence that my professional headshots never do. No matter how much I accomplish, I always feel like an imposter and that insecurity is readily apparent. Marcie Spellman seems to own her success.

I stare at Marcie's green eyes and perfect smile. My replacement even has the same eye color. What do they talk about when they are lying naked in their hotel room exhausted from their exertions? Do they talk about me? About the kids? How can she live with herself? Fuck that, actually. She owes me no loyalty. How can he live with himself?

I'm jerked out of my reverie by the ping of an email hitting my inbox. I glance at the time on the bottom right corner of my screen and am startled to realize it's already after ten. I need to put in some serious hours the rest of the day. Of course, I currently only have three open cases. Since my last maternity leave, the work has been dribbling in. One leave is forgiven and partners will deem to load you up on your return. Two leaves and the general consensus is that it is a waste of time to staff you on cases, because you will likely quit within six months of returning anyway. I returned from my eighteen-week leave ten months ago. Still, that has done nothing to dispel this firmly rooted notion. All three of my current cases involve drafting motions to dismiss class actions filed against the same company for *alleged* violations of federal regulations pertaining to the company's servicing of its student loans. It is hard to be a zealous advocate for your client when one of the reasons you are still working is the six-figure student loan debt you accumulated to finance your own law school education more than a decade ago.

After two hours of massaging the introduction of my first motion to adequately convey to the judge the insurmountable lack of merit on the borrower's part, I can no longer ignore my bladder and must take my once daily trip to the bathroom. Clear evidence of my preference for caffeinated beverages to the healthier water alternative. Halfway down the hall I spy the straight jet-black hair of none other than Elizabeth Townley, the Of Counsel in charge of my student loan matters. While I am certainly grateful she has entrusted me with the work, as none of her male colleagues have done so, running into her is always a stressful experience. It is no secret that Elizabeth has only one client and that if she were to lose that client Mulvaney Stewart would have no problem sending her packing. Of Counsel positions are precarious ones at any large firm. For this reason, Elizabeth micromanages the hell out of her cases. God help you if the briefs aren't perfect down to any widows/orphans at the end of a paragraph. That applies even to the first draft. As my need for the bathroom has now reached emergency level, I try to keep my head down and slip by.

"Maeve, just the person I was looking for," Elizabeth croons. "I was worried I missed you. I can never keep track of what hours you're in anymore what with all those daycare emergencies."

Real nice. I try to keep the contempt out of my voice as I sweetly remind her, "Now Elizabeth, you know I'm in from nine to six every day. And when there are emergencies, I'm always available on email, as per firm policy."

Our firm just announced an obnoxious policy that requires associates to respond to all partner and client emails within two hours of receipt. No exceptions. That includes weekends and evenings. So much for work-life balance.

"Well, call me old fashioned, but I prefer to meet with my associates in person rather than just exchanging emails with them," retorts Elizabeth through her signature hot pink lipstick.

Elizabeth is always impeccably dressed. She must be in her late forties or early fifties and has the post-baby bump most of us mothers sport, but she makes the most of her figure in pencil skirts, bright blouses and designer heels. She must also get keratin treatments because her shoulder-length bob is always impossibly straight and frizz-free. One look at her makes my go-to black stretchy pants and grey cable-knit sweater feel wholly inadequate.

"Anyway, Maeve, I was wondering when I was going to see the first draft of the Gibson motion to dismiss. It is due in fourteen days, after all."

At this point, I'm doing those kegel exercises recommended by my obstetrician like my life depends on it. Which it kind of does. I'm not sure people who pee themselves in the hallway get promoted.

"I've been working on it today and will have it to you by the end of the week, no problem," I promise while attempting to both keep my legs tightly locked and simultaneously slip along the wall in the direction of the bathroom.

Elizabeth puts a hand on my arm to stop my departure. "Oh, that won't work. I need to go out of town this weekend and want a chance to edit it before leaving. Please email it to me by the end of the day tomorrow at the latest."

Shit! For that to happen, I will have to write most of it tonight so tomorrow can be devoted to fine-tuning. Another night with little to no sleep, but at this point I would agree to anything that gets me to a toilet within the next minute. This must be why torture isn't an effective method of eliciting the truth.

"Sure, Elizabeth. End of the day tomorrow it is."

Elizabeth flashes me a Cheshire cat smile and releases my arm. I proceed the remaining way to the bathroom in a half squat so I can keep my legs and thighs clenched together. Not exactly the picture of the glass ceiling shattering, feminist badass I aspire to convey.

Thirty seconds later, I'm enjoying the immense feeling of relief in my bladder region when what catches my eye? Surely that can't be, and yet there it is, gray pubic hair. How can the hair on my head be retaining its mouse-brown hue when my pubic region has multiple silver strands? Is my vagina aging at a more rapid rate than the rest of me? Jesus, that's a depressing thought. Surely Marcie's nether region is gray free and tight. She probably can also sneeze without fear. Demoralized by my aging vagina and shortened deadline, I grab a diet coke from the vending machine and head back down the elliptical-shaped hall to my office. All those researchers comparing the effects of diet coke on your body to that of heroin can go blow themselves for today.

I finish the second of four arguments when I risk a glance at the clock. WTF! How is it five-fifty already? In order to pick up the boys from daycare at six-thirty, I have to be in a cab no later than six. My goal is five forty-five, but that rarely happens. I quickly record my time on my ubiquitous yellow legal pad and power down my laptop. I throw on my staple black, knee-length winter coat I picked up at J. Crew four years ago and am out the door. Six o'clock departures are rather on the early side for associates, so I embark on my *Mission Impossible*-style exit designed to avoid any partner offices. I take the corridor by Jeanine's desk which leads to the inner hallway of paralegal offices before dead-ending at the elevator corridor. As long as the elevator comes quickly, my departure should go undetected. But, of course, as waiting for the elevator stretches from one minute to two I hear the unmistakable sound of four-inch heels clicking toward me. I punch the elevator button three more times in a futile attempt to hasten its arrival, but not before Elizabeth turns the corner and spots me.

"Maeve," she says with concern, "I certainly hope you are leaving yourself adequate time to finish that motion by tomorrow."

The elevator ding saves me and I shout a quick, "Of course, you'll have it tomorrow," before slipping through the doors.

After a quick dinner of chicken nuggets and fruit followed by a bath to hose off the excess ketchup, the boys are snuggled next to me in the oversized recliner rocker in Seamus's room. We are reading *Chugga-Chugga Choo-Choo* for the umpteenth time. While every rhyming line has been seared into my memory, I don't complain. These fifteen-minute reading sessions before bed are the only times I feel like a good parent most days. I'm not begging Declan to eat two bites of broccoli, wrestling with Seamus to put on his snowsuit, or running out of daycare with a quick kiss on their heads. I'm present and relaxed. I put my nose into Seamus's wet messy hair and breathe in the Burt's Bees baby wash. Nestled in my other arm is Declan. Small for his age at not quite five, Declan has delicate features and sports his required glasses to correct his farsightedness. Declan is such a serious boy. Even though he is fully focused on the tale of the train's adventures around the playroom, I can't help but give him a little squeeze. And right then my phone starts ringing. Patrick's regularly scheduled FaceTime chat to wish the boys goodnight.

As Patrick's tired yet handsome face fills the screen, Seamus starts bouncing up and down in excitement. Seamus adores his daddy and both his chubby little arms start flailing in excitement each night during these calls. Declan is also a Daddy's boy and I worry that part of his quiet demeanor is actually sadness over not seeing him enough.

Patrick, who up until Friday I thought I knew so well. A lump forms in my throat, but I force a happy tone.

"Hi, Daddy! Declan, can you tell Daddy about your day?" I prompt in an attempt to keep my part of the conversation to a minimum.

Declan always takes a few beats to collect his thoughts before speaking. "School was fun, but I got a boo-boo on my leg."

Shit! Of all the things Declan could bring up. As Patrick is less than thrilled with our current For Your Child daycare/preschool, I rush to diffuse the situation. "It was nothing serious. Dec's pant leg just came up on the slide and he got a bit of a slide burn. Want to show him, sweetie?"

Declan pulls up the leg of his Superman pajamas and shows Patrick a minor red mark. Patrick blows him a kiss to make it better and Declan seems pacified. I switch hands so the phone is now in front of Seamus.

At fifteen months, Seamus is unable to hold up his end of the conversation so I take over. "Daddy, Ms. Ann at school reported Seamus said 'ball' four times today, but he won't do it for Mommy. Can you say 'ball' for Daddy, big boy? Ball? Ball?"

"Da Da Dada," Seamus babbles.

I laugh. "We know you can say Dada, little man. Can you say 'ball?'"

"Dada."

"Okay, well I don't think we are going to get a 'ball' tonight," I concede. "I'll keep trying tomorrow."

Though these chats usually last more than two minutes, I feel my cheerful facade start to crack and rush to put an end to it. "Can we say goodnight to Dada, boys? It's beddy time."

A mixture of "night, Daddy" from Declan and "Da Da Da" from Seamus fills the room as Patrick waves and blows kisses.

Patrick, surprised, asks, "You going to call me later?"

"Not tonight, hon. I still have a few hours of work to do."

Patrick looks disappointed. "Oh, that's too bad. Zara texted me today. She said you had one of your…ummm…err"—Patrick awkwardly searches for a word before landing on—"attacks and I wanted to check on you. Are you feeling okay?"

I can feel Dec's worried eyes scanning my face and I rush to reassure him…and Patrick, "Oh, yes. You know me. I'm such a worrier." I attempt a light chuckle. "I have a busy week at work and started to stress out. Zara talked me through it. I'm fine now."

Patrick looks unconvinced. "Okay. It's just that Zara made it out to be a bit more than that. And it's not like it's the first time it's happened. Maybe you should consider talking to someone about these events. Like a professional, maybe."

I make a mental note to kill Zara next time I see her. There's a reason I lean on her and not Patrick during these times. And she knows why. Looking to end this interrogation, I strike a conciliatory tone. "Okay, hon. I'll give it some thought. Have a good night."

As I end the call, I wonder briefly what Patrick will do with the rest of his night now that his family obligations are out of the way. Putting that aside, I finish our story and lay Seamus down in his crib with a kiss. I then pick up Declan and carry him to his room next door. Declan sleeps in an actual tree house bunk bed that Patrick insisted on getting him to make up for Seamus's arrival. It's from Pottery Barn Kids and while the bottom bunk is nothing special, the top bunk is enclosed in wood paneling like a tree house. There are four windows for Declan to peek out from and a single open doorway with a ladder to climb in. It is a little boy's dream bed. Seamus is relegated to Dec's hand-me-down crib. I wonder when he is going to realize he got the shaft. Not sure if there is going to be any grand gesture bunk bed in Shay's future either. While Patrick loves him, he was initially dead set against having another baby. But I pleaded for another until Patrick finally caved to my wishes. I experienced the loneliness of only childhood and my son was going to have a playmate even if it killed me. Which on some days I feel it surely will.

A little after two-thirty in the morning, I reach a point where I'm fairly sure any reasonable judge will conclude the borrower did not suffer any actual damages from receiving one monthly statement from her student loan servicer after filing for bankruptcy. And opposing counsel has not met his burden of proof in showing my client has developed a pattern and practice of violating bankruptcy stays. Of course, right as I'm about to power down my laptop, my Jabber pings. Jabber is the work approved IM for quick messages to coworkers. It's from Ethan.

Welcome to the murder squad.

I'm stunned. I hadn't thought about Ethan's pro bono case since our dinner where I felt I had effectively closed the door to any possibility of my participation. I begin to type "what are you talking about" when the status by his name changes to "offline." Just like Ethan to drop a bomb and log off.

Chapter 5

I sneak out of my room, pad quietly down the hallway, and take a seat. Being rather small for an eight-year-old, I have the perfect vantage point from which to snatch glimpses of the holiday party my parents are hosting for Dad's work friends while still remaining hidden from view. I pull my knees up to my chest and wrap my purple terry cloth bathrobe tightly around me. I see Dad's plump partner, Mr. Mullins, talking animatedly with their secretary, Barbara Meach, his hand wrapped around a glass of bourbon and his eyes fixed on Barbara's bosom. I see the dark chocolate buffet table filled with appetizers. Deviled eggs, cheese and crackers, spinach dip in a pumpernickel bread bowl, seven-layer dip, and an assortment of cookies all of which Mom is taking credit for whipping up. I, of course, know she paid Mrs. Collins down the street to not only take care of the spread but also to stay quiet about it. Dad emerges from the kitchen. He's wearing his formal navy blue suit usually reserved for court appearances and seems to be enjoying himself. After clinking the side of his Miller Lite several times with a spoon, he thanks everyone for coming and wishes that nineteen ninety-two will be another good year for their small criminal law firm. Mom takes her place beside him and places her hand on his back. She's wearing a long-sleeve gray dress adorned with an attached gold necklace. Her hair recently permed. Her eyes a bit unfocused.

I must have dozed off because the next thing I know, I'm awakened by the sound of glass shattering. Panic sets in. I steal a peek into the living room. It's late and the party must have been dying down because there are only six or so people still there, including Mr. Mullins and Barbara. I do not see Mrs. Mullins. Dad comes running out of the kitchen toward my Mom. She's crying and appears to be yelling at Mr. Mullins. I hear her say "son of a bitch," but her speech is too slurred to make out much more. From the wet mark on the floral wallpaper next to Mr. Mullins's head, I guess she threw her martini glass at him. Dad grabs both of her arms and begins to lead her in the direction of their bedroom. Mom, stumbling, still manages to aim a few more curses in Mr. Mullins's direction before disappearing into their room.

Once she is gone, the remaining guests recover from their shock and begin to put down their glasses and locate their coats. All the while whispering to each other. A few minutes later my dad emerges. I hear him apologize for my mother's behavior which he explains away as the result of having "overindulged in the holiday cheer." He helps the few remaining women on with their coats and walks them toward the door. As he shakes Mr. Mullins's hand, he seems to whisper another apology into his ear. Once everyone has left, Dad returns to the living room and starts clearing the buffet of its mostly empty platters. He abruptly stops and walks over to the sofa. He sits, puts his head in his hands, and lets out a long sigh. I think he may be crying though I've never seen my dad cry. Not even at Grandma's funeral. I get to my feet, take a deep breath, and walk into the living room. Shaking slightly, I put my arms around my father and lay my head on his shoulder. He instantly recoils from my embrace and stands up.

"What the hell do you think you're doing?"

Shocked, I say nothing.

"Were you spying on me?" he demands.

"I…I…" I stutter. I'm grasping at straws. "The glass woke me up. Is Mom okay?"

A look of utter loathing enters my father's eyes. Whether it is directed at me or my mother, I can't tell.

Dad then grabs my arm and orders, "Get to bed and don't come back out. You hear me?"

I search my father's face for any semblance of love or compassion. Finding none, I walk quietly back to my room.

Chapter 6

I wake up exhausted and emotionally drained, having amassed a grand total of four hours of sleep. Not even four consecutive hours since Seamus woke up fussing at four. Blasted fifteen-month molars. Knowing full well that Patrick wouldn't approve, I ran downstairs, grabbed Shay out of his crib and let him sleep with me the remaining two hours. Patrick thinks we should have a strict no co-sleeping policy. I don't agree but usually go along with it...at least when he's home. When he's away, I let it slide a bit more. They are only going to want to crawl in with their Mommy for a few more years and I want to savor every last snuggle.

I tiredly fumble my way through dressing and feeding the boys their oatmeal and bananas before dropping them off at daycare. Determined to stick with my challenge, I then come home to run/walk a slow three miles on the treadmill in our basement. As I'm throwing on random but clean business casual pieces, my eye catches our wedding picture on the wall above my dresser. Me in my simple, long-sleeved ivory satin dress with a scoop neckline. In the picture, I'm holding hands with Patrick who's clad in a classic black suit. We're walking toward the reception tent. It strikes me how young we both look. I guess that's because we were young. Both twenty-six years old and right out of law and business school. My face is wrinkle-free and glowing, even without a facial. I have a big smile on my face. Patrick looks a bit stiff. I remember him being very nervous during the ceremony. Right up until our vows, that is. Earlier that summer we'd agreed to write our own. Over a few glasses of wine on a patio, it seemed like a brilliant idea. But with work and all the wedding planning it became a source of immense stress for me. Ultimately, my vows were sweet, but nothing special. Patrick, on the other hand, knocked it out of the park. I still remember him looking me in the eyes and saying, "Maeve, in you I have found a place to call home. I have found compassion and love. I have found a kindred spirit. You are my everything." To this day, I still get weepy when I recall them.

We were married at the Chicago Botanic Gardens. It was hot that last weekend of August, but there had been rain the day before and the gardens were green and in bloom, the smell of lavender in the air. Patrick's two brothers gave hilarious co-best man speeches mentioning a few house parties Patrick had thrown when his parents were back visiting relatives in Ireland. His mother stood next to me during her speech and said that while they had all considered me a Shaw for the last three years, I was now officially one of her daughters. Given that my side of the aisle was beyond sparse, having her accept me into their family meant more than she could know. It was the single happiest day of my life before Dec was born. There's no way in hell I'm giving this all up without a fight.

I arrive at the office right around nine. After three hours of tedious edits on Elizabeth's motion I'm starting to fade. I unconsciously find myself back on Marcie's Ernst & Young profile when I'm startled out of my internet stalking by Ethan barging into my office. Although I have pumped in that office twice daily for two six-month stretches, Ethan still never feels the need to do a courtesy knock. I guess a bit of familiarity is to be expected amongst the only two remaining members of our summer associate class. I can still visualize the moment during our initiation when the director of recruiting informed us that of the fifty-two summer associates who had received and accepted offers at Mulvaney Stewart only one or two would eventually be made partner. Both Ethan and I have been passed over for promotion the last three years running. Mine always attributed to a lack of awe-inspiring amounts of billable hours. Ethan's billables are solid. He just needs to impress upon a few more partners his ability to bring in business. He seems committed to kissing the right ass this year and will probably snag that promotion at year's end.

Glancing over my shoulder at my screen, Ethan inquires, "Who's the babe?"

Aghast, I object, "I wouldn't call her a babe. She's passable at best."

Ethan laughs and points out, "You're just saying that because she has bigger tits."

Barely suppressing my rage, I shoot back, "It's not the size that matters, but what you do with them."

Immediately regretting my weak retort, I cringe as Ethan doubles over with laughter. When he recovers, he notes, "I don't think that saying applies to boobs. The size most *definitely* matters."

Annoyed, I quickly close my screen.

Never one to belabor disagreements, Ethan moves on with, "You look a wreck. Let's lunch."

Normally, I turn down lunch invitations trying to cram in as many billable minutes as possible between my arrival and required early departure for daycare. But I put in twelve hours yesterday and deserve a break.

"Sounds good. Where are we going?"

Initially adamant we dine at 69 Chinese Restaurant, his usual haunt, Ethan finally relents to the Protein Bar where he can get a bar-rito and I can get my favorite Southwest salad with tofu. After some initial gossip about who may or may not be leaving the firm, Ethan and I turn back to our usual complaining over how much we hate work/the partners we work for. I lead off.

"Don't get me started. I've been relegated to acting as Elizabeth's main drafter of dispositive motions. It's a thankless job. Literally, the woman has never once thanked me for jumping through her myriad hoops. And the worst part is, I'm forced to smile and say 'thank you, ma'am, may I have another,' because she is the *only* person giving me work. I'm milking these three motions for all they're worth, because who knows what I'll do once they are fully briefed and awaiting a ruling. After last year's maternity leave, I have to bill over two thousand hours this year."

This depressing thought makes me consider going back for a peanut butter brownie to sabotage my healthy lunch.

"Well, you know whose fault that is?" Ethan chides. "As Jabba the Hutt told you, 'babies are luxuries not necessities.'"

"Ugh! Please don't bring him up. I may lose my lunch."

Jabba the Hutt is Ethan's and my nickname for the head of the Chicago office, Chris Bines. An oaf of a man, Chris feels no pressure to conform to the current climate and adopt a more PC approach to dealing with female associates. He routinely "lays off" women while they are still on maternity leave. He has casually hinted I may be next on the chopping block if I don't "redeem" myself this year.

Going for casual, Ethan takes a bite of his steakhouse ranch wrap and tosses out, "I notice you haven't mentioned your newest case, *State of Illinois v. Tammy Sanford.*"

I make Ethan meet my eyes before unequivocally informing him, "That's because I don't have a new case, Ethan. You know I have no interest in criminal law. Besides, even without Nicole, there are already enough lawyers on that pro bono case."

Ethan puts down his lunch and looks serious. "Maeve, we need a woman. The defendant is a woman and Tom doesn't think it will give the right impression if she's defended by two or three men."

I continue as if I hadn't heard him. "Also there is no way in hell Chris would be cool with it. You know I need approval from the office head before taking on any pro bono projects and he won't sign off. He'll say I need to focus on getting my client hours back up. Let's be honest. That guy doesn't give a shit about helping out anyone who isn't paying our $500-an-hour rate."

Ethan starts to fidget and stammer. Most atypical for the always cool and collected Ethan. "I was hoping to win you over with my charm, but the truth is you don't have a choice. Tom's a bit desperate. And he has a pretty big book of business, so Chris kisses his ass. Tom sent Chris an email yesterday telling him he's adding you to our team. Chris will sign off. It's a done deal."

The bite of avocado I just swallowed gets lodged in my throat. I force it down and stare at Ethan aghast. "And you didn't stop him? You know my history, Ethan. You know I can't handle a murder trial. How could you not have suggested another female associate?"

Ethan, looking more uncomfortable by the second, quickly explains, "There wasn't anyone else. Tom wants a junior partner or senior associate who will play a central role in preparing and cross-examining witnesses. You are the only female who fits the criteria. And you know you'll be good at it. Remember you told me you received the award for highest grade in your Crim Law class out of a hundred and ten students!"

I quickly gather my salad bowl and napkins and stand. "Yeah, when your dad is a criminal lawyer, you pick up some stuff. That doesn't mean I want any part of this. How could you let me be put in this situation? After I *trusted* you." I leave Ethan to finish his lunch alone as I fight back tears all the way to the office.

By the time I reach my desk, I've resolved to put this murder case out of my mind. I've received no word from Tom or Chris. For all I know, they could have found someone else to staff the case. Ethan's been known to create drama out of nothing before. I spend another three hours editing a fifteen-page motion to dismiss. I even call for Jeanine's help when I can't get one paragraph to break evenly enough between pages to avoid violating Elizabeth's widow/orphan rule. I draft a curt, "Elizabeth—please find attached the Gibson motion to dismiss for your review. I look forward to getting your edits," (not) and hit send. I'll actually pick up the boys a few minutes early for once. Just as I'm powering down, my phone rings. The caller ID shows Chris Bines. This can't be good. I compose myself and try to answer as cheerfully as possible. "Hi Chris, what can I do for you?"

A deep voice growls, "You can come straight down to my office and explain why you are asking for pro bono work when your billables are shit."

FUCK. "Of course, Chris. I'll be right there."

While all partners receive the larger, cushier offices, those look like hovels compared to Chris's kingdom. When Chris nabbed the office head gig, his first administrative act was to request a double partner office equipped with its own bathroom and shower. The idea that I could walk in here one day and catch Chris in just a towel makes me nauseous. When I get to his door, I take a deep breath to steady my nerves, and knock twice.

"Enter!" Jabba bellows.

I try to gather myself and walk in with as much dignity as I can muster. After all, I'm an almost forty-year-old professional woman who has been practicing law for over a decade. I have proven myself to be more than competent at my job. This asshole shouldn't be able to shake me. And yet, my heart is racing as I wait for him to offer me a seat at one of the three separate seating areas available.

Reading my mind, Jabba informs me brusquely, "Don't bother sitting. This shouldn't take long. Just explain to me why you want to spend your time on a pro bono case outside your specialty instead of devoting that time to developing your client relationships and justifying your salary."

I take a deep breath and as calmly as possible clarify, "Chris, there seems to be a misunderstanding. I didn't ask to join the murder team and I don't actually want to join the murder team. I am keenly aware that I need to have a high billable year and so I agree it makes sense for me to accept only billable work."

Chris seems momentarily confused but regains his composure and resumes the interrogation. "If that's true then explain why I got an email from Tom Gaines requesting you specifically for his team."

It dawns on me that Chris might actually be able to save me from this disaster of an assignment. "My understanding is Tom is looking for a female junior partner or senior associate to replace Nicole on his team. Ethan probably offered my name. I'm sure Tom would happily accept any other candidate you suggest that fits that criteria." I smile and begin to turn toward the door.

Then I hear Chris mumble, "I see. Well, unfortunately, there is no one else then."

Knowing I must have misheard, I turn back to Chris and ask, "Excuse me?"

"You and Nicole are the only two females at Mulvaney Stewart with the requisite experience. I'll have to allow it."

While this situation seems to have caught Chris off guard, he quickly reverts to his asshole default setting and bellows, "But don't think this means you're off the hook in terms of your hours. I'm going to be keeping an eye on your billables. If they dip below one seventy-five in any month, we'll need to have a tough conversation about your future here."

Panic rising, I plead, "But that's impossible. I can't bill a hundred seventy-five hours *on top* of prepping for a trial. Please, just tell Tom I can't do it."

Chris fixes me with a steely glare. "Ms. Shaw, other associates routinely bill over two hundred hours. Either step up your game or get off the field."

Sufficiently chastened, I acquiesce, "Of course, Chris. Understood."

The lump in my throat tells me I need to make a quick departure. I don't want to give Jabba the pleasure of making me emotional. As I walk back to my office, I take a quick glance at my Fitbit Alta. Almost six. Guess the boys won't be picked up early after all.

Chapter 7

Patrick flew in late last night. I have no idea when he got home because I was so tired from the week I basically fell into a coma as soon as I got the boys settled. But I wake around midnight and he is next to me. Looking at him lying on his side with nothing but his Northwestern sweats on evokes so many emotions. How I love curling into his toned, bare chest. I desperately want him to turn over, give me his shy little smile, pull me close and whisper his usual, "I missed you, babe" into my ear. But then an unwelcome vision appears of an exhausted Patrick and Marcie spooning post-coitus, and my stomach begins to churn. Too disturbed by that visual to go back to sleep, I grab my iPhone and start scrolling through my Facebook feed. After a few minutes of scanning my friends' typical posts of political outrage punctuated by kid updates, it occurs to me Marcie may also have a Facebook page. I type Marcie Spellman into the search line and scroll through a half page of erroneous results before spotting her. It seems Marcie is the athletic type too. Her profile picture shows her on top of a glacier in Iceland. While her account is private, there are a few other pictures visible on her newsfeed. Marcie crossing the finish line of the New York City Marathon. Marcie next to a giant redwood in Sequoia National Park. It strikes me that Marcie is the better version of me. Me if I hadn't become obsessed with work and insisted on having children. Me if I hadn't stopped obsessively dieting and exercising. Me if I wore a C cup instead of an A. Marcie is the version of me that Patrick wants. I put down my phone a little too aggressively on the nightstand causing a crack to form on the screen.

After tossing and turning the rest of the night, I let Patrick handle the daycare drop off and head into the office early. I need a distraction from the *Real Housewives*-level drama I'm dealing with on the home front. Nothing better to kill all thoughts of sex than drafting mind-numbing legal arguments. Since Elizabeth still hasn't given me edits to the first motion, I turn my attention to outlining her second. To complete my whole "woman done wrong" mood, I select the Tori Amos station on Pandora for background. Just as I'm starting to get into a groove, an email pops up in my inbox from none other than Thomas Gaines. The subject reads "Welcome to the Team." Heart plummeting, I reluctantly double click on the message.

Ms. Shaw - Thank you for agreeing to jump on the Tammy Sanford case. As Ethan may have mentioned, we have a hearing at nine on Monday to set a trial date. Plan to attend. We will of course request as much time as possible, but I expect the judge will set a date within the next six months. Begin to familiarize yourself with the case file before Monday's hearing so you are ready to hit the ground running. Best, Tom

I sarcastically draft a response in my mind, "No, Tom. Ethan conveniently forgot to mention we have a hearing in *three days*. Maybe that's because he's a prick." Dejected, I realize there is no putting this off any longer. I open up the firm's electronic file organizing software creatively titled WorkSpace and quickly locate the Tammy Sanford file. Ethan is clearly devoted to this case, as he has created an "attorney notes" folder containing detailed outlines of the facts, profiles on the victim and accused, a summary of the prosecution's theory, and a quick reference of key evidence and potential witnesses. Sipping my coffee, I start skimming for highlights.

Tammy Sanford is a forty-four-year-old grandmother accused of strangling her only daughter, Kyleigh. The file contains several photos of Kyleigh as a child—all from what appear to be dance and talent competitions. Kyleigh was your stereotypically blond-haired, blue-eyed child with just the right amount of baby fat. She was billed as a triple threat—she could sing, dance, and act. It appears she raked up a substantial amount of first place trophies and prize money over the years. She even nabbed small spots on television commercials for Gap and Carters brands. The photos and news clippings seem to peter out when Kyleigh hits her teen years, but it's hard to accurately gauge her age under all that makeup. Nevertheless, at some point, Kyleigh stops winning prize money and turns to drugs. Specifically, opioids. As the story usually goes, Kyleigh developed an addiction to the prescription drugs she received for a back injury. When the doctor stopped signing scripts, Kyleigh turned to heroin. There are frequent domestic violence calls to the police by concerned neighbors. Tammy also called the police on Kyleigh on three occasions when she stole from Tammy's house to feed her habit. Toward the end of her short life, Kyleigh had a baby boy named Garrett. He was present at several of the domestic violence incidents and ultimately at the murder scene.

This has all the markings of a heat of the moment, passion crime. A voluntary manslaughter charge at worst. But the prosecution claims Kyleigh's murder was premeditated. Their theory is that Tammy is not some long-suffering mother driven over the edge watching her only daughter fall deeper and deeper into addiction. Instead, they paint Tammy as a disappointed pageant mom whose adorable little paycheck burns out and starts stealing more than she's bringing in. Once Tammy realizes Kyleigh is more Lindsay Lohan than Anne Hathaway, she decides to cut her losses. They say Tammy went to Kyleigh's dealer's house that night. Remained in her car for over an hour waiting for the dealer to go off on a run. Then she gained access into the house, probably through promises of cash, and strangled Kyleigh.

The prosecution's theory strikes me as a bit too Lifetime movie of the week. Nothing more so than the murder weapon. According to the prosecution, Tammy waited until Kyleigh lay down on her dealer's bed and dozed off. No doubt too high to stop herself. Tammy then allegedly crawled on top of Kyleigh and strangled her. I click back through the case file to find a subfolder of crime scene photos. It easily contains over a hundred thumbnails. All too small to reveal their image so I have to quickly click through each one. The majority depict a squalid apartment littered with drug paraphernalia. The crime scene photographer seemed determined to capture each powder-filled baggie, burnt spoon with accompanying lighter or candle, scale for weighing quantities, and discarded needle. As I feel my anxiety level start to rise, I start clicking through more quickly. I don't need a lesson on the various instruments and implements of an addict. I've had enough real-world experience to qualify as an expert.

The last twenty-five thumbnails are of the bedroom crime scene and are hard to stomach. Kyleigh is pictured face up on top of the comforter. She is wearing only gray boxer briefs and a dirty, light pink camisole with bits of the lace torn in places. She is thin, but not in a healthy way. One of her forearms is facing the ceiling and the track marks are clearly visible. She has a mass of tangled bleached blond hair with two inches of visible dark brown roots. There are spatters of dried brown blood on multiple spots of the comforter. Around Kyleigh, the bedroom is in the same shape as the rest of the house. Clothes are flung haphazardly. Various beer and liquor bottles are visible on the floor as well as more drug paraphernalia. There are a few pieces of broken glass on the floor near the beaten-up dresser that could be indicative of a struggle. But given the state of the remainder of the house, it would be hard to say that conclusively. The most heart-wrenching images are saved for the end. An empty Costco car seat sits on the kitchen table, if you can call a cheap folding table that. And the car seat appears to be a hand-me-down. There are multiple stains on the hot pink fabric. Not a color I can see Kyleigh or Tammy buying for their little boy unless they are more genderfluid than I assume. I shudder to wonder how long Garrett sat in that chair after his mother's death before someone found him. I unconsciously wrap my arms around my chest for comfort.

I'm still staring at the dirty kitchen stacked with pizza and takeout boxes in the middle of which sat little Garrett when my Jabber pings. It's Ethan.

Tom told me he emailed you about Monday's hearing. I know you're still pissed, but I think after you meet Tammy you'll be glad you took the case.

Nice try.

I didn't take the case, Ethan. It was thrust on me.

A minute goes by before Ethan responds.

Listen, Tammy needs us. The prosecution has it all wrong. Sure, Tammy is uneducated. Greedy even. Maybe undeserving of a mother-of-the-year trophy, but she's not a calculated killer. She tried over and over to get Kyleigh clean. You of all people should understand how hard that is and the toll addiction takes on the family.

My blood pressure spikes. I need to nip this shit in the bud.

Listen. Whether I like it or not, it seems I'm on this case, but we will only remain friends if we get something clear right now. You are never to use my drunken confession against me. There will be no more references to my sob story. Understood?

Instantly Ethan responds,

You're right. I'm sorry. Understood.

I decide what's good for the goose is good for the gander and change my Jabber status to offline. I glance at the clock and am shocked to realize I have whiled away over two hours on Tammy's file. I now need to work through lunch on Elizabeth's second motion to salvage a decent billable day. I set to work dismantling the borrower's argument that a single failure of my client to respond to a qualified written request demanding irrelevant information such as the name of the investor on his loan, the origination file, and the name and title of every customer service representative he'd spoken to over the last five years constitutes an evil plot to defraud him and others similarly situated. I have a pretty solid outline completed when a new email brings me back to reality. Comments from Elizabeth on her first motion. Sent at a quarter to five to blow up my weekend no doubt. But as I scroll through I'm pleasantly surprised to conclude these edits should deprive me of only about four hours. Not a bad first draft after all.

I decide to end my day on that high note. It's Friday after all. I text Patrick and see if he wants to grab a drink at the bar next to For Your Child before picking up the boys. Not even two minutes pass before Patrick responds with:

I'm actually already on my way out for drinks. College acquaintance is looking to get into consulting. Don't wait up.

My stomach plunges and my heart starts racing. Is he going to meet Marcie? No. Marcie lives in New York. What would she be doing in Chicago on a Friday night? Especially since Patrick said he'd be home tonight. Don't freak out, I tell myself. He has gone out for drinks and career counseling before.

Still, unable to stop myself, I text back,

Really? Where?

This time five full minutes pass before Patrick texts back,

Not sure. We're going to meet at his office and decide from there.

Knowing I'm risking coming off clingy or worse, I text back,

Oh, where does he work?

Another five minutes pass before Patrick shuts down the conversation with,

Google, Maeve. See you tomorrow.

Google is in Fulton Market. With Friday traffic it could take twenty minutes to get there by cab. By that time, Patrick and his friend (or Marcie) may already be off to a bar. But before I can pull the crazy train back into the station, I'm throwing on my coat and heading for the elevator. Upon entering the cab, I tell the driver in no uncertain terms the faster he gets me to Google the bigger his tip. The driver is thankfully sufficiently motivated by my offer and we pull up to the internet giant's front doors in thirteen minutes flat.

I get out, toss four fives at the driver, and scan my surroundings. It's a veritable bar and restaurant mecca. One I've never been to. I have no idea where Patrick would take his friend. Just then a bro in a long black coat and cosmetic glasses exits the building staring intently at his phone. I take a chance.

"Excuse me. Do you work at Google?"

He nods barely taking his eyes from the screen.

Bingo! "I'm supposed to meet a friend for a drink but before he could give me the name, my phone died. Do you guys have a favorite bar I should try?"

Now frantically responding to a text, the bro grunts. "Aviary. Up the street. Amazing cocktails."

I offer a cursory thanks before sprinting in the direction indicated. Just up the next block I spy a grey awning with The Aviary written in script. Once outside, I slow my pace and scan the bar through the large front windows. There are dozens of virtually identical young, well-dressed men sitting at the bar enjoying fluorescent-colored drinks. But none of them appear to be Patrick. Undeterred, I turn around and make a second pass. Still, no sign of my husband. I take a deep breath and on my third pass, open the heavy front doors, and enter the drinking establishment. Unsure of my next step, I approach the hostess and ask for a drink menu to peruse. Using the menu as a mask, I make one more pass around the restaurant. No dice. I then chance a glance at my watch and see it is now a quarter past six. A curtain of shame descends. I'll be late for daycare pickup. And for what? A wild goose chase. Jesus, Maeve. You're better than this. I do the walk of shame back to the hostess station to return the menu. Just then out of the corner of my eye I spy Patrick's lithe frame emerging from the bathroom. I freeze, but he makes a beeline to the bar. I dart outside and peer through the front glass. A waitress has positioned herself to the front and left of Patrick, blocking my view of his companion. The Ludacris line about a bitch being in his way goes through my mind. A moment or two passes before the waitress heads back to the kitchen, revealing the nondescript head of a brown-haired man sitting next to Patrick. So he was telling the truth. He wasn't meeting Marcie after all. I exhale deeply before frantically hailing a cab to pick up my boys.

***

After apologizing profusely to the daycare director for my tardy pickup, I speed through the usual bedtime routine. In record time, I'm pouring myself a glass of Meritage and ordering an old favorite, *Bed of Roses*, on Amazon Prime. Patrick hates this movie, but I'm a sucker for Mary Stuart Masterson's character. The type A corporate executive who never lets anyone get close to her until a strange florist played by Christian Slater sends her flowers. Awwww romance.

After pouring myself a second glass of wine, I become nostalgic for the early days with Patrick. We met at Tommy Nevin's Pub, a popular Northwestern hangout. We were both in our first semester—him in the business school and me in law school. Patrick knew a 1L, the slang term for first year law students, from his college days at Notre Dame and came over to our table to say hello. I was instantly attracted to him. He seemed to pick up that I was interested and asked if I wanted to play darts. We spent the rest of the night talking about our pasts. I gave the sterilized version. I grew up an only child in a boring suburb outside of Indianapolis. My father was a lawyer and my mother a homemaker (at least that was the image she projected to our friends and neighbors). Both had since passed away. Patrick grew up in a big Irish Catholic family in Chicago. And he was funny. I remember almost falling off my bar stool laughing at his stories of trying to sneak past his mother, Mary, and join his friends' plot to sneak into Wrigley.

After a few dates, Patrick invited me to Sunday dinner at his parents' and I fell hook, line and sinker. They were exactly the type of family I had been looking for my whole life. All four siblings gathered around the table swapping stories. Mary in the kitchen making a meal large enough to feed twice as many people. Patrick's dad, Cormac, ribbing his kids about childhood embarrassments while drinking a beer and holding a grandbaby. I think I fell in love with Patrick's family before him. But I did fall in love with Patrick. And we had a great relationship...at one point. Long Sunday afternoons in our apartment in Evanston watching marathon sessions of *Law & Order* on our cheap tube television set. Our post-bar trip to Costa Rica. Ten days of zip lining, hiking, swimming in hot springs and sunbathing on gorgeous beaches. Not to mention the many passion fruit margaritas we imbibed while talking for hours about how we could stay in Manuel Antonio forever and support ourselves by opening a decent coffee shop.

With these rosy memories floating through my head, I tell myself that our current state of affairs isn't that perilous. Patrick was just feeling a bit lonely. It may have even been a couple night fling with Marcie that's already over. I turn off the movie and go to bed.

When I wake and check my Fitbit, I see it's almost four. Patrick is to my right lying spread eagle on his stomach clad only in his tighty whities. I wonder when he finally made it home. Seems like quite a late night for drinks with a college acquaintance. I get up and use the bathroom so I can hopefully sleep another three hours before the boys wake. As I pass the dresser on my way back to bed, I notice Patrick's jeans and sweater tossed on the floor next to it. He must have had quite a few drinks. He always puts away his clothes unless he's had a few too many. My type-A personality can't stand the clutter, so I pick up his things and start folding. As I make the second fold in his

Bonobos dark wash stretch jeans, my hand feels something hard. Patrick must have left his ID in his pocket. But as I fish the card out, all my suspicions are confirmed. Patrick was in room 648 of the Intercontinental Hotel tonight. He must have met Marcie after I left him at The Aviary.

Chapter 8

The bell rings and my third grade teacher, Miss Devlin, instructs us to get up from our desks quietly and slowly walk to our cubbies to retrieve our things. I pull my self-portrait down from the top shelf where I stored it so it wouldn't get rumpled in my backpack. I can't wait to show Mom. I worked on it over four art classes. Whereas other kids had moved on to landscapes, I sat at my table mixing colors to get my green eye color and light brown hair just right. I had drawn and redrawn my mouth at least six times so that the shape was natural and not cartoonish like the other kids. I knew if Mom could see how hard I worked and how pretty I am, it would make her less sad.

"Maeve, please get in line, dear," Miss Devlin calls. "We mustn't keep your parents or the buses waiting." We all know it is Miss Devlin who doesn't want to wait. Having been written off as a spinster by the school moms, dumpy Miss Devlin with the garish floral dresses found herself a boyfriend at the age of forty-three. He picks her up every day at precisely three-fifteen.

I quickly throw on my backpack, but keep my drawing in my hands turned toward me so as to not attract any attention. Lea already called me a "slowpoke" after she had finished her own drawing on day two. I politely didn't mention that in her portrait her right eye is about an inch higher than her left. When I reach the end of the line, Miss Devlin starts the procession out the door and down the hall to the entranceway. We file past the mint-green lockers of the middle graders and out the large double doors.

Outside, the line splits in two. One group goes off to the awaiting yellow school buses. I remain with the other group: those of us who live close enough to the school to be picked up by our mothers at the end of each day.

For a few minutes, my friend Sara and I recount the fight that happened at recess after Bobby hit Joe in the face with a dodgeball. Joe was so mad, he ran at Bobby and tried to shove him to the ground. But Bobby, who is twice as big, stayed on his feet and punched Joe right in the stomach. Coach Wilson took Bobby to the principal's office while Joe was sent crying to the nurse. Joe came back during readers' workshop with an ice pack on his cheek where the dodgeball hit, the outline of a developing bruise already visible. Principal Keller must have sent Bobby home. Our class couldn't stop speculating as to the extent of his punishment. Becky even bet that Bobby had been expelled!

Then Sara is picked up by her silver-haired grandma in her green plaid house dress who can't stop apologizing for her tardiness. She lost track of time while making blueberry pies. She promises to bring Miss Devlin one tomorrow as an apology. That leaves just me and Miss Devlin on the stairs. A few more minutes pass and I can tell she's getting antsy. Miss Devlin is glancing at her watch with increasing frequency and letting out longer sighs each time. All the while keeping her eye out for a certain Audi Quattro driven by her car salesman boyfriend.

Finally, I spy our silver Chrysler New Yorker coming down the street and say a silent thank you to God for answering my prayers. But then it strikes me how slow Mom is driving. It's odd because Mom is never one to obey the speed limit. After what feels like an eternity, Mom slows to a stop right in front of the school. As she opens the door, I turn to say goodbye to Miss Devlin. Before I can say anything, Miss Devlin gasps. I follow her gaze back to my mom who is on all fours in her white tee and jean skirt. She must have tripped getting out of the car. The world seems to move in slow motion, as I watch my mom reach for the driver's door for help getting back to her feet. Slowly, she gets to one knee before being able to drag herself back up to vertical. She sways briefly before backing up and lowering herself down to the driver's seat. She takes a deep breath, lifts her sunglass-covered eyes and slurs, "Come on, Maevey. Time to go home."

I take a step, but Miss Devlin grabs my arm.

"Maeve, honey, go back inside. I'm going to talk to your Mom for a minute."

My Mom will be furious if Miss Devlin embarrasses her, so I try to break her grip and continue. "Miss Devlin, my mom is kind of in a rush. I better go."

Miss Devlin tightens her hold, looks me in the eye and orders, "You are not to get in that car, Maeve. Go to the office and call your father for a ride. I'll talk to your mom."

Knowing how angry my father is going to be when I pull him away from work again, I drag my feet down the hallway. I foresee how the night will progress. My dad screaming expletives while my mom stammers out some pathetic excuse for why she couldn't be trusted to drive me home from school on a Wednesday afternoon. The front door slamming as my dad returns to the office. Mom crying herself to sleep on the couch. It is only then that I realize I'm still carrying my self-portrait. I look down and for the first time see how truly pathetic it is. My eyes are much too big. My mouth isn't centered and my nose takes up half the page. I sit with my back to the middle grade lockers and tear the picture over and over again. I am still shredding it into increasingly miniscule squares as my father ascends the front stairs, fuming.

Chapter 9

After three tentative rings of Zara's doorbell, I depress the button fully and let it continue to ring until I hear a sleepy but angry voice answer the intercom.

"Listen, asshole. I have no problem calling the cops. Go sleep it off elsewhere."

I take a deep breath to steady my voice before responding apologetically, "Zara, it's Maeve. I know it's late, but please let me in."

"Maeve!" Zara exclaims. "Are you okay? Come straight up."

The door buzzes and I hurry through the entrance to the elevator bank. Zara lives in a hip two-bedroom flat in the newly revitalized Fulton Market district. Not far away from where I was stalking Patrick earlier this evening. A fresh flash of anger surges through me. When the elevator doors open on the fourth floor, Zara is standing there wrapped in a cute monogrammed white, silk robe that falls to her knees. The sight of her waiting with open arms undoes me. Tears stream down my face as she envelops me in a hug and squeezes tightly. As I start to sob into her shoulder, she gently ushers me across the hall to her apartment.

Once through the door, Zara morphs into caregiver mode. She leads me to her comfortable aubergine couch where I immediately curl up in my usual corner. Zara throws a warm wool blanket over my legs and sets off to the kitchen. She returns minutes later carrying a wooden tray filled with two wine glasses, an open bottle of pinot noir and a large Hershey's bar. She pours approximately a third of a bottle into a wine glass and hands it to me. She then gets herself settled with a similarly large pour before curling into the opposite end of the couch.

Taking a bite of chocolate and washing it down with a sip of wine, she bluntly inquires, "So, your 'save my marriage' plan isn't going as well as you had hoped?"

Her brutal honesty breaks the ice and makes me laugh, a feat I would have thought impossible a moment ago.

When I recover I admit, "I guess you could say that. Patrick apparently snuck out to shag Marcie tonight."

"Marcie? I thought it was Macy?" Zara questions.

"I think he was using a pseudonym to give me the slip. I found a Marcie Spellman on his company's web page who seems to fit the bill: same practice group as Patrick, attractive, athletic, successful. Basically just better than me." With that I take a long sip of wine.

"Stop it!" Zara orders and slaps my leg. "I'm sure she's a bitch and I'd hate her," she says, giving me one of her sarcastic grins.

"Well, bitch or not, it seems my husband enjoys fucking her." Saying it out loud makes the hurt that much more intense. Without realizing what I'm doing, I grab one of the white marble throw pillows behind me, bury my mouth in it, and emit a long primal scream. Once Zara recovers from her shock, she sits her glass next to mine and crawls over to my corner to wrap me in a big hug. After a few minutes, my frustration subsides and I relax into Zara's embrace resting my head against her shoulder. We lie like that for what seems like an hour. Finally, as I'm starting to doze off, Zara gets practical.

"You need to text Patrick and let him know you're here. Tell him I had boy trouble and asked you to come stay with me. Tell him I'm in a right state and you're staying through Saturday. He can handle the boys for once. We'll have a girls' day."

Happy to let her take care of the details, I hand her my phone, pull the blanket up to my chin and close my eyes.

I awake at almost ten to the same tray as last night, but this time filled with two steaming mugs of coffee and accoutrements. Zara is wearing a Lululemon ensemble of black leggings and a green strappy-back tank, her pixie hair held back from her face by a merlot headband. I'm now acutely aware of my swollen, red eyes and puffy face. Zara sits down purposefully at the far end of the couch to lay out the day's itinerary.

"I know that movement makes you feel better so I've signed us up for the ten forty-five hot yoga class at Zen. Then a boozy brunch before our two o'clock massages at The Peninsula." As I start to interrupt, Zara reads my mind and adds, "You can borrow clothes." She then looks me in the eye and raises her index finger. "One rule: No talking about Patrick until we're back here for dinner and movies. You deserve an afternoon of pampering and no stress. Deal?"

I let out a sigh of relief. "How can I resist? I can't recall the last time I've had a day off. Thank you." My love for Zara swells in my chest as I wrap my hands around her large "What Would RBG Do?" mug and take my first sip of coffee.

Zara stands up and commands, "We don't have much time so start getting ready." She then tosses me my cell phone and informs me, "Patrick texted back. He's fine with you staying over again."

I let the facial recognition open my iPhone to read my texts. There are a couple from Patrick responding to Zara.

That's fine. I can handle the boys today. And tell Zara those losers don't deserve her. Love you.

Reading those last two words feels like Patrick stabbed a knife straight into my heart. A text from less than an hour ago is more practical:

Remember Sunday lunch at my parents. Will you meet us there?

The monthly family gathering at the Shaw house. Usually one of the things I look forward to. At least there will be plenty of people there to minimize any awkward alone time. I text back quickly:

Yep. See you there. Give kisses to the boys.

I decisively put all thoughts of Patrick away as I enter Zara's walk-in closet to get dressed for the day. Turns out when you don't spend all of your money on daycare, you use it to buy super cute clothes.

***

Sitting on Zara's couch eating veggie sushi feels like the perfect ending to a surprisingly relaxing day. Zara signed us up for the Purva Karma at the Peninsula Spa, which involves two massage therapists using multiple different body oils to achieve the "ultimate in tension release." Sure, it was almost five hundred dollars, but I may never need a man again. No wonder Jennifer Aniston insists on staying at that hotel when she's in Chicago. The Purva Karma is far superior to Brad Pitt and Justin Theroux put together!

The night got even better when we stumbled across old episodes of *The Practice* on Netflix. Zara and I obsessed over this show during our freshman year of college. Both wanting to be attorneys at that time, we idolized Lara Flynn Boyle's ultimate badass character. She was hot, smart, ruthless, and got to flirt with Bobby Donnell aka Dylan McDermott. Unsurprisingly, Zara and I did both follow legal paths. Although Zara didn't attend law school, she's happily employed as the director of legal recruiting at a large firm. As Zara returns from the kitchen with a chilled bottle of sauvignon blanc to finish off our dinner, I remember that spring is the start of her busy season. She's responsible for wooing the stars of the top law schools to choose Brown & McKay as the place to begin their promising legal careers.

"Is your summer class full of youthful candidates wearing rose-colored glasses and dreaming of becoming the next Alan Dershowitz?" I inquire.

"Give me a break," Zara responds, rolling her eyes. "These millennials are so entitled. They just want to know how much money they can make putting in as few billable hours as possible."

"Well, they need that money to pay for their expensive blow habits," I point out, referencing one of the stickier situations Zara had to disentangle in her years babysitting third-year law students. A certain cocky Harvard student slipped Zara a one hundred-dollar bill at a firm-sponsored happy hour and asked her to score him some coke. Zara had to walk the tightrope of making sure the junkie law student didn't receive an offer from Brown & McKay while maintaining a friendly relationship with Harvard, which expects all of their law students to receive offers at the end of the summer.

"Ugh!" Zara pushes herself upright so she can reach the coffee table. "Knock on wood there are no Bryces in this year's summer class."

I giggle. "But seriously, I say more power to them," pausing to take a sip of my cool, crisp wine. "Maybe the millennials can finally figure out a way to get the heads of these firms to take work/life balance seriously. When firms realize they can't find anyone willing to work twenty-five hundred hours a year, even for exorbitant salaries, maybe they'll become a bit more reasonable about their expectations."

Zara laughs heartily spilling a few drops of wine on her red and green plaid flannel pajamas. "Not likely. They'll always be able to find people like you. People willing to kill themselves in order to see the word 'partner' underneath their name."

"Ouch," I wince.

"That's not a dig," Zara hastily assures me. "It's just a fact. There will always be ambitious people."

"Yep," I say bitterly. "People like me willing to flush a wonderful marriage and family down the toilet in search of a title."

"Hey now." Zara puts down her glass and shoots me a serious look. "That's not what I was saying and you know it's not true. You work hard, sure, but so does Patrick. And you're a wonderful wife to him and mother to those adorable boys. He's the one who flushed your marriage down the toilet by screwing a coworker."

I take another sip for courage before retorting, "Well, nothing is flushed yet."

Zara's jaw drops. "You're not seriously staying with Patrick after Friday night, are you?" She throws one of the couch cushions at me and scolds, "Maeve, you're better than this."

I was prepared for this reaction. I knew this day of decadence was a pre-divorce-filing present. I didn't challenge her assumption because I wasn't ready to deal with her disappointment. But I knew eventually this had to be said. "Zara, nothing has changed since I called you last weekend. I knew Patrick was cheating then and I was committed to winning him back. I still am."

Zara's shock quickly turns to anger. "Then why the hell did you show up weeping on my doorstep at four a.m. if you're just going to continue letting Patrick treat you like a doormat!"

I close my eyes to absorb the impact of Zara's words. We're silent for a couple of minutes while I compose myself. "I'm sorry I've been such a mess this last week and have been leaning on you so heavily. That wasn't fair and it won't happen again. I won't keep putting all of my emotional crap on you. But I am going to keep my family together," I say firmly. "Those three are the only family I have."

After a few minutes of awkward silence pass, I add lightly, "Jesus, Beyonce didn't file for divorce when Jay-Z cheated and she's fucking Beyonce."

Zara manages a weak chuckle before noting, "Yeah, but I don't think Patrick is worth half a billion." A minute or so passes and I can tell Zara is struggling with her next response. I also know Zara has never chosen the tough love approach when it comes to me. I see her shoulders slump before she concedes, "I'm always here for you, Maeve. Show up at my door at any time. Call in the middle of the night. I'll be here."

With that she gives my leg a quick squeeze and we both pick up our wine glasses to return to the fictional drama of *The Practice*. But after a bit Zara can't help but add quietly, "You of all people should know growing up in a two-parent household doesn't always guarantee *Family Ties*. Sometimes it turns out more like *Breaking Bad*."

***

I arrive at the Shaw house on Sunday morning after enjoying a slow three-mile jog along The 606. During the half hour I was on the converted train track, I thought back to when I started running. It began simply as an excuse to escape my house. But as I kept at it, I started to revel in the strength and confidence running gave me. As I pushed my screaming legs mile after mile, I started to believe there may come a day when I wouldn't cower in fear of my father's rages and my mother's meltdowns. I would finally choose to fight back. While that ultimately hadn't worked out with my parents, I needed the same strength and courage to fight now. Fight for the kind of family I had prayed for as a child.

The exact type of family I had married into. Mary and Cormac have lived in the same bungalow on Marshfield Street in Lincoln Park for the last fifty years. Of course, when they bought their house the average price was less than six figures. Now, all of the new builds are firmly in the seven-figure range. As soon as I walk through the doorway, Declan and Seamus run, or in Shay's case, toddle, into my arms as if it's been a week since they last saw me. Cue mom guilt. Looking around, it appears the rest of the family has already arrived. Patrick and his brothers Connor and Aiden are sitting together on the living room couch watching *SportsCenter*. The couch is a relic from the seventies, velour with a farm scene pattern, but still comfortable. It fits well in the room with its faux wood wallpaper. Aiden's daughter Erin runs by holding her bear lovie and searching for Mom. For some reason, I've never bonded with Aiden's and Connor's wives. I've always felt, maybe unfairly, they didn't approve of my decision to continue working after Seamus was born. Susan and Allison were both teachers who quit their jobs shortly after having their first child. It made sense given the cost of daycare. And they are amazing moms who volunteer at all the school events. I pale in comparison. I've always gotten along well with Patrick's sister Megan, a yoga instructor. But since she lives in Denver, we only see her over holidays.

I give Patrick a little wave as I pass through the living room and let him continue his in-depth analysis of the pathetic goalie who has been subbing for Corey Crawford as of late. That the Blackhawks are unlikely to make the playoffs has been the main topic of Patrick's family group texts. As I enter the kitchen I see Mary with her apron over her house dress at her usual spot in front of the sink washing dishes. Through the window she watches the children play at the park that abuts their house. Mary loves washing dishes. She told me once she found the repetitiveness therapeutic. I grab a drying towel and take my usual spot next to her. Mary, who is all of four foot eleven inches, looks up at me with a kind smile.

"Oh, Maeve, honey. So glad you could make it."

"I wouldn't miss one of your Sunday lunches, Mary. I've already got my eye on your spiced apple cake. Diet be damned." I laugh.

Mary lightly smacks me with her dishrag and scolds, "Don't let me hear you talking about dieting. You're too thin as it is. Now, how is our sweet Zara doing? Patrick told me you stayed with her last night because she's having some boy trouble."

Zara has attended a few Sunday lunches and Mary always dotes on her. "Oh, she's fine," I say truthfully. "She just needed some pampering and is back to her usual fiery self."

Mary looks thoughtful and we clean and dry a few sauce-pans in silence before she continues, "You know boys come and go, but family is forever. Whether that be family you are born into or the ones you adopt as your own. Look at you and Zara. You both didn't have siblings, so you adopted each other. And just like you were a part of this family long before you and Patrick were married."

I look at the ceiling to compose myself. Mary drops the coffee mug she was washing back into the sink and puts her arm around my waist.

"There, there, Maeve," she comforts. "No need to get upset. I'm always here for you."

I wonder if that's true. Would Mary still think of me as a daughter if Patrick and I were divorced? Or would Marcie take my place by the sink washing dishes? Before I can go down this rabbit hole, I feel Declan's hand on my leg. And then a warm, moist mass sprays across the bottom of Zara's boot-cut jeans. Declan, now crying, has just purged his breakfast of what looks like eggs and sausage onto me.

Declan belatedly informs me, "Mama, I don't feel good."

"Oh, sweetie." I pick him up while Mary tries her best to salvage Zara's jeans. Patrick comes into the kitchen a few seconds later carrying Seamus.

"Shit, Maeve," he says, assessing the damage. "You want to go home?"

Seeing an opportunity to avoid Patrick a bit longer, I decide to appear magnanimous. "That's okay. I'll take the boys home. You enjoy the game with your brothers."

"Are you sure?" He hesitates. "What if Dec gets sick again? I should be there to help."

"I can handle it," I assure him with a large smile. "You've taken care of them all weekend. I need a little snuggle time with my guys."

"Well, if you're okay with it, I did bring my suitcase in case lunch ran late. I could head straight to the airport from here."

Perfect. I can use the next couple of days to reconfigure my marriage-saving game plan. I give quick kisses on the cheek to Mary and Patrick, take Seamus's hand, and am out the door and into a waiting Lyft in less than five minutes. Bet our driver wishes he'd taken a pass on this ride, as the smell of vomit wafts from my jeans. With one boy in the crook of each arm, I consider my next move. After the events of Friday night, I think something dramatic is in order to recapture Patrick's attention.

Chapter 10

Since daycare will not take Declan less than twenty-four hours after a vomiting incident, I drop the boys off with their grandparents and am sipping coffee from my Yeti while navigating traffic down to the Cook County Circuit Court. I always feel like such a stereotypical mom driving my maroon Honda Odyssey. I try to counteract the effect by listening to what the "cool kids" like on the radio. Currently, that's "God's Plan" by Drake. I sing the line about only loving my bed and mamma to Seamus in the bath to make him laugh. Yeah, I'm hard like that.

I arrive at the courthouse better known by its location as "26th and Cal." A large, square, brick building with eight columns strangely located in the middle of the facade above the large entrance doors. The neighborhood is a bit on the sketchy side, so I park in the jurors' lot across the street. Entering the front doors, I flash my attorney registration card at the security guards so I can bypass the long line and metal detector and proceed toward the courtrooms. I spot Ethan and Tom Gaines waiting for me by the benches outside the last courtroom on the right. I would guess Tom to be around fifty-five years old and six four with a linebacker's build. Ethan must be telling the truth about Tom's book of business because here he is in criminal court surrounded by legal aid attorneys in Target suits wearing a custom-made Michael Andrews Bespoke creation, a two-button navy twill suit with a coordinating vest that costs more than what these lawyers pull down in a month. I had been feeling pretty confident about my own Calvin Klein gray sheath dress with black pumps, but no longer.

As I approach them, I extend my hand to Tom. While I'm not happy about this assignment, I won't let my personal feelings get in the way of me schmoozing someone who could play an integral role in me obtaining partnership.

"Thank you for requesting that I be staffed on this case," I say in what I hope sounds like an ambitious tone. "I've read through the case summaries and reviewed the crime scene photos. Pretty sordid stuff. But charging a mother with the premeditated murder of her only daughter seems unwarranted. And their heartless pageant mom theory is weak. I'm excited to finally meet Tammy and hear her side."

Tom firmly shakes my hand while declaring in his deep, baritone voice, "She's heartless. They got that right." Tom drops my hand before reconsidering his position and adding, "Doesn't mean she did it, mind you. But she's no Tami Taylor." With that he retrieves his coat and Tumi briefcase from the bench.

I was prepared for this. Well, maybe not for the *Friday Night Lights* reference, but for the rest of it. Tom has a reputation for being a hard ass. Many associates avoid him, but I never held his rumored rudeness against him. Tom is African American and was a federal prosecutor before deciding to make money by moving to Big Law. It isn't easy being a minority lawyer now, let alone thirty years ago when Tom was making a name for himself. I assume he had to be tough as nails to climb the ladder as quickly as he did.

I follow Tom and Ethan as they stride into the courtroom. It's empty save for the deputy on duty. Tom announces he's going to meet our client Tammy Sanford in the holding cell. The deputy nods and returns to his magazine. Oddly enough a copy of *Marie Claire*. Go figure. We exit the courtroom through the farthest door and enter a hallway leading to the lockup. There are two large enclosures, one for the male and one for the female prisoners. The men's cell is first on our right. We arouse their interest immediately, figuratively and literally. Tom comes into their view first and a few yell comments about him being a "fancy ass lawyer" while others ask him to take their case. The second I come into eyesight the heckles switch to overtly sexual. "Nice ass." "You ever been fucked by a real man?" Etc. I risk a quick glance into the cell and notice an open urinal that is currently being used by an inmate. I also notice a man at the bars with face tats sticking his tongue between his index and middle fingers and simulating oral sex.

Feeling like I've taken more than my fair share of shit from men as of late, something inside me snaps and I shock myself as I turn to Face Tats and say, "Why, now that you mention it, I don't believe I have been fucked by a real man. Can I give you my number and you can call me in what…say, five to ten years?"

There's a moment of shocked silence before raucous laughter fills the jail. Even Face Tats is laughing before yelling something that sounds like, "Give me a pen, sweetheart."

Tom, on the other hand, is pissed. He walks back, grabs my arm and hisses, "Please control yourself," while quickly escorting me to the women's side.

Embarrassed, I scan the women seated on the benches against the wall to find Tammy. I don't see her. Tom looks to the far left corner of the cell and calls to an overweight woman with stringy dyed blond hair and three-inch brown roots. Just like her daughter, I note. She looks up, but doesn't react until she spots Ethan. Once she locates him her face lights up and she shimmies her way over to the bars. I realize the reason I didn't recognize her is because she's at least fifty pounds heavier than she was in her mugshot. In the picture she'd appeared a bit gaunt, perhaps from worrying about her heroin-addicted daughter. Seems like now she's eating her sorrow. Can't say I blame her.

While Tammy is pointedly making a beeline to Ethan, Tom steps in front of him and cuts right to the point. "Tammy, as you know, we are here today to set a trial date. Most likely the judge will want us to proceed within the next three months, but we'll push for as much time as he'll allow so we can retain and prepare our expert. We won't be able to talk after the hearing as I'd hoped because something popped up on another case that requires my attention. We'll come to the jail on Thursday. Does that work?"

Tammy is visibly upset and whines, "I don't want to push the trial date. I want my trial now. I *need* to get out of here."

"Don't we all, sweetie," one of her fellow inmates chimes in. They're all staring at us and hanging on our every word. Seeing as there is no television in the cell I guess we're the entertainment.

Tom ignores his fan club and reasonably explains, "You won't be getting out at all if we don't have adequate time to prepare your defense. But, as I said before, the judge is also anxious to set a quick date. Your case has been pending for two and a half years after all. He wants to clean up his docket."

Clearly having said all he intended to, Tom makes a move for the exit. Tammy stops him in his tracks with, "You going to at least introduce me to your secretary?"

Tom and I are stunned silent, but Ethan steps toward Tammy and smoothly introduces me as his fellow senior associate Maeve Shaw. "She'll be taking Nicole's place on our team now that Nicole's out on sick leave. Maeve is brilliant and already well versed in the facts of this case. I think you'll find her a strong advocate for your innocence."

As Tammy is still sulking, Ethan puts his hand over hers on the bar and amps up the charm. "I know you're anxious to have some closure to this tragedy, but try to be patient. The trial will be here before you know it and we'll be able to talk over our defense strategy on Thursday." Ethan's plan works. Tammy smiles adoringly at him as he releases her hand.

We begin to follow Tom back to the courtroom when a female inmate catches my eye. She looks to be about fifty and she's seated away from the other inmates. Her hair is a pretty shade of brown with light red highlights and it's styled in a fashionable bob. Her hands were recently manicured, but they are shaking. She's also sweating even though the holding cell is quite cool. Classic signs of drug withdrawal. I can tell she's doing her best to hide it, but her eyes are wide with fear.

A vision of my own mother flashes before my eyes. Having been caught forging scripts, she sat in a similar holding cell praying my father would use his influence to make the charges go away. I push the memory away and instead walk back to Tammy to give her a firm handshake. "I'm excited to join your defense team and look forward to talking with you more on Thursday."

Tammy refuses to acknowledge me. Instead, looking at Ethan, she inquires anxiously, "How's Rapscallion? Have you been to see him lately?"

Ethan's cheeks flush pink with embarrassment. "He's fine, Tammy. I saw him this weekend and took him a bone."

"Thank you," Tammy says breathily and adds, "you're a peach."

As we re-enter the courtroom, my curiosity gets the best of me. "So…who's Rapscallion?"

Ethan tersely responds, "Her award-winning Papillon. He's boarded at a kennel in nowheresville. Every couple of months I rent a car, drive down there, and bring back proof of life pictures."

My interest has peaked. "So after Kyleigh stops winning trophies, she replaces her with Rapscallion? Dogs are probably easier to train than teenagers," I concede.

Ethan lets my comment hang and we take our seat behind the counsel's tables to wait for our case to be called. Tom turns to Ethan and gruffly admonishes, "I get you're playing good cop to my bad cop, but we can't set unrealistic expectations. There's a good chance Tammy will see jail time from this. If you blow smoke up her ass until trial, she won't be prepared for losing and could start throwing around words like"—air quotes—"'inadequate representation of counsel.' You can stay on her good side while ensuring she's aware of the risks."

Ethan just nods his head. I get the feeling this isn't the first time he's heard this lecture.

Tom then rounds on me. "As for you, Ms. Shaw. Learn to control yourself. I expect to witness no more childish outbursts."

I nod my head as my face burns hot with shame. So much for schmoozing. I'm thankfully saved from any further scolding by the entry of Judge Timothy Howard. A middle-aged man of smaller stature. My guess would be no taller than 5'5, with a receding hairline. Judge Howard has the air of a veteran of the bench. He scans the rows of lawyers waiting for their cases to be called and nods at a few. His expression noticeably brightens when his gaze falls on Tom. Clearly they have history.

"Mr. Gaines, you brought your entire trial team for a simple scheduling hearing? Doesn't Mulvaney Stewart have any billable cases these young associates can attend to?" Judge Howard taunts.

Tom stands in greeting. "Good morning, Your Honor. The hearing just gave us a chance to speak to our client. We wanted to introduce her to a new associate on our team, Maeve Shaw," Tom says, indicating me. I nod nervously.

Judge Howard smiles at me while picking up Tammy's case file. "Well, let's get you on your way then. Calling the case of *The State of Illinois vs. Tammy Sanford*."

A tall, thin lawyer from the state's attorney's office, whom I've been told is Al Porter, rises. Ethan said he has a hard-on for seeing Tammy behind bars for life. We all proceed to the bench. I've appeared at probably a hundred or so status hearings over the course of my twelve-year career and yet my stomach still tightens whenever approaching the formal wood desk behind which a judge looks down ominously. Even when, as today, I will no doubt play a non-speaking role. We wait a few moments for the deputy to fetch Tammy and bring her out to stand behind us. I venture to give her a sympathetic smile, but she continues to ignore me. Guess I'm no Ethan.

Once the deputy gives the thumbs up that the prisoner is secured, Judge Howard greets us, "Good morning, Mr. Porter and Mr. Gaines. As you know we're here today to set a trial in this matter. I propose thirty days from today or April thirtieth. What say you?"

Mr. Porter is immediately agreeable. "That works for the State, Your Honor."

Tom's eyes widen to the size of saucers and he sputters, "Your Honor, the defense can't possibly be ready in that short of time frame. Let me remind you, we only entered our appearance on behalf of Ms. Sanford in December. We've been reviewing evidence and contacting witnesses the last few months. We have yet to retain an expert to refute the findings of the medical examiner. We won't be ready to proceed to trial before the fall."

Now it's Judge Howard's turn to look outraged. "Let me remind you, Mr. Gaines, that this isn't a multi-million-dollar civil case you can drag out for a decade. This case has been pending for two and a half years. During that time, Ms. Sanford has remained in custody without having her guilt established.

I'm sure she's more than ready to have her day in court."

Tom is growing more agitated by the second. "And let me remind you, Your Honor, the reason my client has remained behind bars is because she was appointed a legal aid attorney who spent the first six months trying to convince her to plead guilty to first degree murder and, when it was apparent Ms. Sanford wouldn't take the plea, spent the next year missing court dates and avoiding my client's calls. It is unfair to punish Ms. Sanford's current counsel for its predecessor's unethical behavior."

Tom's depiction of prior counsel's misconduct seems to strike a chord with Judge Howard. He takes a moment before proceeding more calmly. "Be that as it may, Mr. Gaines, you have the resources of one of the top law firms in the country at your disposal and a team of top associates to do the grunt work. While thirty days may have been a tough deadline, I will not keep Ms. Sanford in prison another six months. Trial is set for June ninth and no future requests for continuance will be granted. I trust that date works for the State, Mr. Porter?"

Mr. Porter, clearly enjoying watching Tom squirm, answers, "It does, Your Honor."

"Good. Next case." With a bang of his gavel, our hearing concludes.

Tom barrels past Tammy, grabs his briefcase from the benches, and storms out of the courtroom. Ethan gives Tammy a quick, "See you, Thursday," before hurrying to catch up.

Seeing as I'm newest to the team, and probably the last person Tom wants to talk to at the moment, I linger while retrieving my purse. As Tammy is being led back to the cells she briefly turns her head toward the courtroom exit doors and I'm surprised to see a big smile across her face. Seems she got exactly what she wanted out of the hearing. When Tammy sees me watching, the smile fades and she turns away.

By the time I leave the courtroom, Tom and Ethan have both vanished. Once I'm safely inside my mom-mobile, the feelings I'd kept repressed all morning surface with a vengeance. My whole body is shaking, I'm sweating profusely, and I hurriedly re-open my door as I begin to dry heave. A middle-aged prospective juror sees me and offers help, but I wave her off. Another ten minutes pass before my stomach settles enough for me to get back in the car. Then another ten before my hands stop shaking enough to grip the wheel. My drive back to the office takes a bit longer than it should as I employ some meditation techniques I learned from my college counselor. At one time, I was employing these techniques daily, but over the years I find I need them less and less. Now I only need them when I've encountered a trigger…a prison for example.

I'm finally parking in the garage across the street from my building when I hear the pings of what sound like ten emails hitting my inbox at once. When I'm in park, I grab my phone and see a number of new emails all from Tom. As I start opening them, I realize they all comprise a big to-do list. He must be emailing tasks as they occur to him. The first email orders Ethan to call the four potential experts and schedule interviews within the week. The second one directs me to go through the evidence and gather all documents, photos, reports, etc. that the experts will need to form an opinion as to cause of death. The third item is again for Ethan and requests that he contact the prison where "the boyfriend" is currently incarcerated and schedule a visit. The emails go back and forth assigning Ethan and me tasks such as beginning to identify witnesses to subpoena, tagging helpful photographs for use at trial, contacting the head of support services and requesting a paralegal be staffed on the case. And on and on. The sheer enormity of work that remains to be done before trial begins to dawn on me. How am I going to get all of this done and still bill a hundred and seventy-five additional hours to paying clients? What have I gotten myself into?

As my stress level shoots from its normal "barely keeping it together" all the way up to "losing my shit," I give Jeanine a curt hello and scurry into my office. The most time sensitive item on my to-do list is gathering the documents for the experts' review. Multitasking, I eat my tofurkey sandwich I packed this morning, while re-reading the medical examiner's report. Not exactly the best reading material when trying to enjoy a meal. If a few slabs of soybean conglomerate on wheat bread can even be described as a meal.

Doctor Lauren Fagen conducted Kyleigh's autopsy. The report starts off in the usual way: "The autopsy is begun at 8:30 a.m. on August 5, 2015. The deceased is wearing gray Hanes boxer briefs and a pink, lace camisole." The report goes on to note that the body is that of an undernourished twenty-four-year-old white female measuring sixty-four inches and weighing one hundred and five pounds. "Lividity is fixed in the distal portions of the limbs. The eyes are open. Petechial hemorrhaging is present in the conjunctival surfaces of the eyes." That fits with what little I know about strangulation. Petechiae or tiny red spots in the eyes are the result of ruptured capillaries. Common in strangulation cases, but not conclusive. But what is noteworthy is what Dr. Fagen didn't find. Namely finger marks or bruising around Kyleigh's neck. How did Tammy strangle her, but fail to leave a mark? Even if she used something like a belt or pillow case, it should still leave some marks or scratches. Also, Kyleigh's hyoid bone remained intact. This small horseshoe-shaped bone in the neck is almost always broken in these cases. Why didn't Dr. Fagen mention this anomaly?

The rest of the report doesn't add much. Dr. Fagen notes recent abrasions to Kyleigh's arms that could be indicative of a struggle. I posit they could have also been sustained by Kyleigh falling into furniture while high. My theory is bolstered by the fact that there are several minor contusions on Kyleigh's shins and knees that Dr. Fagen's states were sustained days prior to her death. Dr. Fagen also documented multiple needle marks on Kyleigh's arms, feet, and alarmingly, neck. I recall that addicts try their feet after the veins in their arms collapse. But only the really hardcore ones can stomach sticking a needle into their jugular. Not surprisingly, the toxicology report came back positive for opioids. I note Dr. Fagen's ultimate opinion, asphyxia due to strangulation, and drag the medical report into the file I've created cleverly entitled "docs for expert."

I spend the next two hours dragging relevant crime scene photographs into the same file. I don't want to overwhelm the expert with too many repetitive drug den pictures, so I include only a select sampling. All of the photos documenting how Kyleigh was found go into the folder. I then click open the police report of Detective Donald Myles.

Detective Myles arrived at the home of Simon Harr located on the 1300 block of Central Avenue at 10:13 a.m. He thoroughly documents the drug paraphernalia present in the home and notes that Simon Harr was known by the Chicago Police Department as a small time peddler of heroin and prescription drugs. Kyleigh's body was found in the first bedroom Detective Myles entered. Interestingly, Kyleigh's entire body had been wrapped tightly in a comforter. The police pulled the comforter off to attempt resuscitation, but quickly determined it was too late. Because of the police officers' haste in attempting to save Kyleigh, no photographs were taken of her while encased in the comforter. Still, how is the prosecutor going to explain that? Tammy jumps on top of a drugged-up Kyleigh and chokes her. Without leaving any marks, mind you. Then she climbs off and rolls her lifeless body into a burrito? For what purpose?

I glance at the time and am startled to realize I've spent six hours working on a non-billable matter with nary a billable hour to show for my day. I quickly close the Sanford file and open the document containing my second motion to dismiss for Elizabeth. I'll need to work on it the remaining two hours of my workday and maybe two or three hours after the boys are in bed to ward off Jabba's wrath.

Before opening Westlaw to locate a few cases supporting my lack of damages argument, I pick up my phone. An idea has been percolating since last night and I decide to run with it. I quickly text Zara.

If a girl is getting her first Brazilian what should she ask for?

I have always been staunchly opposed to waxing my nether regions. Partly because I'm afraid of the pain. Partly because I'm embarrassed. But mostly because I didn't think I needed to do anything to make my vaginal area more attractive. In the past, I've found that men are pretty much always up for sex. I didn't need to put a bow on my vajayjay to coax them into it. Now I'm not so sure. There has to be some reason Patrick wants Marcie's punani and not mine.

Zara immediately responds.

You're pathetic.

I'm grasping for what words to put into Google to elicit this information without summoning a tsunami of pornsites when I see the telltale three dots in our text string.

Tell them you want a full Brazilian but leave a landing strip.

Not sure what that means exactly, but trusting Zara's judgment, I pull up the Avieve website and book an appointment for eight a.m. tomorrow.

Chapter 11

After going old school and working out to my *Cindy Crawford: The Next Challenge* DVD, I lie down next to my boys. I let Declan sleep with me last night to ensure he was feeling better and for easier access to the bathroom in case of emergency. Seamus, sensing the injustice, woke up screaming at midnight and so also snagged a coveted spot in our bed. Rubbing their backs gently, I attempt to initiate the wake-up routine. Declan in his fleece gingerbread man pajamas from Christmas and Seamus in his fire truck-footed pjs make me smile. As I tousle their identical chestnut brown hair, it hits me, not for the first time, that I would literally do anything for them. The intense love I feel would make me jump in front of a car to save them without hesitation. Remaining in a potentially sexless marriage to give them the opportunity to grow up to be happy, confident adults is a no brainer. With that thought, I steel myself for this morning's unpleasantness and kissy monster the boys awake.

Waiting in the waxing room at Avieve, I'm a ball of nerves and anxiety. Kerrie has been my esthetician for the last six years, but until now that has only involved eyebrow waxes every six weeks. Nonetheless, Kerrie is a no nonsense, sturdy, middle-aged woman who has been at the salon for fifteen years. There is no one else I would entrust with my vaginal waxing virginity. As the door opens, I decide to lay it all out there:

"Kerrie, I have no idea what I'm doing. I've never even gotten a bikini wax before. You'll have to talk me through it," I blurt.

Kerrie professionally hides her shock, but tentatively questions, "If this is your first time, are you sure you want the full Brazilian? Maybe we should start with something easier and work our way up."

"No," I say adamantly, "I want the full treatment." I need something drastic to get Patrick's attention. Maybe he'll even be inspired to try some oral action. Something he's never really been into.

Swayed by my conviction, Kerrie gets practical. "Okay. Take off your jeans and put on this paper underwear. Then have a seat on the table and I'll be back shortly."

Sitting on the paper square in the middle of the treatment table with only the barest of coverage, I feel like I'm back in my obstetrician's office. When Kerrie returns and starts describing the breathing method we will employ before each "removal," the similarity is even more striking.

"Okay, now you are going to lie with your legs open in a butterfly position. Before each removal, I will ask you to take a deep breath in. I will pull the wax as you exhale. This breathing technique really does make it less painful," she assures me.

I feel the warm sensation of wax being painted near my labia. After Kerrie lets it dry for a moment she instructs, "Okay, breathe in."

I take in a deep shaky breath.

"Now exhale."

As I blow out, I feel the pain of hundreds of hairs being ripped out by the roots. Holy shit!

"How many more times are you going to do that? Ballpark?" I ask, while silently praying…please say ten or less. Please say ten or less.

Kerrie just laughs. "Oh, honey. We're just getting started. Now pull your right leg up toward your armpit."

I do as I'm instructed and my already fragile self-esteem heads decidedly south. Kerrie decides to lighten the mood by making chitchat.

"Do you have any summer vacation plans with the kids? Exhale." Rip.

Sweet Jesus! "Ummm…nothing planned yet," I fumble.

"Well, if you are planning on renting a lake house in Michigan, you better jump on it. Now, exhale." Rip.

For the love of God! I scream in my head as I try to coolly respond,

"Noted. I'll get on that straight away."

After thirty minutes of Lamaze breathing with my hands firmly clutching the sides of the table, I'm sure we must be near the end. Just when I've mustered enough courage to ask again, Kerrie appears at the head of the table looking slightly embarrassed.

"Okay, we're nearly done." Her gaze drops to the floor before she adds, "But...I'm going to need you on your knees and elbows for this last part."

As I crawl into position with my butt up in the air for the wax application near my anus, my dignity is in the toilet. Who the hell came up with this procedure and why do women subject themselves to it? Patrick sure as hell better appreciate this.

I text Zara the second my Lyft arrives to take me to the office.

Okay, you could've prepared me a bit better for that. Even just a heads up about the doggy-style position at the end would've helped.

OMG! I never thought you'd go through with it or I would have.

There is a pause for several seconds before another text pops up.

How exactly did you think they were going to yank the hair from there?

I concede the point. The truth is I was too uncomfortable with the concept to dive into the details. But, now that it's over, I have to admit I'm enjoying the results. Even the tiny V-shaped section of hair at the very top of my vajayjay known as a landing strip. Makes the results seem slightly less extreme. Now to implement part two of my scheme after work tonight.

I planned to spend most of the day on Elizabeth's work to try to make a dent in my billable hours target, but find my attention keeps being drawn back to the Tammy Sanford file. I guess murder is slightly sexier than student loan defaults. As I run through all the material in my "docs for expert" file, one anomaly keeps nagging at me. Why would Tammy wrap Kyleigh tightly in her comforter before making an exit? After strangling her only daughter, Tammy's adrenaline would have been through the roof and she would have fled the scene immediately, right? Unless she's a psychopath, that is, and Tammy didn't exactly strike me as the type. Anyone who is that concerned about a dog must have some capacity for empathy. I'm just about to run this idea by Ethan when my Fitbit vibrates: "It's step o'clock."

My watch does have a point. I've been sitting motionless for over four hours. I'm surprised it didn't instead text: "Do you need an ambulance?" I decide to take the stairs down two floors to Ethan's office. And since I'm feeling snarky, I give him a taste of his own medicine by opening his door without first knocking.

Ethan looks up from his phone, startled, "Maeve. Shit. Don't you knock anymore?"

I'm surprised by his curt response and give a little laugh before reminding him, "No, Ethan. I took that straight from your play book."

Ethan is looking away and shoving his phone into the top desk drawer. He'd never been one to hide his personal business, so I boldly inquire, "What's going on? Who were you texting?"

Ethan forcibly recovers his usual nonchalant persona and guffaws, "Oh, it's nothing. Just my newest boy toy. Totally closeted and wants to be discreet."

Typical Ethan. But I still chide, "You're such a slut."

"Thank you," Ethan says with a shit-eating grin.

"Anyway, I just came by because I know you're talking to our four potential experts. I have all of the material they need to review in the folder, but I want to highlight a couple of things for you to pass along."

"Look at you, Marcia Clark," Ethan smirks. "I thought you hated Crim Law."

I begrudgingly concede, "I have to admit the dramatic subject matter is inherently fascinating." Regaining my conviction, I add, "This will still be my one and only case in this area."

Ethan looks annoyingly dubious. "Noted. What did you find?"

"Well, thanks to the police's rescue efforts, we don't have any pictures of how Kyleigh was found."

"Yeah, can you believe their audacity? Confirming death before photographing the scene? Complete assholes," Ethan interrupts.

Undeterred, I request, "Can you just bring up the police report?"

Ethan obligingly clicks open the Tammy Sanford file and scrolls down to the report. Once it is open on his oversized monitor, I continue.

"Note that Detective Myles found Kyleigh wrapped tightly in a comforter. So, the State's theory is what?" I posit. "Tammy rolls up her daughter like a sausage after murdering her? Seems unlikely."

Ethan nods his head while reading the relevant section. "Yeah, that does seem odd now that you mention it. I hadn't really thought about it before."

My face flushes pink with pride and excitement. "She is calm and collected enough to sushi wrap her daughter, but leaves her only grandson in the garbage-filled kitchen? Unlikely. And another thing, bring up the autopsy results."

I wait until Ethan locates this document in the file. As soon as it's open though, I move around to his side of the desk, lean over, and take his mouse. It'll be quicker if I do it since I know exactly where these details appear on the page.

"Look here," I direct him. "The hyoid bone is still intact. And the medical examiner doesn't even bother to explain why there are no marks around Kyleigh's neck."

Ethan leans back in his chair. "Yes, Tom and I have talked about this several times. This is the weakest part of their case. That's why we need a really good expert to shred Dr. Fagen's theory as to cause of death."

I realize I've been holding my breath for the last few minutes and let all my nervous energy out with the stale air. "Okay good. Just wanted to make sure we're on the same page and the experts have been properly briefed before the interviews on Friday."

I walk around Ethan's desk to let myself out, but before I go his voice stops me. "Good work, Maeve." His face hangs a bit as if he's feeling sad or guilty about something.

I mean it was totally shitty the way he got me on this case knowing my history. But feeling magnanimous, I decide to let him off the hook…a little. "Ethan, I'm not going to lie. This case has been giving me some severe anxiety. But if it somehow results in me making partner, it will have been worth it."

***

I'm so excited to execute the rest of my plan that I rush the boys through their usual bath and book routine. No bubbles and only two books. Quick smooches and lights out. I want to be ready for Patrick's scheduled FaceTime. I run upstairs and rifle through my underwear drawer for a pair of black crotchless panties to show off my wax job. I locate the matching lacey, see-through bra and recall that this pair was a gift from Zara at my bachelorette party. Seems like a lifetime ago that the two of us, along with a couple other college and law school friends, spent the weekend in NOLA. We'd awaken to coffee and beignets at Cafe Du Monde, do a bit of sightseeing, and then enjoy happy hour at The Columns before hitting the bars on Bourbon Street. Awww…youth. Now, three hurricanes would land me in the hospital.

In just my bra and pointless-but-for-sex panties, I proceed to my vanity to frantically search through my box of cosmetics. I know there is some sexy makeup under all of this wrinkle cream and foundation. I first apply a light brown eyeshadow accented with a darker brown in the corners just like *Cosmopolitan* magazine taught me in high school. I then get out the liquid black eyeliner I never use and do my best to attempt a cat eye. Harlot red lipstick and a little rouge complete the look. This is what I imagine high class escorts look like. Although, that image is based solely on having watched *Pretty Woman* twenty times. Who doesn't want the fairy tale?

It's almost time for Patrick's call when I remember I took our Mac downstairs to look up an enchilada recipe for this weekend. Why did I have to pick tonight to also try to improve my culinary skills? I tiptoe down the stairs past the boys' rooms like a damn ninja. Please God, don't let them wake up. Please God, don't let them wake up. My prayers are answered and I retrieve the laptop off the kitchen counter and make it back to our room unheard.

Now to choose my pose. Going for sexy with no visible cellulite. That means any seated position in front of the computer is automatically eliminated. If I lie on my back, I'll have to hold the computer over my head. That's awkward. Then I have an idea. I run to our closet and grab the black-and-white stilettos I purchased for my Cruella de Vil Halloween costume in college. I lie down on our bed on my stomach with the computer in front of me. I push my boobs toward the camera and have my legs bent behind me to show off the shoes. A check of my reflection in the webcam confirms I look pretty sexy…or as close to sexy as I'm going to get. Four minutes until eight.

Patrick is supposed to call at eight. I want to call him first so we can use the bigger computer webcam rather than the dinky iPhone camera.

My heart is racing as I open the FaceTime app, find Patrick's name, and select "make a video call." He's going to be so surprised. This is brilliant. As soon as I see the call has connected, I say in my sexiest voice, "Hey, there stranger. Want some company tonight?" The video feed connects and a conference room fills my screen. A conference room containing not only Patrick, but also several of his colleagues. I can see Patrick's boss, Peter Gibson, filling a glass with Diet Coke over at the refreshment area. Patrick must have his computer connected to the room's big screen TV. He was probably planning on saying goodnight to the boys before continuing his meeting. As comprehension sinks in, I scramble for the "end call" button.

Where is that button? Where is that button? Patrick must have just figured out what is going on because he emits a small nervous laugh. Bad move. His reaction causes everyone else in the conference room to turn slowly toward the screen. Oh, holy hell! Okay, I locate the red button. I just need to click on it. But wait. Who is that walking into the room? None other than Marcie freaking Spellman. I've spent enough hours obsessively stalking her website bio, LinkedIn profile, and Facebook photos to positively identify her within three seconds. As I stare at her, frozen, Patrick switches into damage control mode.

"Well, Maeve! This is certainly not the goodnight I was expecting." More nervous laughter. "Probably should've given me a heads up that this call wouldn't be the usual PG version. I was all warmed up for a rousing rendition of 'Twinkle, Twinkle Little Star.'"

I know Patrick wants me to hang up or say something witty, but I can't stop staring at the next Mrs. Shaw. She has an almost defiant persona. Like she's obtained an illicit preview of her opponent in action and is now confident she will easily win. Just then my bedroom door swings open. An elated Declan runs in screeching, "Is that Daddy? I want to say goodnight."

How could I have forgotten to lock my door? I snap back to reality and slam my computer closed.

Declan begins visibly surveying me and the surroundings. "Mommy, what are you wearing?"

I dive under the sheets and wrack my brain for a cover story.

"Oh, sweetie." More stalling. Think, think! "Ummm…Mommy just bought some new makeup today and wanted to show Daddy."

Looking confused, Declan points out, "But why did you hang up before I could say goodnight?"

More stalling. "It…turns out…he was in a meeting. So…he had to go." I see Dec's face fall, so I rush to salvage the end. "But he told me to tell you goodnight and that he loves you to the moon and back."

Disappointed but satisfied, Declan starts to climb under the covers.

I pull the sheets around me tightly and implore, "Dec, honey, could you go back to your room while I take this makeup off?"

He looks ready to protest. I must offer a carrot.

"If you go back to bed now, I promise I'll come down and read a chapter of *Charlotte's Web* when I get done."

I just started reading chapter books to Declan whenever I have an extra fifteen minutes after putting Seamus down. Which isn't often. Dec is loving the story of Wilbur and Charlotte's quest to save his life. He takes the bait and starts making his way slowly back to his room. While I don't think he understood what he walked in on, I worry this might become a repressed memory that resurfaces when he's in therapy in his twenties. Trying to understand why he can't hold down any job that requires the use of webcams.

Mortification doesn't begin to describe my feelings as I pour makeup remover on a cotton round and attempt to de-hussy myself. I'm such an idiot. Why didn't I text Patrick first to make sure he was in his hotel? In my excitement over my stupid plan I've managed to make the situation worse. I now look like a desperate fool while Marcie is the penultimate professional. She'll also be there tonight to soothe Patrick's bruised ego.

I grab my phone and text Zara.

I can't go into details now, but suffice to say both Marcie and Declan saw my boobs tonight. You're right. I am pathetic.

As I change into comfy Gap flannel jammies, my phone vibrates multiple times. I can't bring myself to read any of the incoming texts. Instead, I head down to Dec's room to hold up my end of the bargain.

Chapter 12

I sit in the back seat of Dad's black Pontiac Bonneville watching the snow fall outside my window. We've been driving for what feels like an hour already, so I entertain myself by looking at all of the Christmas decorations. With Mom gone, we didn't put up any this year. Not that Mom has put up many decorations in years past, but she usually helps me string a few lights along the porch. This year there is nothing. I imagine what Christmas must be like in these houses bedecked with lights and inflatable snowmen and reindeer. Does their mom sing carols with them before bed on Christmas Eve? Does she help them pick out frosted sugar cookies for Santa and carrots for the reindeer? Does the whole family go to bed in matching pajamas? Does their dad wake them early on Christmas morning so they can all go downstairs together and discover what Santa has delivered? I know that some of my fellow fifth graders have started acting like Christmas is no big deal. They must have had the luxury of enjoying a prior decade of amazing Christmases to be so dismissive of their eleventh.

We take a left and pass a sign reading Paths of Hope. We drive down a long lane with large swaths of snow-covered grass on both sides. The forecast was accurate and we awoke to three inches of fresh Christmas snow this morning. Of course, at our house that just meant a silent breakfast of Aunt Jemima waffles with plenty of syrup before getting dressed in our church clothes to come visit Mom. Santa must have forgotten our house this year. As did Mom and Dad, apparently. There were no presents festively wrapped and adorned with bows under our tree. Although, this morning I did wrap a present for Mom. A small rectangular gift in green paper with a shiny red bow on top. I am excited and a bit nervous to give it to her. Mom has always been hard to buy for so it took me until Christmas Eve to come up with the perfect gift. Something to let her know how much I miss her.

We exit the car, me holding my gift close to my chest, and enter the front doors of Paths of Hope. Dad walks up to the receptionist while I take a seat in the waiting area. It's nice and cozy with comfortable chairs, a gas fireplace keeping the room toasty warm, and a small fake tree decorated with red ornaments and tinsel. I take off my black wool jacket and straighten my red-and-black plaid Christmas dress with black sash. It's the one I picked out last year. It's getting a bit short, but it was the fanciest dress in my closet.

Dad appears next to me and reaches down to take my hand. He leads me into a larger sitting room furnished with several couches and armchairs. This room has a Christmas tree too, but it's much bigger. Probably at least eight feet tall. And this tree is decorated with white lights and blue and silver ornaments. It's magnificent. As I'm admiring the tree, my mother enters the room wearing jeans and a black turtleneck, her hair swept back by a black headband. She looks stylish, but gaunt. She takes a seat near the Christmas tree and immediately lights a cigarette without saying a word. Dad and I shuffle nervously for a few seconds before he puts his hand on my back and pushes me forward a few steps. I take the hint.

"Merry Christmas, Mom," I say timidly.

Mother takes a moment to give me the full head-to-toe inspection. I'm found to be lacking and she shakes her head in disappointment.

"Maeve, you're too old to be wearing such a short dress. What were you thinking?"

Wanting to divert attention away from my clothes, I hand her my gift. Mother considers it critically before finally taking her manicured red fingernail down the seam and slicing the Scotch tape. Although not one to reuse anything, Mother hates ripping wrapping paper. She turns down the folds of the paper to reveal a hardcover copy of The Lion, The Witch and The Wardrobe *by C.S. Lewis. She looks up at me questioningly.*

"Thank you, Maeve, but you know I've never been much of a reader."

I was prepared for this. "I know, Mom, but I thought it would give you something to do during your free time here." I take a deep breath before continuing with my real reason. *"I also just finished reading this for school. Did you know it's an allegory of Jesus's life? I thought we could talk about it when I come back to visit."*

Mother turns the book over and flips through the pages as if expecting to find the real gift hidden inside. I have one more idea.

"It's also about Christmas. You know in Narnia it's always cold and wintery, but they never have Christmas until Aslan returns."

"Oh, that's a nice idea, I guess. But I would have preferred some recent issues of People *or* Vogue.*" She tosses the book on the coffee table in front of her and turns to Dad.

"And what housekeeping gift did you get me this year? A new Dirt Devil?"

Dad gives her a sarcastic smile before retorting, *"Why, dear, your gift is two months in this expensive rehab. Enjoy."*

Mom picks up the book and throws it at him. Hitting him right in the stomach. As he bends down to pick it up, I hear him mutter, *"Ungrateful, bitch."*

Clearly the nurse supervising the visitors' area overheard it as well, as she instantly appears at my side leading me into a smaller room with a couch, coffee table and TV. I sit down as she picks up the remote and scrolls for Christmas shows. She stops at A Charlie Brown Christmas.

"This is my favorite Christmas special. I watch it every year with a cup of steaming hot chocolate. Can I get you one, sweetie?"

I shake my head. I'd recently discovered consuming calories was one of the few things I could control at home. Now any time my father rages or my mother is drunk before dinner, I forgo food for the next twelve hours.

The nurse looks like she wants to say something else, but thinks better of it. Instead, she grabs the throw blanket behind me, spreads it across my lap, and departs.

On the screen in front of me, Charlie Brown just opened his mailbox to discover he once again hasn't received any Christmas cards. He laments about how he already knows nobody likes him. Why does there have to be a holiday season to rub salt in the wound?

I hear the argument between my parents escalate, with my father asking my mother, *"What did you want me to give you? Booze and pills? Unfortunately, they are kind of frowned upon here."* I realize I understand exactly how Charlie Brown feels.

Chapter 13

On Thursday morning, I arrive at 2717 South Sacramento Avenue, better known as division four of the Cook County jail. Division four is a two-story, sixteen-wing building housing all security classifications of the female general population. Walking inside, I quickly assess that waving my bar card will give me no special treatment here. I'm subjected to the same thorough search all visitors are put through. My briefcase is scanned and my person is subjected to both a metal detector and full body pat down. Damn you, metal in my nude pumps. Once I clear security I'm escorted to a hallway where I find Ethan and Tom already sitting on a metal ledge against the white, brick wall. They both look up from their ubiquitous yellow legal pads and nod in greeting. I take a seat next to them and wait for the guards to retrieve Tammy.

The smell of Cook County jail is overpowering. It's a mixture of sweaty, unwashed bodies and urine. The smell must be pervasive among prisons, as it had been the same in the Indiana Women's Prison where my mom had resided for a time. While we wait, at least twenty women file past us going to who knows where. I know from experience that some of the programs offered include substance abuse counseling and domestic violence group therapy. I also think my mom took an art class to add a hint of summer camp to her incarceration.

Tom and Ethan in their high-priced, fashionable suits of gray and black, respectively, come off unmistakably as legal counsel and so several of the passing women ask them for representation. The women aren't quite as sure about me. My mid-range navy long-sleeve dress with a brown accent belt could be the attire of a well-compensated paralegal. I do get a couple of "you'd be popular in here, sweetie" which I guess is nice to know. If my life ever goes so sideways I end up an inmate, at least I won't be a lonely one.

Not surprisingly no one seems in a hurry in prison. When Tammy finally arrives, she's in a blue prison jumpsuit and her two-tone hair doesn't appear to have been washed this week. Her pungent body odor also suggests she's missed a few showers. The guard motions for us to follow him down the long corridor. A few minutes later, he stops and unlocks a door to our left. He motions for us to proceed inside while he positions himself to stand watch. I follow Tammy, Tom and Ethan into a minimally furnished conference room. Minimal means a flimsy table chained to a metal loop in the concrete floor and six folding chairs. Tammy takes a seat and Ethan and Tom pull up chairs on either side of her leaving me to sit across. I reach into my Kate Spade Vivian bag and pull out what else but a yellow legal pad and a pen to take notes.

Tom is as efficient and to the point as ever. "Tammy, as you're aware, today is April fifth and your trial is scheduled to begin on June ninth. That doesn't give us much time to prepare. This week we've been scheduling expert witness interviews and preparing case summaries for the potential experts to review."

Tammy, noticeably upset, interrupts with, "What for? What are these experts going to say? My daughter was a drug addict and died. End of story."

Tom has clearly been through this before and impatiently reminds Tammy, "Now you know Kyleigh didn't die from an overdose. She asphyxiated. The prosecutor is going to argue that you choked her. We need to present an alternative theory. So, we are going to have these experts review Kyleigh's autopsy report, police report and the crime scene photos and tell us if there is another explanation for Kyleigh's death."

Again, Tammy interrupts. "Well, there must be because I didn't do it. I went to that shithole she stayed at with her dealer because she wanted money. As usual, I might add. We got into a fight because I told her I was cutting her off. I wasn't going to keep handing over my paycheck so she could get high. And then she went crazy. Screaming that I didn't care about my grandson.

He'd go hungry. She hit *me*." Tammy points to her right cheek as if evidence of a slap is still there. "Not the other way around. I finally had enough and split. That's the last time I saw her."

Apparently satisfied at having given her side of the story, Tammy leans back and starts biting her nails. Tom takes a moment to regroup and consult his notes. I know I should stay quiet and wait for him to refocus, but curiosity gets the best of me.

I invoke my sweetest most unassuming tone meant to, hopefully, encourage Tammy to confide in me. "Tammy, as you know, I'm new to the team. While I've read the police reports, including the statements you made when you were questioned, I know they're biased. I'd really like to hear from you what happened that night with Kyleigh."

Tom looks startled to discover I have working vocal chords, but doesn't object. Tammy still looks wary, but her defensive posture relaxes a bit. She turns to Ethan and asks, "If I'm going to do this, did you at least bring me some smokes?"

Ethan instantly reaches into his jacket pocket and pulls out a box of Marlboro reds and slides them to Tammy with a lighter on top. Tammy slowly selects a cigarette, lights it and takes a few puffs. Then she looks at me.

"I'll tell you what I can remember, but it was two and a half years ago. The details are a bit fuzzy. I don't know how much help I can really be."

Tammy is hedging. She's not ready to cooperate. Then an idea pops into my head to engender trust and I run with it. "Why don't we start a bit farther back. I have two young children, and I'd really like to hear what Kyleigh was like growing up."

Bingo. A smile slowly spreads across Tammy's haggard face as images of a young Kyleigh emerge.

"Oh, Kyleigh was a beautiful child. Just gorgeous. She had long blond ringlets and big blue eyes. By the time she was five everyone could see she was destined to be a star. I signed her up for dancing and singing lessons. She was a natural. Best kid in her class. Voice like an angel. One year she sang "Silent Night" at the school Christmas pageant. Everyone in that auditorium was wiping away tears, I tell ya. And it just so happened that one of the dads there was also a judge for a pageant in southern Illinois. Came up to me that very night and told me I should sign Kyleigh up. So I did. And Kyleigh won. First place. I couldn't believe it. After that, I signed her up for as many pageants as I could find and she brought home all kinds of awards. Helped pay for all those lessons."

"Wow. Sounds like she was really talented," I add encouragingly.

"She was. That girl was destined for great things." At this Tammy takes a long puff on her cigarette and seems to get lost in bitter memories. After a few moments, she continues, but with a rueful tone.

"Then she hurt her back in cheerleading. She was the top of the pyramid her junior year. And that idiot Bobby Pratchett didn't catch her right on one of those throws. I think he did it on purpose. He liked Kyleigh since the fourth grade and she never gave him the time of day. I don't know what he expected with that terrible acne. Anyway, after that Kyleigh started having back spasms. They hurt so bad she was missing school. We started seeing a chiropractor two and three times a week, but it didn't help. And the Miss Illinois Teen pageant was coming up. Kyleigh had been working for that all year. So her doc told her to take a Vicodin and a muscle relaxer at night the couple of days leading up to the pageant. Worked like a charm. Kyleigh finished in the top ten. We just knew next year she'd win it all."

After Tammy takes a drag this time, she seems reluctant to pick up the thread.

I give her a prod. "But then Kyleigh kept taking the pills?"

Tammy just nods her head.

She needs a scapegoat. I give her one. "That happens all the time. These doctors are so quick to prescribe opioids even though they are extremely addictive."

Tammy takes the bait with relish.

"Exactly! It wasn't Kyleigh's fault. She was only sixteen. What was the doctor thinking giving a young lady such strong drugs? He should've known better."

"I completely agree." I see Tom out of the corner of my eye doodling on his notepad. His patience with Kyleigh's back story is wearing thin. I need to get Tammy talking about the night Kyleigh died before he reins me in.

"Well, I don't want to make you relive too much of Kyleigh's struggle with addiction. I know this is hard, but can you tell me how much you remember about the last time you saw Kyleigh."

Tammy looks up at the ceiling as if trying to decide where to begin. "Well, Kyleigh died on Monday, August 3, 2015. A mother doesn't forget the day her only child died." Tammy exhales a big puff of smoke toward the ceiling.

"I had worked the day before. I was the manager of the Walmart in Evergreen Park. Kyleigh had been texting me all day asking me to come over after work. I knew she wanted money so I kept putting her off. But then she said she thought Garrett had an ear infection and wanted me to take a look. I knew she was probably lying, but I couldn't risk Garrett being sick and not looked after. I agreed to go over. See, she never had Garrett dressed properly and he was always getting colds that turned into ear infections. And then she didn't have insurance, so she'd just let it go on for weeks…"

To get Tammy back on track, I prompt, "And what time did you get off work?"

Tammy looks a bit miffed to be cut off, but responds, "I got off at seven. But then I needed to go home and change and get some dinner. And Rapscallion needed to be walked and fed. So, I didn't get to that asshole Simon's place until nine or ten."

This discrepancy has been bugging me. I jump in, "It was after ten. See, in the police investigation notes, it says that film from a 7-Eleven down the street shows you arriving at Simon Harr's house around ten thirty-five p.m., but text messages show that you were texting back and forth with Kyleigh until eleven nineteen p.m. Why did you wait in the car? Why didn't you just go in?"

Tom and Ethan exchange looks indicating they are mildly impressed with my attention to detail. Tammy, on the other hand, snaps back into defensive mode. She stops gazing at the ceiling and looks right at me, pointing with the cigarette in her hand.

"I was waiting for her dickhead dealer to leave, obviously."

I expected this response, so I push back. "Right. That's what you told the police, but that same video camera shows Simon left his house at ten fifty-seven. Why did you wait another twenty minutes?"

Tammy seems unprepared for this question. "To make sure he didn't come back, of course. How did I know he wasn't just making a delivery around the block?"

Something still bothers me about this delay, but I decide to let it go for now. "Okay. I guess that makes sense. What happened after you went into the house to see Kyleigh?"

Tammy takes a deep breath to compose herself and lights another cigarette. "Well, I remember the place was filthy. There were broken bottles and needles strewn all over. It wasn't fit for anyone to be in, let alone a child. Garrett had just turned a year old in July. At eleven o'clock at night, he should've been asleep in his crib. Not stuffed in a car seat while his Mom gets high."

Again, looking to end the tangent, I prompt, "And what happened between you and Kyleigh after you went inside?"

Tammy can see what I'm doing and gets visibly annoyed. She appeals to Ethan to end the interrogation.

"I've already answered all of these questions. Can you just catch her up later?"

Ethan starts to respond, but Tom cuts in. "Tammy, this is good for us to go through again as we start prepping for trial in earnest. Please continue."

My face flushes with excitement as Tammy sighs and lights another cigarette. She's going to make me wait a little while before answering.

"Well, Kyleigh starts asking for money, of course. She knows I'd do anything for Garrett, so she starts going on and on about how diapers are so expensive. How she's going to need to go to urgent care for his ears and will need money for that. It was total bullshit. I got a discount on diapers and wipes at Walmart and would bring her over new boxes every week or so. And, when I went and looked at Garrett in his car seat, it was clear as day that baby didn't have no ear infection. He wasn't fussin'. He was sleeping just as sound as could be. So I told her no. She wasn't getting any more money from me. And that's when she got hysterical and slapped me."

"Kyleigh slapped you because you wouldn't give her money?"

"Well…" Tammy pauses and takes another drag. "She slapped me because I called her a liar and a junkie and wouldn't give her any money. She started screaming about how Simon makes her pay for drugs with sex. Sometimes even passing her around to his friends. She said that I was turning her into a prostitute! Can you believe that? This is my fault?" Tammy looks to me to share her outrage.

"That must have been very hard for you to see Kyleigh that way."

Tammy nods her head. "And then she basically told me to go fuck myself and picked up a baggie and a needle to get high. That's when I left. And the next thing I know, the police are coming to tell me she's been found dead." Tammy sits back indicating she's come to the end of her tale. But I can't let it go quite yet.

"When you left you knew Kyleigh was going to get high?"

"Of course. That's all Kyleigh ever did," Tammy answers with a short laugh.

"And you didn't take Garrett with you?"

Tammy looks like she's been slapped again. Her face is red with outrage. Then she stands up and leans over the table to get closer to me, cigarette right in my face, and shouts, "You don't think I wanted to take him! You don't think I begged Kyleigh for months to just let me have him? But she wouldn't let him go. Even called the police on me once for 'interfering with her parental rights.' Parental rights, my ass. That girl didn't have a maternal bone in her body. She didn't care about him. She just wanted to use him as leverage to keep extorting money from me. She was never going to be a mother to that baby when all she cared about was her next hit."

The guard outside must hear the yelling and abruptly opens the door. "Sit down now or this meeting is over," he orders Tammy.

Tammy reluctantly obeys and takes another few drags from her cigarette in an attempt to regain her composure. "So, yeah, I left Garrett there in his car seat. I didn't have no other choice."

As we exit the foreboding prison gates adorned with barbed wire, Tom turns to me with a surprised but pleased expression on his face.

"You conducted yourself well in there. Got some good information and touched on a couple of weak points we'll need to work out before trial. I'm impressed with your command of the facts after only being staffed on the case for a week. You show real promise."

I feel a surge of pride rise within me. "Thank you, Tom. I'm enjoying being part of the team." As I say it, I realize it's true. I'm enjoying this case more than I've enjoyed any of my other work these last few years. I decide not to overthink it and just enjoy the moment.

"I don't think Tammy's delay going into the house is as big of a deal as Maeve is making it. It makes sense she would wait to see if Simon was coming back," Ethan interjects petulantly.

He's jealous. I thought he might be put out by the unexpected competition. I let the comment go unanswered, but have a feeling Ethan will continue to make me pay for showing him up. For his part, Tom just nods as he walks off in the direction of his black BMW 230i.

As I climb back into my mom-mobile, I grab my phone to see what I've missed the last few hours. Another text from Zara asking for details behind Tuesday night's mortification. I still can't bring myself to tell her the whole story.

And a text from Patrick:

Plane is delayed. Won't land until midnight.

My response is curt and to the point as it's been the last two days:

Thanks for the heads up. See you tomorrow.

Another night's reprieve until I'll be forced to address the elephant in the room. Or, in my case, the scantily clad woman on the monitor.

Chapter 14

The feeling of dejection in the forty-seventh floor conference room on Friday afternoon is palpable. Tom is angrily flipping through his case file and occasionally scribbling notes while Ethan contemplatively stirs the cream into his fourth cup of coffee. I prefer to swivel my chair and stare at the twinkling skyscrapers visible through the floor-to-ceiling windows. The conference room floor has the best views and is thus the only floor where clients are permitted.

We've interviewed three experts today via video conference and none of them were promising. Sure, they all admit there are weak spots in the prosecution's case, namely Kyleigh's intact hyoid bone and lack of strangulation marks, but none of them put forth an alternative theory as to the cause of death. If the best we can get is an expert to point out inconsistencies in the autopsy report, Tammy better get used to life behind bars. Our last interview of the day is with a doctor from Wisconsin who is regarded as one of the country's foremost experts on strangulation. If he offers nothing more helpful, we may need to reconsider our entire case strategy including whether to try to negotiate a last-minute plea rather than preparing for trial.

The phone in the middle of the twelve-person table rings, startling all three of us from our contemplation. I reach for it already knowing it is Tom's secretary informing us the last expert is ready. Tom reaches for the remote to turn on the screen and Dr. Daniel Smart appears. Dr. Smart is a thin, balding, bespectacled, middle-aged man. He's wearing a tan suit jacket over a plaid oxford shirt. He looks virtually identical to our last two experts, the third being our token woman. Tom, clearly frustrated, cuts to the chase.

"Dr. Smart, we've interviewed three potential experts today. While they agree the state's evidence is weak, they can't rule out Kyleigh died by strangulation. Do you share their opinion?"

Ethan and I both hold our breath as Dr. Smart considers Tom's question. As much as I resisted being staffed on this case, I'll be heartbroken if this is the end of my playing Nancy Drew. Dr. Smart seems to sense we are all on edge and decides to toy with us. He takes a long sip of what looks like tea. The mug cheekily reads "Please don't confuse your Google search with my medical degree." He then takes a deep breath before offering his opinion.

"Well, Tom, I can't rule out strangulation entirely."

Tom lets out an audible sigh and Dr. Smart is visibly irritated by the interruption.

"But, if you will kindly let me finish my sentence, I was going to say it is my expert opinion that it is more likely that Ms. Sanford died from asphyxiation."

Tom, Ethan and I exchange confused glances. Tom then leans forward to clarify.

"Dr. Smart, are you saying Kyleigh choked to death?"

Dr. Smart leans back and smiles. He enjoys flaunting his expertise.

"No, Tom. While choking is a typical form of asphyxiation, it is not the only form. Asphyxiation describes many circumstances in which a person finds themselves deprived of a sufficient supply of oxygen."

Tom does not appreciate the doctor's apparent attempt to educate the team.

"Unfortunately," Tom says, "arguing Kyleigh was smothered rather than strangled, doesn't get Tammy off the hook for her murder." His frustration elicits another condescending smile from Dr. Smart. I'm starting to hate this expert.

"You misunderstand me, I'm afraid. I don't believe Kyleigh was smothered or strangled. My theory is Kyleigh died from positional asphyxiation."

More confused looks from the murder squad. Dr. Smart continues.

"Positional asphyxia, also known as postural asphyxia, occurs when someone's position prevents them from breathing adequately. This can happen by force, for example, when a police officer hogties a suspect. But this can also occur by accident."

The good doctor is getting into lecture mode. He leans his chair back and rests his feet on the desk before continuing.

"People can die from positional asphyxia by simply getting themselves into a breathing-restricted position they cannot get out of. It can also happen to babies who are laid in their crib in a position where their mouth and nose are blocked or their chest is unable to fully expand. Hence the 'back to sleep' campaign."

My patience is spent and I have kids to pick up from daycare, so I strive for brevity.

"You're saying Kyleigh died of SIDS?"

Ethan laughs exaggeratedly at my apparent ignorance all the while looking to Tom for approval.

But Dr. Smart simply nods. "Essentially."

Now it's Tom's turn to interject, "Dr. Smart, you are going to ask the jury to believe a twenty-plus-year-old woman died of sudden infant death syndrome?"

"Again, essentially."

Dr. Smart can sense he's losing his audience and plows on.

"Babies die of SIDS because they don't have the muscle strength to turn themselves over into a position where their breathing is no longer constricted. While Kyleigh's muscle tone was sufficient, she ingested an ample amount of heroin before rolling herself into a comforter and falling asleep. The heroin deadened the synapses in Kyleigh's brain rendering them unable to signal to her muscles to unwrap herself. Instead, she remained cocooned in her blanket receiving increasingly insufficient oxygen flow until she perished."

I sit back in my chair, astounded. This theory makes much more sense than the prosecution's version of events. Tammy didn't jump on her daughter, strangle her ninja-style without leaving a mark, wrap her up for no apparent reason, and then leave her infant grandson to fend for himself.

Kyleigh's death was an accidental byproduct of her drug addiction. The jury will swallow this lock, stock and barrel.

Tom seems to agree. He is smiling for the first time today.

"This makes a lot of sense, Dr. Smart. We will want to retain your services for the trial."

And now it is Dr. Smart's turn to grin.

"I assumed you would. I've cleared my calendar for that week. But I must warn you, my testimony does not come cheap and I don't work pro bono."

Tom was prepared for this.

"I didn't assume you did, Doctor. We work for a multinational law firm that invests heavily in its pro bono practice. Your hourly fee will not be an issue."

"Glad we understand each other, Tom," Dr. Smart acknowledges as he removes his feet from his desk and prepares to stand. "I'll finish drafting my expert opinion over the weekend and will send a draft to your team early next week for review."

"We look forward to receiving it," Tom responds as he shuts down the monitor.

Tom then turns to me and Ethan, wearing a victory grin.

"This is excellent progress. Nothing more needs to be done on this case before Monday. Why don't you take the weekend to catch up on your billable work."

A relatively stress-free weekend is the best gift I can receive. I gather my things and am out the conference room door before Tom can change his mind.

Later, my spirit still buoyed by our retained expert's ingenious theory, I pour myself a celebratory pinot noir and bring up the latest episode of John Oliver to watch. The boys, exhausted after a week in daycare, went down easy and I'm ready to relax. Of course, just then the front door opens. Patrick is home. I can no longer avoid the dreaded conversation sure to come.

"I'm downstairs," I call.

"Okay, let me get changed and I'll be down."

About five minutes later, Patrick emerges in the basement wearing his

Northwestern sweats and a white tee. He helps himself to a beer before joining me on the couch. He then takes a big sip before diving in.

"Are we going to talk about what happened?" he asks, straightforward.

I set my glass down and bury my head in my hands.

"I'm sorry. I wanted to show you I can be sexy, so I got a bikini wax and put on some lingerie to spice things up. Instead, I humiliated us both."

Tears spring to my eyes as I keep my head buried. I can't bring myself to face Patrick's reaction. He must be so pissed. Patrick takes his job very seriously. A long minute passes and he doesn't respond.

Then, "Wait, you got a bikini wax?" Patrick asks incredulously. "That must've hurt."

I laugh in spite of myself and toss a throw pillow playfully in his direction.

"It did fucking hurt! I don't know how women in Brazil do it more than once."

Patrick's deep laugh is infectious. It's one of the first things I fell in love with. Once our laughter subsides, he pulls me closer and wraps his arms around me.

"Maeve, you don't have to try to be sexy. You're naturally sexy. And you didn't humiliate anyone. You just gave my coworkers something to be jealous about."

I feel the tension in my chest dissolve as I allow myself to bury deeper into Patrick's embrace. I nuzzle my way up to his neck where I can smell his Old Spice aftershave. Patrick is his father's son. What's good enough for Cormac is good enough for him. Patrick then leans down and gently kisses my forehead. I can't remember the last time we've been this close and I've missed it terribly. Before I can help myself, I pull Patrick into a long kiss. The bitter taste of Revolution Brewing is still on his lips. As Patrick kisses me more deeply, I can feel his hands running up my side. Gently, he begins to massage the side of my breast. My breath quickens.

It's been so long and I'm so turned on, I don't need much foreplay. I'm aching for him. I want Patrick inside me. I lay back on the couch and pull off my nightshirt all in the same movement. Thankful I chose my cute red-and-white polka dot bikini briefs this morning, I reach for Patrick's hand to pull him onto me when he freezes.

"What's the matter?" I ask.

Patrick gets up from the couch and walks toward the stairs. He listens for a moment.

"You should get dressed. I think I hear Declan."

I'm confused, as I have excellent kid-dar and didn't hear a thing. But Patrick has already started up to check on them.

I pull my nightshirt back on and Patrick returns a few minutes later. But the mood has definitely shifted. Patrick takes a seat on the far end of the couch.

"I could've sworn I heard something, but they are both asleep. I pulled the covers up and gave them both goodnight kisses."

He glances at the television. "Oh, I haven't seen this week's episode of *Last Week Tonight*. Let's watch."

As John Oliver explains the massive impact of the Equifax security breach, I try my best to mask my disappointment. But my head is full of questions. I surreptitiously recover my phone from the coffee table while Patrick takes another sip of his beer. I need my BFF right now.

I know this is TMI, but Patrick and I were this close to doing it on the downstairs couch when he froze and went to check on the kids. WTF!

Zara's response is immediate.

DUDE! My tofu pad thai just arrived and now I have no appetite!

Me: Hilarious, but I'm freaking out right now. Am I that hideous that the mere sight of my naked body sends Patrick running??????

I look up to see if Patrick is aware of my texting, but he's too busy laughing at a dick pic joke.

Zara: Okay, how did this…intimate encounter happen? Did you go out to dinner? Do some serious talking?

Me: Ummmm…no. Patrick came home. I was in the basement in my jammies. We talked for a minute about my webcam fail and I kind of jumped him.

Zara: Jesus, Maeve. You reek of desperation. Maybe that's what turned Patrick off. You're coming on too strong.

I pause. Zara did have a point. I'd been avoiding Patrick all week and the second he comes home, I'm ripping off my clothes. Maybe I did come off as desperate.

Me: Point taken. What do you suggest?

Zara is never one to equivocate on her true feelings.

What I suggest is you grow some self-esteem and dump the guy…but since that isn't going to happen, how about you stop throwing yourself at Patrick and maybe reconnect. Dinner? Movie? Normal date stuff.

I look up to see Patrick turning off the TV and starting to stand. The episode must have ended. I stow my phone in my nightgown pocket and follow him up the stairs. After brushing our teeth, we lie down side by side, both unsure where this will lead. As I roll over to lie on his chest, Patrick preemptively kisses my forehead, says goodnight and turns toward the far side of the bed.

I'm not sure any amount of dinner dates will be enough to bridge the abyss that's somehow opened between us. The faded scars on my legs begin to prickle, begging to be reopened, but I push the idea out of my mind and roll back to my side of the bed.

Chapter 15

My school-books are spread out taking up half of the large wooden table in the back of the Carmel Public Library. I've studied chemistry for over an hour even though I already felt prepared for tomorrow's test. Finding the mass percent to find the molecular formula of a compound is pretty basic. I grab my homework notebook and double-check, already knowing I've completed all the assignments due tomorrow. And I'm right. The only other assignment due was fifteen problems in precalculus and I'd completed those in study hall. So, I root through my backpack to find my copy of The Great Gatsby. *Ms. Casterly has given us another week to finish the novel, but I'm almost done and might as well get it over with. I'm not particularly enjoying the classic Roaring Twenties story, but anything is better than facing the drama that awaits me at home. F. Scott Fitzgerald did have a way of aptly describing vain, self-centered people. I will give him that. Tom and Daisy destroyed lives, retreated to the safety of their mansions, and let others clean up the mess.*

I gasp loudly when Mrs. Anderson puts her hand on my thigh. The pain is so intense, I stand up too quickly and the chair topples behind me.

She draws back confused. "What's wrong, honey? I just came to tell you it's closing time. Are you hurt?"

Flustered, I begin frantically grabbing books and jamming them back in my backpack.

"No, Mrs. Anderson, I'm all right. You just scared me."

Her confusion soon turns to fear. She points and quietly says, "Maeve, there's blood running down your leg. What happened?"

I pray that she's wrong, but as I look down past my red plaid checkered skirt I see that she's not. A thin trickle of blood is running from my thigh down my calf. My mind races for a believable story. I go for nonchalant, but my voice is shaking. "Oh, that's nothing. Just cut myself shaving this morning."

Not my best lie and I can tell Mrs. Anderson isn't buying it. But I can also tell she's unsure how much more she should press. My father is a big fish in a small pond. And no one likes to make waves.

I hurriedly pack my last book away and zip up my bag. "Goodnight."

I see Mrs. Anderson steel herself and she grabs my skirt before I can stop her. We both freeze as not only the five fresh cuts on my right thigh are revealed, but also the dozens in various states of healing. When my parents' fights escalate from screaming to glass breaking to slapping, I retreat in my bathroom with my razor. It sounds crazy, but the pain calms me down.

She puts her hand over her mouth and sounds as if she might cry. "Oh, honey. What have you done?"

Panicking, I grab Mrs. Anderson's free hand and plead, "Please, don't tell anyone. I've only done it a few times. I'll stop. I promise!"

She is out of her league. A young wife with a small child. Her husband just recently graduated from law school and joined a local firm. Her father-in-law is a respected judge who has presided over many of my father's cases. All three go to the same bar association events. She wouldn't dare tell.

Now it's Mrs. Anderson's voice that's shaky. "Okay, honey. You run along home now. And don't let me catch you doing this ever again. You promise?"

My heartbeat slows. "I promise. Thank you."

Looks like I'll be finding a new place to study after school.

Chapter 16

I'm slightly embarrassed of my mom-mobile, as I pick up Ethan from his hip flat on Berwyn Avenue in Andersonville. This neighborhood is perfect for young, attractive singles. In a two-block radius, there's Hop Leaf Brewery, a kitschy novelty T-shirt shop, a local bookstore, amazing Mediterranean, Mexican, and Italian restaurants, and no less than five boutique gyms to work off those calories. In the few minutes I've been idling, I've seen no less than two women walking with yoga mats and a man drinking Intelligentsia coffee because Starbucks isn't on trend in this hood. Lincoln Park, on the other hand, is Whole Foods, Target, Costco, family friendly restaurants, tutoring services, and gyms offering "mommy and me" classes. I take a moment to mourn the loss of my youth before refocusing on why I'm here at eight-thirty in the morning. Last night, Tom sent us an email directing us to go to Stateville Correctional Center this morning to interview Kyleigh's drug dealer boyfriend. Simon Harr was charged with one count of possession of narcotics and one count of being a felon in possession of a weapon a week after the police catalogued the crime scene. He pled guilty in return for a five-year sentence. Simon is serving that time in Stateville, a maximum security men's prison about an hour's drive from Chicago.

I see Ethan emerge from the front door of the newly constructed three flat, an increasingly common style for condominium buildings in Chicago. Ethan has the top unit complete with hardwood floors throughout and a large master bedroom suite with a cozy gas fireplace. Perfect for romantic nights in. Ethan strolls to my van clad in a slim fit Hugo Boss navy checked suit with a light blue oxford shirt peeking out and coffee in hand. My embarrassment increases exponentially.

As Ethan is buckling his seatbelt, I decide to preempt his snide remarks. "I know my car screams suburban soccer mom and is covered in goldfish crumbs. Let it go."

Ethan raises his hands in a gesture of surrender. "Whoa, whoa. Don't shoot. I was going to say thank you for the ride since I don't own a car, goldfish covered or otherwise. What's got you so touchy this morning?"

My face flushes. Maybe I did start off a bit aggressively. I take a deep breath and try again. "I'm sorry. It was a crazy weekend. A response brief was filed in one of Elizabeth's student loan cases, so I spent about ten hours on Saturday and Sunday nights after putting the boys to bed drafting the reply. I didn't sleep much. How was your weekend?"

Ethan fidgets with his suit before responding, "Pretty low key."

I laugh. "Does that mean only one sleepover per night?"

Ethan shoots me a dirty look before snapping, "Why don't you try worrying about your own love life for a change."

A dagger right to my heart. I inhale audibly and fumble around for an equally painful retort, but nothing comes to mind. After a few tense minutes, I quietly ask, "What did you mean by that?"

Ethan runs his hand through his hair, before responding, "Now it's my turn to say sorry. I'm just incredibly frustrated. I really like this guy, but he won't commit. I'm not sure how much longer I can settle for sloppy seconds."

I feel like an idiot. I just assume Ethan likes playing the field. I've never really thought about whether he might like to fall in love and settle down one day. "Well, then that guy is stupid because you're a huge catch. He'd be lucky to have you all to himself."

Ethan nods appreciatively in my direction but lets another several minutes pass in silence. I carefully merge from I-90E to I-55S toward Joliet where we'll stay for the majority of the hour-long trip. Thinking back over my response, I realize it was a bit trite. Ethan opens up to me and I give him back a Hallmark soundbite. I take a deep breath and try again. "Hey, relationships are tough. Patrick and I have been married for almost a decade, but most days it feels like we're roommates rather than spouses. You aren't wrong to suggest I should worry about my own love life."

Ethan takes a sip of his coffee before sheepishly inquiring, "I take that to mean not much is happening between the sheets these days?"

Of course, Ethan focuses on sex. But I concede, "You could say that. How long do you have to abstain before you can be deemed a born-again virgin?"

Ethan chuckles and seems to take solace in our mutual dissatisfaction. He turns his attention to trying out all my pre-programmed radio stations. I allow my mind to wander as an endless landscape of farmland takes the place of skyscrapers. It always amazes me how quickly you can leave the third largest city in the country and enter the rural Midwest.

As Ethan and I car dance to Electric Feel by MGMT, the imposing concrete monstrosity of Stateville enters our vision. The prison sits on sixty-four acres of land completely enclosed by a thirty-foot high wall. The land immediately surrounding the prison is barren and desolate. I pull into the visitors parking lot adjacent to the enormous red brick reception center. Ethan and I look at each other and I take a deep breath. "Let's get this over with."

Ethan and I are assigned a table in the visiting room, as they call it, and we wait for the guards to bring Simon down. Ethan turns and asks, "What exactly is Tom hoping to get out of this visit? The cops know Simon wasn't home when Kyleigh died. They have video from the 7-Eleven of his car leaving his house before Tammy enters and then not returning until the following morning."

I concede, "I think Tom just wants us to confirm that Kyleigh was wrapped up tight in the comforter when Simon found her."

The large metal doors leading out into the hallway clang open loudly and the guards lead a painfully thin young man into the visiting room. Simon is about average height with stringy, unwashed reddish brown hair that's been pulled back into a ponytail. He also sports an unruly beard and mustache. The skin that's visible has the unhealthy pallor and pock marks typical of a user. Simon is wearing the de rigueur orange jumpsuit and his hands are cuffed in front of him.

He sits down at table three opposite Ethan and me and immediately gets to the point. "What the fuck do you two want? I waived my right to an appeal in the plea agreement."

Ethan takes the lead. "Good morning, Mr. Harr. I'm Ethan Colopy and this is my colleague Maeve Shaw. We represent Tammy Sanford. We want to ask you a few questions about her daughter, Kyleigh."

Simon gives us a nasty grin revealing several missing teeth. The remaining ones are discolored. A condition referred to by medical professionals as "meth mouth."

"I hope that bitch rots in jail."

No love lost between the formerly potential in-laws. Maybe some sympathy will make Simon more willing to cooperate.

"I'm sorry for your loss, Simon," I say. "How long were you and Kyleigh together?"

Simon turns his attention to me and blatantly conducts a slow appraisal from my legs up. Indicating his appreciation of my Houndstooth pencil skirt and white blouse, he flashes me a hungry smile.

"Ky and I are ancient history, sweetheart. I like to live in the present."

Why does it seem that all the prisoners I meet have Don Juan delusions? I attempt to cover up my distaste. "Understood. But if you remain uncooperative, I'll walk out of here and you won't get the pleasure of ogling me. If instead you tell me about the night Kyleigh died, I'll stay a bit longer and give you some new visuals for your spank bank. Deal?"

Simon throws back his head and cackles at the ceiling, drawing the guard's attention. The guard tenses and grips his nightstick in anticipation of trouble. But Simon quickly recovers and seems more relaxed. He awkwardly puts his shackled hands on his head and leans back. "Fair enough. Fire away."

Ethan seems surprised at Simon's one eighty, but plows ahead. "Can you tell us a bit about Tammy and Kyleigh's relationship? Did they get along?"

Simon guffaws. "Not since Ky stopped bringing in the pageant money. Say what you want about me, but that woman pimped out her daughter for *years* before I had my turn with her."

My protein shake starts to make a reappearance, but I want to keep Simon talking. "Is that what Kyleigh thought?"

Simon leans forward. "That's the truth. Tammy put Ky in every pageant she could find within two hundred miles. Ky had to dance and sing like her little puppet. She put lipstick and mascara all over her face. Ky showed me pictures. She hated that shit. She was happy when she hurt her back and had to quit. Her ma was sure pissed though. She actually had to get herself a j-o-b at Walmart. After that, Tammy got herself that little mutt and started pimping him out instead."

Simon will make a perfect witness for the prosecution painting Tammy as an overbearing pageant mom. Of course that's all hearsay. Simon didn't know Kyleigh before she needed his drugs. "Is that when you met Kyleigh? After she hurt her back and stopped performing?"

Simon thinks for a moment before responding. "Can't say I remember exactly when I met Ky. She just started showing up at the house and getting high. After a while, her and her baby just started living there."

I cringe at the mention of Garrett living in that crack house. Simon doesn't seem bothered by it though. Quite the opposite. I feel dirty and my skin tingles. I want to get Simon talking about the comforter so I can get the hell out of here. I prompt, "Can you tell us what you remember about the night Kyleigh died?"

"You mean the night her mom killed her," Simon snaps. "Yeah, I can tell you about that. The baby had been screaming all damn day. It was driving me nuts. I couldn't sleep. I tell Ky to shut him up and she says something about his ears hurting. So, she calls her mom for money to take him to the doctor. Bitch owed her after all the pageant money she stole. But when Ky told me her mom was coming over after work, I bounced. I hated that bitch." Simon smiles to himself before continuing, "She hated me too, I guess, 'cause when I left I saw her in her fucking Dodge Charger waiting for me to go."

Funny Simon noticed that. Maybe it wasn't the first time. "Was that usual? I mean, did Tammy usually wait in her car until you left?"

Simon shook his head. "Nah. Tammy had no trouble barging into my house and cussing me out. Made her feel better to blame me for Ky's problems instead of looking in the goddamn mirror."

I pause for a minute to think about this, and Ethan jumps in. "And then you didn't come back to the house until around nine the next morning?"

"Yeah, something like that," Simon says vaguely. "I remember it was early. I knew something wasn't right when I walked in the door. I found the baby sleeping in his car seat, so I knew Ky had to be home. That's when I went into the bedroom and found her."

Simon looks away from us. He seems sincerely shaken by the memory. Ethan asks the million-dollar question, "Can you describe how Kyleigh looked when you found her?"

Simon turns back. "Well, at first I didn't know she was dead. She was all wrapped up in this big blanket on her side like she was trying to get warm. But when I got closer, I could see her face was bluish. Something wasn't right. I called nine-one-one. To be honest, I thought she'd OD'd and just needed a shot of Narcan."

Having gotten what we needed, Ethan and I begin to put our legal pads and pens back in our respective bags. Simon looks anxious at the prospect of losing the only visitors he's had for a while.

"Don't you want to know why Tammy killed her?"

Ethan and I jerk back to attention. "What are you talking about?" I ask.

Simon gives a triumphant grin. "After the police left, I found the adoption papers ripped in half and thrown in the garbage. Tammy had been badgering Ky to let her have that baby for months. But Ky didn't want Tammy to fuck up Garrett like she'd fucked her up. When I saw that Ky had torn up the adoption papers, I knew Tammy did it."

My mind's reeling. How has the adoption never come up? I scramble for an alternative explanation, stammering, "But you don't know Kyleigh tore the papers up in front of Tammy. She could have torn them up before Tammy came to the house and never told her."

Simon's grin becomes joker-esque. "Nope, because Ky and I were looking at those papers before I left the house. Tammy had dropped them off the last time she gave Ky money and diapers. She told Ky she either signed them or she was cut off. Ky was going on and on about whether she should go ahead and let Tammy have him. She knew she wasn't the world's best mom. I told Ky, if you do it make sure you get something out of the deal. Tell Tammy you'll sign for five grand. Tammy wants the baby so bad, let her have him. But make her pay. When I walked out the door, Ky said she wasn't giving her baby up for less than ten."

I feel sick. Not just because of Simon's baby blackmail scheme. But because he can give the State their missing motive.

Chapter 17

"Don't we have a duty to tell Porter about this?" I prod.

Ethan and I dropped Simon's little bombshell on Tom the minute we got back to my car. We are receiving his less than satisfying response via Bluetooth as we haul tail back to the office.

"Absolutely not," Tom emphatically declares. "You didn't uncover new evidence, exculpatory or incriminating. What you got was a theory from a convicted felon. A convicted felon who admittedly hates our client."

Ethan and I exchange skeptical looks, before I counter, "I think you're minimizing the impact of this, Tom. There's no mention of Tammy's proposed adoption in any of the police reports. Tammy never mentioned wanting to adopt Garrett in any of her interviews. Even when she was directly asked by the police whether she ever considered taking Garrett away from Kyleigh given her drug abuse, she demurred. Her omission alone lends credence to Simon's theory."

Tom sighs like a professor frustrated by his subpar pupils. "Listen to yourself, Maeve. You just admitted what this is. A *theory*. Nothing more. We are under no ethical obligation to make the State's case for it. If Porter hasn't found the time to drive out to BFE and interview Simon, that's his fault. We simply cross Simon off of our potential witness list and move on."

Undeterred, Ethan enters the fray. "Tom, while I see your point, we did potentially uncover incriminating evidence. Simon said the ripped-up adoption papers were in his trash can. He said he saw them after the police processed the crime scene. And then he was arrested two days later. They may very well still be there. Given the state of his apartment, I doubt he bothered to clean up."

The line falls silent. Ethan's point is brilliant. Those papers are probably still at the crime scene just waiting to be discovered.

Tom recovers himself and issues a directive. "You two are not to go anywhere near that apartment. We don't know whether Simon discarded them or not. And we are under no obligation to investigate further. Leave them be. Do you understand?"

I look at Ethan and can tell from his furrowed brow and thoughtful expression that he is as uncomfortable with Tom's demand as I am. But what else can we do? It's Tom's case. We're just his minions. I take a deep breath before emitting a perfunctory, "Understood," and disconnect the call.

Ethan and I maintain silence for the remainder of the ninety-minute drive back to Chicago. The long stretches of pasture and open highway slowly give way to concrete and standstill traffic. Ethan appears to be alternately responding to email and browsing social media and I find myself mindlessly cycling through the five pre-programmed radio stations unable to settle on one. I finally admit to myself that I'm not going to be able to let this go. I need to find out if Tammy and Kyleigh argued about Garrett's adoption on the night of her death. But I can't directly disobey Tom's order to stay away from Simon's place. Then it dawns on me. While I can't visit the crime scene, Tom's prohibition doesn't extend to questioning witnesses. I spot the Armitage exit and quickly merge onto Ashland Avenue going south.

"Where are you going?" Ethan inquires. "This isn't Monroe."

"I know," I respond nervously. "Up for another prison visit?"

Ethan smiles approvingly. "Let's see if I can get us added to today's visitors list."

***

Tammy looks suspiciously at Ethan and me as she takes her seat across from us. This unexpected visit seems to have her nervous and I have a hunch that we may be able to get some useful information. Before I can dive in though, Tammy turns to Ethan and asks, "Do you have any pictures of Rapscallion?"

Ethan grins and obligingly pulls out his iPhone 11. He scrolls through his camera roll before landing on a picture of a dainty-looking dog with a white body and mostly brown face and ears. A streak of white fur runs down the center of his face. His large brown eyes beam back at the camera.

Tammy gets misty eyed as she lovingly strokes the picture. *I need to put an end to this photo sesh.*

"Good afternoon, Tammy. Sorry for the unexpected visit, but Ethan and I went to see Simon Harr this morning and a few things came up that we wanted to ask you about."

Tammy's disposition changes from nostalgic to pissed in a hot second. "Why the hell did you go see him?"

Ethan unsurprisingly jumps in to calm Tammy down. "Tammy, if we are going to competently defend you at trial, we need to speak to all of the witnesses. We have to make sure there are no last-minute surprises."

Tammy shakes her head. "But Simon ain't no witness. He wasn't even there when Kyleigh died. Off selling drugs, of course."

"Right, but Simon was Kyleigh's boyfriend," I reason. "And, even more importantly, Simon is the one who discovered Kyleigh's body and called the police. You see why we would want to get his story?"

Tammy begrudgingly grunts, "I s'pose," so I continue.

"Ethan called you last week and told you about our expert's theory that Kyleigh died of positional asphyxiation, right?"

Tammy manages a half-hearted nod. "Didn't understand most of what he was talking about, but Ethan said this expert will testify I didn't kill her."

"Right. Our expert, Dr. Smart, will testify Kyleigh wrapped herself so tightly in her comforter she couldn't get enough oxygen. And because of the drugs she had taken, her brain couldn't tell her body to change positions. Understand?"

Again, Tammy gives a small nod. "Sounds right."

"Well, Simon corroborated many key facts our expert is relying on, including that Kyleigh was still wrapped tightly in her comforter when he found her."

Tammy picks a hangnail from her left thumb until it bleeds. She then puts her thumb in her mouth and sucks it.

Apparently Tammy is unimpressed by Dr. Smart's theory. I plow forward. "Unfortunately, after speaking with Simon we don't know if we'll be able to call him as a witness at trial."

Tammy's interest peaks. "Why's that?"

Time to pull the pin from the grenade and lob it in her direction. "Well, because he could also testify that Kyleigh was trying to bribe you in exchange for custody of Garrett."

Tammy's stunned silence speaks volumes.

"What happened that night after Kyleigh demanded ten thousand dollars in exchange for signing the adoption papers?"

Tammy leans toward Ethan and, without uttering a word, Ethan is getting the pack of Marlboro reds from his briefcase. He lights one, takes it out of his mouth, and hands it across the table. She takes a slow drag and exhales the smoke in my general direction.

"I knew Simon put her up to it. Kyleigh'd done a lot of bad stuff by then, but she wouldn't have thought to try to sell her baby. Kyleigh was a good mom, when she was sober. You know, Garrett was taken by the state for three months after his birth because he was born with opioids in his system? Kyleigh had to submit to weekly drug tests in order to regain custody. She even went to rehab for six of those weeks. I visited her at Rosemont. She said she threw up every day for the first two weeks. It was hard, but she was determined to get him back. And when she finally did, she was so happy. She'd play with him and read books to him. Hell, she even co-slept because she couldn't stand being away from him. But then she went out with some friends for her twenty-third birthday and got high. A month later she moved in with Simon."

Tammy wipes away the tears at the corners of her eyes with the back of her shackled hands. While I empathize with Tammy's situation and truly believe she loved Kyleigh, that, unfortunately, only makes it more likely that she murdered her. After all, seventy-nine percent of all homicides are committed by friends or loved ones. It was time to turn Tammy's focus back to the night in question.

"So, what did you do when Kyleigh offered to give up the son she loved so much for less than the price of a used car?"

Tammy's eyes flash with rage. "What do you think I did? I tried to talk some sense into her. I didn't have that kind of money. I worked at Walmart. Any money left over after paying my bills went to Garrett. I told her she should do the right thing for her son and left."

No way this is the whole story. A person with Tammy's temper doesn't just "try to talk some sense" into Kyleigh and leave without a fight.

"Things never got physical?"

Tammy's simmering temper begins to boil. "I already told you, *she* hit *me* when I told her I wasn't giving her the money."

"And you didn't lay a hand on her?" After a deep breath, I take a calculated risk. "Even after she tore up the adoption papers in your face."

Tammy throws down her cigarette and jumps to her feet. "That bitch thinks she can rip up my generosity and laugh in my face. I didn't touch her, but, you want to know the truth? She got what she deserved."

Two guards are on either side of Tammy within seconds. "This visit is over," they needlessly inform us as they drag Tammy out the doors to her cell.

Before I can say anything or even begin to pack up my notebook, Ethan is in my face. "This doesn't prove anything, Maeve. Yes, Tammy was pissed. Do I think Tammy might have given Kyleigh some of those bruises? Sure. But there are no physical signs of strangulation. No marks around Kyleigh's neck. Kyleigh's hyoid bone was intact. This doesn't prove she killed her."

I mull this over before finding myself agreeing with Ethan. If Tammy killed Kyleigh in the heat of a fight over Garrett's adoption, she would have taken Garrett with her. And she wouldn't have had the foresight to stage the scene with the comforter.

Chapter 18

It's as if I'm swimming thousands of miles below the ocean's surface. I hear voices, but the words come to me muffled and distorted as though from a great distance. I'm aware of bright lights above me, but my eyes are closed and I'm unable to open them. I'm also unable to turn away from them, my body no longer responding to my brain's requests. I try to remember how I got here. Snippets of events flash before my eyes. I'm looking through a crack in the door to my parents' bedroom. They are slewing vitriol at one another. My father lands a verbal blow and my mother spits in his face. He slaps her and she falls back on their bed. Then I'm in my own bedroom. I'm writing a letter at my desk. "I can't live like this any longer. The hurt is too deep to bear." A bottle of my mom's Percocet sits across from me. The last thing I remember is lying on my bed to sleep, the pill bottle now empty in my hands.

I can feel a woman take my head and reposition it toward her. She brushes my hair away from my face and opens my mouth. I hear the words "gastric lavage." A few moments later I feel a plastic tube being inserted into my throat. It scrapes my esophagus raw as it descends. I gag, but am helpless to stop it. My eyes are watering and I feel like I'm going to retch. Then something cool, like water, hits my stomach. But that same water is immediately sucked back out. This process continues over and over for what seems like an hour. Water hits my stomach and is then sucked back out again. I want to die. Finally, the tube is yanked from my stomach. My throat is on fire. Those same hands lift my head up and press a plastic cup to my mouth. I take a sip of what tastes like a bitter slushie and immediately begin to vomit. I keep vomiting and vomiting until it feels like there is nothing left inside of me. I'm just an empty vessel. Then I slip into darkness.

The next time I wake up, I'm in a hospital bed wearing the traditional gown. A white blanket covers my legs. An IV is inserted into my right arm and is connected to what looks like a saline bag. I hear the soothing beeps of the heart rate monitor next to it. I look around for my parents, but no one else is in the room. On the wall across from me is a white board. Across the top border it reads Ascension St Vincent's Carmel. In the middle of the white board in red erasable marker, a nurse has written, "I'm Angie. How can I help?" Angie's offer may be a bit late, but it's all I've got. I'm searching for the call button when my parents enter the room carrying matching Starbucks cups. They freeze as our eyes meet.

My father, dressed in a gray suit and white oxford for work, is the first to recover. "Maeve, you're awake. Thank God." He looks genuinely relieved.

My mother is less impressed. "What in the hell were you thinking?" she seethes.

I try to respond, but my throat feels like it's been rubbed raw with sandpaper. "Water," I croak.

My father scans the room and finds a small pink pitcher on the windowsill next to a pink plastic cup. He hurries over, fills the cup, inserts a straw and hands it to me. Just a sip of the cool liquid provides much-needed relief.

My parents fidget nervously as I carefully continue drinking. My mother picking invisible lint from her lavender blouse. My father straightening his navy blue tie. But after a few more minutes pass in silence, my mother can no longer bear it. She rushes to take a seat at the foot of my bed and resumes her interrogation.

"Seriously though, Maeve, what were you thinking? You could have died." She says it less out of concern and more out of offense.

I don't know where to even begin. Then I remember the letter. "Did you read my note?" I rasp.

My mother looks stricken and steals a glance at my father. His expression is one of shock.

"What is she talking about, Joanna?" There is danger in his voice.

"Oh, Michael, it was nothing. The usual sixteen-year-old girl drama." She then feigns what I assume is meant to be a stereotypical high school girl tone of voice. "My life is so hard. I can't go on. My parents don't understand me." She

drops the voice before concluding, "You know, the usual stuff."

My father utters his next words in the very low, very slow pattern that usually preceded their screaming matches. "I'm sorry, Joanna. I'm not sure I'm familiar with what is 'typical' in high school suicide notes these days. You told me you found her in her room and you had no idea what she had done. You said she looked pale and her breath was shallow. What are you not telling me?"

My mother looks away and starts smoothing down the blanket around her. "I just didn't want to upset you."

"Didn't want to upset me??? I watched my only daughter get her stomach pumped last night!" he explodes.

A nurse peeks into the room, I'm assuming it's the helpful Angie. "Everything all right in here?"

My mother and father instantly compose themselves. My mother flashes Angie one of her signature happy housewife smiles before saying, "Everything is fine. Thank you."

Angie looks in my direction, brightening "Oh, you're awake. That's wonderful. Let me come in and take your vitals."

My father takes three giant steps toward the door and blocks her way. "Miss, can you give us a few minutes to speak in private?" It's phrased as a question, but before Angie can respond, my father is closing the door in her face.

He rounds on us. "Maeve, where did you get the pills?"

I'm struck mute at the abrupt change in the conversation. I stare back at him open mouthed.

My father closes the distance between us. He is now next to my bed, one hand firmly on my arm, staring directly into my eyes. He demands, "Tell me where you got the pills."

I don't want to tattle, but my eyes betray me. I look directly at my mother. Without another word, my father storms from the room slamming the door on his way out. My mother slowly turns toward me making sure we have direct eye contact before unabashedly declaring, "I hate you."

Chapter 19

I sit down at my desk on Tuesday morning feeling unusually alert and confident, having managed to fit in a thirty-minute jog down Fullerton Avenue to Lake Michigan and back after dropping the boys off at daycare. Running along the path watching the sun reflect off the waves and feeling the wind whip my ponytail gives me an instant mood reset. It even motivated me to apply eyeliner and don a skirt before catching a cab to the office.

I take a big sip of my Starbucks skinny vanilla latte before mentally going over today's to-do list. Six hours revising and finalizing Elizabeth's reply brief for her review will leave me with a little over an hour to start outlining the opening statement for trial. Tom emailed me last week that he thinks it would be the best optics to have a woman deliver Tammy's defense to the jury. I jumped at the opportunity and want to get a good start on it even though the trial is still two months away. I'm rudely pulled from my reverie by the high-pitched ringing of my office phone. Tom's name appears on the screen. Funny, he always emails.

"Morning, Tom. Is there something I can help you with?" I answer brightly.

"You can get your ass upstairs pronto," he growls and abruptly hangs up.

What is that all about, I wonder. I mean he wasn't exactly thrilled to hear we visited Tammy on the DL. But after we relayed the conversation, he agreed with our assessment that this wasn't a heat of the moment killing and Tammy's outburst about the adoption scam only lends credence to her claim of innocence. What could have happened in the last sixteen hours to get him fuming?

After taking the stairs two at a time to reach the forty-sixth floor, I breathe a small sigh of relief upon seeing Ethan enter Tom's office only seconds before me. If I'm about to get reamed at least I have company. Immediately upon my entry, Tom bellows, "Shut the door."

Seeing Tom standing over his desk slamming various folders and legal pads I get the distinct impression I'm not going to like where this conversation is headed. I strive for casual. "Morning, Tom, what's up?"

Tom's neck snaps to attention and his expression is undeniably furious. "What's up?" he mocks. "You want to know what's up? I'll tell you what's up. Judge Howard has skin cancer. He apparently had a biopsy of a spot on his neck this past Wednesday. His doctors say it's stage three and has spread to the nearby lymph nodes. Judge Howard will be starting a chemo regimen shortly."

While this must be troubling for Judge Howard, I'm at a loss to explain Tom's impassioned reaction. I tread lightly. "I'm sorry to hear that," I say sympathetically before adding, "What does this mean for Tammy's trial date?"

Tom rounds his desk, takes two giant steps in my direction and points his index finger aggressively at my chest. "That's the million-dollar question, Maeve. It means we've been assigned a new judge."

"What?" Ethan blurts out. "That's terrible. Judge Howard was friendly to our side. He *loved* you. Who knows what this new guy will think of our big shot law firm taking on a pro bono case for training."

"Or new gal," I mutter irritably.

Tom ignores me, takes a pen from his pocket and whips it toward his desk. He misses his mark by a few feet and the pen buries itself into Tom's abstract cream and grey area rug. This must be a common form of stress release for Tom as I notice several other pens lodged in various spots near his desk.

"Our new judge is Clarence Tyler and I'll tell you what he thinks." Tom advances on Ethan, now invading his personal space. "I just got off the phone with his clerk. He thinks Judge Howard has been too lenient with us. Granted us too many continuances. Trial is rescheduled to Judge Howard's originally proposed date of April thirtieth."

"What?" Ethan and I exclaim in unison.

Tom continues ranting. "That means we have less than three fucking weeks to write opening and closing statements, prep our expert, and draft cross examinations of the medical examiner and police officers. Not to mention identify any other witnesses we may want to call. I hope you two didn't plan to sleep in the next twenty days because that's out of the fucking question. You will eat and breathe this case, is that clear?"

Ethan and I exchange stunned glances before murmuring our agreement.

"Good. Get back to your offices and I'll email your assignments."

I descend the two floors in a state of shock. How will we prepare a winning defense in only twenty days? We'll be lucky to clear the low bar of effective assistance of counsel. Roughly ten minutes after returning to my desk, I receive Tom's list of assignments. The tasks seem Herculean at this juncture:

Confirm Dr. Smart is available - Ethan
Draft questioning of Dr. Smart - Tom
Set up a meeting with Tammy to discuss new trial date and strategy - Maeve
Rough draft of opening statement to Tom by end of the week - Maeve
Rough draft of closing statement to Tom by end of the week - Ethan
Draft cross examination of medical examiner - Ethan
Identify and prepare exhibits for jury - Maeve
Draft cross examinations of police at crime scene - Ethan
Identify any helpful witnesses to call for trial - Maeve
Draft motion in limine to exclude testimony about previous altercations between Tammy and Kyleigh - Maeve
Draft motion to exclude media from courtroom - Ethan
Prepare jury voir dire - Tom

By the time I reach the end of the list my palms are sweaty and my heart rate is over one hundred beats per minute. Tom is right. Between completing these tasks, finishing Elizabeth's brief, and taking even mediocre care of my kids, there will be little time for rest in the next three weeks. What have I gotten myself into? I rise from my chair and walk across the hall to Jeanine's cubicle. One thing I can always count on from my assistant is an ever-present supply of chocolate. Once having been given a large handful of Hershey kisses in exchange for showing Jeanine a couple recent photos of Dec and Shay, I'm ready to start chipping away at the tasks.

I've just secured a visitation appointment with Tammy for Thursday and am emailing the pertinent information to the murder squad, when my phone rings again. I thought we'd all collectively agreed to limit our forms of communication to texts and emails. I throw an annoyed glance at the caller ID and my heart skips a beat. It's none other than Jabba the Hut. Today can't get any worse.

I pick up the receiver and before I can even stammer hello, Chris commands, "Shaw. My office. Now."

I feel like Sean Penn in *Dead Man Walking* as I slowly make my way from the lowly associate side of the forty-fourth floor to the large partner offices. Chris is finishing off what looks to have been a custard-filled donut when I cross the threshold into his kingdom. I notice a bit of filling remains on the right corner of Chris's mouth and choose to make that my focal point for the remainder of this conversation.

"Maeve, long time no see," Chris begins sarcastically. "Now, correct me if I'm wrong, but I seem to remember us having a conversation about your hours expectation when you were last here."

I give a slight nod of my head in response.

Chris continues, "Good, good. We're on the same page. I was beginning to think I was delusional. Do you know why I might have thought that?"

This time a slight shake of my head in response. My eyes are laser focused on the custard glob which expands and retracts as Chris delivers his clearly rehearsed browbeating.

"Well, let me enlighten you then. You see, I remember being quite clear about a certain one hundred and seventy-five monthly billable hours requirement during our last conversation. And yet in the two weeks since our meeting, your billable hours have only declined. Were you somehow confused about my expectation?"

The small voice that I'm able to muster in response is pathetic even to my ears. "No, sir. I wasn't confused. I've just been billing the bulk of my hours to Tom's murder case. If you add those to my billable ones, I'm working over eighty hours a week."

Chris slams his hand on his desk so hard the crumbs jump. "I thought I made it clear to you last time that I don't give a shit about pro bono hours. I want you working for clients who *pay* their bills."

Now I'm in full grovel mode. "Please, Chris. Just let me get through this trial and I'll pull my billables up to where you want them to be. Our trial date was moved up to the end of April, so I just need three more weeks. Please." Tears spring to my eyes and I change my focus to my feet. Chris remains unmoved.

Sighing, he responds, "Maeve, I'll be honest. If I were you, I'd be updating my resume. You just aren't Mulvaney Stewart partner material. Please close the door on your way out."

***

The rest of the day I alternate between concocting a persuasive opening statement and dry heaving into my garbage can. Countless times I find myself reaching for the phone to call Patrick, but something always stops me. We used to be each other's main confidants. In graduate school we'd lie for hours in bed discussing politics, television shows, books, and our hopes for the future. The only topic I clammed up about was my childhood, for obvious reasons. But after the boys arrived, we were both so busy just trying to tread water that we came to an unspoken understanding that the boys were the only real topic of conversation between us. Any work stress one of us might be under was for that person to resolve. Not shockingly, I've felt more alone in the last few years than I've felt since I left for college.

A wave of relief rushes over me when my phone alarm goes off at four forty-five reminding me of "parent teacher conferences" at daycare. First, it's a ridiculous requirement given the boys' ages of six years and sixteen months. The most they "teach" them at daycare is how to craft and play nicely with others. Second, Declan and Seamus are never any trouble for the staff, so this should be a breeze. After grabbing my things and hailing a cab, I manage to even arrive a mere five minutes late for my conference. Winning.

Miss Sarah takes the boys into the art room while I sit uncomfortably across from Miss Yolanda at a toddler-sized desk. Needing to get the boys fed and to bed quickly so I can get back to trial prep, I cut to the chase.

"Miss Yolanda, Declan and Seamus love it here at For Your Child. The teachers are all so friendly and kind. The boys arrive each morning with smiles on their faces and at night Dec can't wait to tell me about the day's activities. Unless you have any concerns, I think we can cut this conference short."

I presumptively begin to stand when Miss Yolanda responds, "Actually I do have some concerns I need to address with you."

I freeze mid-rise. Miss Yolanda's face looks so grave that I find myself taking a shaky breath and sitting back down.

Miss Yolanda continues. "As a daycare, we are sensitive to the demands placed on working parents. Most of our children at For Your Child have two working parents who are doing their best to balance the responsibilities of work and home. And for the most part, our parents seem to conduct this balancing act beautifully." At this, Miss Yolanda pauses and takes a sip of her tea. She then focuses her gaze on me before delivering the verdict. "Unfortunately, it doesn't seem that you and your husband are able to balance these demands as well as some others."

My stomach clenches as if I've been punched in the gut. Which I believe I have been in an emotional sense. I stammer, "Where is this coming from? I drop off the boys every day and pick them up every night. Just like every other parent here."

Miss Yolanda shakes her head sadly. "I'm just telling you what the boys are telling us. Well, Declan really. He says he only gets to see Daddy on the weekends and he misses him. He says you're always in a rush to get them to bed so you can get back to work." Miss Yolanda pauses as if considering whether to add the next part. She ultimately decides it's necessary to do so. "Declan also said, more than once, that he's heard you crying at night."

I interrupt unconvinced. "When? When did he tell you these things? He hasn't said anything like this to me."

Miss Yolanda shakes her head sadly. "You know we have a counselor on staff that we call Ms. Feelings, right? The children are free to go to her office at any time and talk about their big emotions. These can be issues with the other kids in school or issues at home. I'm sad to say, Ms. Feelings sees Declan daily. And even little Seamus is clingier and more emotional than the other kids his age."

I clasp a hand over my mouth and fold in half as the world crumbles around me. How have I allowed myself to become so wrapped up in a stupid job that Dec has to seek out a counselor to talk to about his loneliness? That Seamus has to cling to maternal stand-ins? Of all the things I set out to be, a good mother was at the absolute top of the list. And I'm failing. Failing miserably. My chest starts to constrict and my breathing becomes ragged. I have to get out of here. I rise so abruptly, I send the toddler seat tumbling behind me.

"I need to leave," I manage to squeak as I stride to the art room and yank open the door. Declan, Seamus and Miss Sarah are coloring pictures of The Incredibles. They all look up, startled at my aggressive entrance.

"Boys, we have to go," I pronounce shakily.

Declan begins putting back the crayons as they've been taught, but my panic continues to rise. I can't have a meltdown here. "Now, boys. We're leaving now!"

I pick Seamus up and we walk the block back to our house in silence, tears streaming down my face the entire way.

Chapter 20

As I wait for the water to hit the boiling point necessary to add the fusilli noodles, my mind is spinning. How do I fix this? How do I make this right? One thing I know for sure is that Patrick and I need to make some major life changes. We need to forget about our romantic complications and unite for the boys' sake. We both need to slow down at work and be more present at home. I may be out of a job soon, so that shouldn't be too hard on my end. But Patrick is going to need to talk to Ernst & Young about only being onsite three days a week or maybe every other week. The weekends aren't enough. Clearly. The more I think about the necessary adjustments, the more I realize I need a face-to-face discussion with Patrick. And soon. But when will I have time with all the trial tasks?

I put planning aside and sit down to actually share a meal with the boys. Most nights I sit the boys' plates on one side of the kitchen island and return emails from the other side. I then eat the leftovers as I clean up. Tonight I get my own plate of pasta with steamed broccoli, leave my phone on the counter, and seat us all at the reclaimed wood dining room table. Declan tells me about the plastic eggs he helped fill with jelly beans in preparation for the daycare egg hunt in a few weeks. Seamus gets down from his booster seat and shows me how the bunny hops into the house each Easter. He even gets pretty close to saying "bunny" with "bunda." Declan is excited about a new yoga program they're offering at school. He already knows downward facing dog, tree, and happy baby poses. He laughs as I tell them about a yoga class I once took where a woman emitted a loud fart while attempting happy baby. Thank goodness for the lavender essential oil they diffused soon after that during savasana. As I feel the day's tension begin to release with each minute I share with my boys, I admonish myself for ever missing out on moments like this.

After getting them both into jammies and reading *Where's Baby's Belly Button* to Seamus, I give him a big squeeze and kiss on his forehead before laying him in his crib. I then walk with Declan to his room to read our chapter. When Wilbur laments that he's not terrific but average for a pig, I can relate. Although according to Miss Yolanda, I'm not even batting average as a mom.

With Dec in bed, I climb the stairs, laptop in hand, to put in a few more hours on this opening statement. But as the minutes tick by, I find myself unable to concentrate on anything other than my burning desire to talk things through with Patrick. And I know this is a conversation that needs to take place in person. The phone won't substitute this time.

How do I make this work? Let's see. The murder squad is going to see Tammy on Thursday. And Tom wants a draft of this statement on Friday. But tomorrow Tom's in an all-day mediation for one of his City of Chicago lawsuits, this one involving alleged bribery in exchange for jobs with the Department of Streets and Sanitation. Might not seem like an ideal job, but it comes with a City pension so it's apparently in high demand. I open a new browser window and go to the Southwest Airlines site. There's a five-thirty a.m. flight that would get me to Boston by eight-forty. Patrick usually takes calls from his hotel in the morning before heading into the office, so I should be able to catch him. I would just need to drop the boys off with his parents by four. I'll tell Mary I had something come up and need to fly out for a one-day client visit. I can also work on the opening during my flights. This is perfect. It's the only chance Patrick and I will really have to talk (sans kids) before the trial ends. I book the flight and call my amazing mother-in-law for a favor.

As I lie in bed and try to force myself to get at least four hours of sleep, my mind starts to spin. Is this a smart move with all that's going on at work? To be honest, it isn't. If I want to keep my job, I should drop the boys off early and make sure Jabba sees me toiling away on Elizabeth's brief for one of our top-paying clients. But I couldn't care less about that now. My boys are more important than a promotion. The next question that plagues me is why I haven't given Patrick a heads up about my trip. The truth to that one is harder to face. It's because I want to see if he's alone tomorrow morning. If I arrive and he's with her, then I will finally admit that things are unfixable and I need to start planning for the next phase of my life with the boys and sans Patrick.

***

My flight is on time and my cab pulls up to the Boston Marriott Long Wharf just after nine. I don't know what room Patrick is in, so I stop by the front desk. I pulled on yoga pants, a long-sleeve running shirt, and sneakers for the flight. I just remove my jacket, drop it on a lobby chair, and am ready with a story.

"Hi, I'm Maeve Shaw. I was on my way back to my room when I realized I left my room key on the treadmill. Could you give me a new one?"

The petite red-head behind the desk with the nameplate "Emma" punches some keys at her computer. She looks like a walking advertisement for Aer Lingus. "Maeve Shaw you say? I don't see your reservation."

I laugh. "Of course. The reservation is under my husband's name, Patrick."

More clicking at the keyboard. "Oh yes, here you are. Patrick Shaw. Platinum Member. Room 610." Emma feeds a keycard into the magnetizing machine and hands it over to me.

The elevator seems to be moving in slow motion and my palms begin to sweat. I try to put the image of walking in on Patrick's face between Marcie's legs out of my mind and instead focus on my reason for coming. As any good litigator would do, I try to anticipate Patrick's reaction to hearing Miss Yolanda's comments at the parent teacher conference. He has never been a huge fan of For Your Child. He had wanted to send the boys to a Montessori school farther north of the city, but the additional twenty-minute commute each way didn't seem worth it to me. Still, I don't see how he can dismiss her concerns entirely. If he's dubious, I'll offer to set up an appointment for us both with this counselor woman, Ms. Feelings. Given the extent of Declan's visits with her, we should really make an appointment regardless of Patrick's reaction. I need to hear if Dec has other worries he talks to her about beyond Patrick's and my absence.

I take a deep breath as I slide the key into the card slot and pull it back out. This isn't going to be a fun conversation, but our boys need us to be adults. I say a final silent prayer that Patrick is indeed on his morning conference calls and not with Marcie and push the door open. Instant confusion. Is my mind playing tricks on me? Ethan is sitting on the edge of the bed, iPhone in hand, with just a towel around his waist.

He looks up and starts to say, "Excuse me. Who the—" but then stops, shock written all over his face.

My mind still can't process the visual stimulation. Did Emma give me the wrong room? Why is Ethan staying at the Boston Marriott? Shouldn't he be in Chicago working on the closing statement?

"What are you doing here?" I manage to stutter.

Just then Patrick comes out of the bathroom, towel wrapped around his waist as well. He doesn't see me. He walks straight to Ethan and lays a hand tenderly on his shoulder.

"I called the office and told them I'm not feeling well. We have the whole day free. What time is your flight tonight?" I watch him lean down and kiss the top of Ethan's head. All the while Ethan hasn't taken his eyes off me.

"What in the hell is going on here?" I blurt.

Patrick sure notices me now. He drops his hand from Ethan's shoulder, but remains mute. The fear in his eyes tells me all I need to know. All this time, Ethan was Marcie.

"So what? Are you two together now? Are you a couple?" I ask. Even though I know the answer.

Patrick regains the ability to speak but can only run his hands through his hair and mutter, "Shit, Maeve. I'm so sorry. You were never supposed to find out this way."

The shock and disbelief begins to dissipate and be replaced by pure unfiltered fury. "Look, I'm not stupid, Patrick. I knew you were cheating on me, but I assumed it was with some skank from work. Not one of my best friends."

Patrick shakes his head sadly, but doesn't respond. I keep going. "And Ethan, how could you look me in the eye every day at work. Ask me out for shitty Chinese food. Push me to take on a pro bono case that is actively ruining my career. And then sext my husband each night? I trusted you!"

Ethan does what he always does when he's backed into a corner. He comes out swinging. "Cut the crap, Maeve. Don't act like you're innocent in this."

I find myself physically taking a step back in response to this outrageous accusation. "Wait. You think *I'm* somehow to blame for this? *I* turned my husband gay? *I* made you a backstabbing slut?"

Ethan spits back, "You two don't even know each other. You've remained blind to your husband's sexuality for years even though it was immediately obvious to both me and your bestie."

Patrick, never one for confrontation, steps in between Ethan and me and tries to defuse the situation. "Hey, there's no need for mean-spiritedness here. Let's calm down and talk about this like adults."

I push Patrick aside with my forearm and get right in Ethan's face. "Wait, you've talked to *Zara* about this?"

Ethan laughs. "Oh yeah. Zara and I've had *many* conversations on the subject. Way before Patrick and I started sleeping together. It was like our running joke. We both wondered how long it would take for you to wake up. I knew you'd never admit it unless the proof was right in front of your face."

My voice is raised now and I can feel my face flush with anger. "What a couple of great friends you two turned out to be. You're nothing but gossipy bitches. Instead of talking to me you decide it would be best just to screw him! Prove your point. Did you have money on this?"

Patrick grabs my arm to pull me back from Ethan, but I whip it out of his hands and in doing so end up accidentally slapping Ethan in the face. He puts his hand to his cheek and his mouth hangs open. I'm just about to apologize when he spits, "It's not like you've ever wanted to talk about hard things, Maeve. I mean, Jesus, Patrick didn't even know about your parents' murder-suicide until I told him."

Stunned silence. From the look on Ethan's face, even he knows he's gone too far.

"Ethan, that was uncalled for," Patrick says as he tries again to take my arm.

I drop the key card and begin backing from the room. Ethan's conscience seems to have awoken as I vaguely hear him say, "Shit, Maeve. I'm sorry."

I run to the elevator and jump in the first door that opens, not caring if it's going up or down. I just need to get away from them. Right as the elevator doors are about to close, I see Patrick standing two feet away, still in his towel. I think he says he's sorry, but it's too late.

Chapter 21

I turn left at the corner of Brookshire Parkway onto Spruce Drive. Only a quarter mile to my house to complete my three miles. I'm getting faster. When Nancy, my therapist, suggested I start exercising to reduce my anxiety, it took me a full thirty-five minutes to complete this loop. Today I should clock in at around twenty-eight. I'll give it to Nancy, this half hour a day is when I feel my best. It hasn't hurt that it's been an unseasonably warm and dry spring. It'll be harder to keep this habit up during the winter months in Chicago, but I'm determined not to gain the freshman fifteen.

I slow down as the dark blue A-frame comes into view. When we had the house repainted a few years ago, I somehow convinced my parents to paint the front door yellow. It's still my favorite feature of the house. Who wouldn't want to knock at a house with a cheery yellow door? Not that we have many visitors outside of Mom's booze crew. They call themselves "the ladies who lunch." That's true if you consider chardonnay and valium a balanced meal. As I walk up the two front stairs and pause at the white railing, my eyes drift to the old-fashioned porch swing. The swing seems to be waiting for a couple to sit and enjoy a lemonade while catching up with the goings-on of the neighborhood. It'll have to keep waiting.

Before I can slip my key into the lock, I hear loud voices inside the house. So much for the anxiety-relieving effects of my run. I turn the key as quietly as I can and slip inside, closing the door soundlessly behind me. Mom and Dad are in the kitchen. As I tiptoe down the hallway to my room, I hear glass shatter. One of them has thrown a plate or a cup. I see another trip to Crate and Barrel in our future.

My mom slurs, "That's it. I've had it. I want a divorce."

I freeze at my bedroom door, my hand on the knob, my heart pounding in my chest. I've overheard a lot of fights, but I've never heard either of them use the "d word."

My father's voice is raised but flat. "We are not getting a divorce."

My mother laughs harshly. "I'm getting a divorce and there's nothing you can do about it."

My mother stumbles toward their bedroom. She'll see me if she looks down the hall. I tiptoe to the living room. There's a small space between the china cabinet and the wall just big enough for me to squeeze into. No one can see me unless they're at the dining room table. This hiding space has come in handy during numerous arguments. I squeeze around the china cabinet and slide down the wall, my knees pulled against my chest, my heart still pounding. Will Mom actually leave me here alone with Dad? Will she abandon me? I hear drawers opening and closing in their bedroom.

My father bellows, "Put that shit away, Joanna. You aren't going anywhere."

"The hell I'm not."

"What about Maeve?" Dad hollers. "Have you completely forgotten you have a daughter?"

"You were the one who wanted her, Michael. Not me. You wanted a wife and a kid to show off with pictures on your desk. While sticking me with the job of actually raising her. Well, she's your problem now."

Mom's revelation knocks the air from my lungs. So that's why she doesn't love me. She never wanted me in the first place.

The door to their bedroom opens with a bang. From my vantage point, I can only see Mom from the waist down. She's wearing cream linen pants with navy high heels. In her hand she clutches her brown overnight bag. Dad's right behind her. Still in his black suit pants from the office. He grabs her arm.

Pleading, he says, "You haven't thought this through, Joanna. Where are you going to sleep tonight?"

Mom pauses. Then she giggles. "Oh, this is rich. You really don't know? You haven't even guessed? Bob and I've been seeing each other for six months."

Silence. Dad stutters incredulously, "Bob? Bob Mullins? My partner?"

Mom smiles cruelly. "That's the one."

Dad is out of his element. He's not used to being on the receiving end of surprise revelations. "What does Tess think about all this?"

More giggling. "You really are clueless. Bob moved out of the house last month. He's renting a place two blocks from the office. I've been a frequent visitor. It's over, Michael."

I hear Dad almost whisper, "Do you love him?"

Mom whips around. She's enjoying this. She takes her time responding. "Well, I love having his big, fat cock in my mouth during his lunch breaks. And I love that he's more interested in fucking me at night than prepping for court. And I love that I feel alive when I'm with him, instead of feeling like I'm married to a fucking corpse."

Mom walks to the front door, my dad unmoving. She stops and turns to deliver the final blow. "Oh, and Michael. You're going to have to replenish Maeve's college fund. I've been dipping into it the last few months when you've been stingy with my spending money. I withdrew the last three thousand dollars this morning. Bob and I are going to Mexico next week."

In a flash, Dad darts into their bedroom. I hear the front door open and the screen door slam behind Mom. My dad reappears in my line of vision. He's running after her. I see his handgun in his right hand. The one he always keeps in his bedside table for protection against all the burglars roaming the mean streets of Carmel, Indiana. I need to stop him. I need to scream and warm Mom. But I do neither. I'm frozen. Still reeling from Mom's confessions. I hear the screen door slam again. Then a loud explosion. Then another. Then silence. I remain frozen.

Chapter 22

I travelled back to Chicago on autopilot. I completed the outward motions of hailing a cab from the Marriott, changing my flight departure to noon, walking to the designated gate, sitting next to an elderly gentleman in seat 13D and pretending to sleep to avoid continuing the already too lengthy conversation about the hassle of getting a CPAP machine through security ("Don't they know it's a medically necessary device! The difference between life and death, really!"), and hailing a Lyft from Midway home. But inside I felt frozen.

When I finally open the door of our townhome, I sit my purse down on the top stair leading from the front door to the living room like always. It's how the boys know that I'm home when they are out with Patrick. If they walk in and see my purse on the top step, they immediately start calling my name.

My gaze drifts to the family pictures decorating our walls. Patrick with his arm around me sitting on the arm rest of our love seat while I cradle a six-week-old Declan. The picture was taken in this very living room. Declan was outfitted in blue-and-white striped overalls with a tiny white onesie underneath. I remember I had to bunch up the excess fabric in the back as I held him so the outfit looked more fitted. Declan was born at six pounds three ounces and didn't fit into any of the one-to-three month clothes I had pre-purchased. Yet, I was determined he was going to wear those adorable overalls for his first pictures, sizing be damned. The photographer placated me for a few shots, but then suggested we take the rest of the pictures with Declan just in his diaper. They were perfect.

I remember how nervous and excited Patrick and I were during those newborn months. Being an only child, I had no clue what I was doing. Patrick had a bit more common sense when it came to babies, having learned some things from his siblings. I smile in spite of myself as I remember our early morning walks to Starbucks with Declan in his stroller. The only people in the coffee shop before seven on a Saturday morning were other parents with small children. And of course, all the late night diaper changes and feedings. Patrick was a trooper. Even though he didn't have the generous law firm maternity leave I had, he still got up and changed Declan two or three times a night before handing him back to me to nurse. He was basically running entirely on caffeine in those days.

I next look at the most recent family photo hanging above our dining room table. This time of our family of four at the Chicago Botanical Gardens. The same place we were married. We had spread out a blanket near the lake there. Declan was engrossed with his green stuffed teddy bear, Orso Verde, he brought along as an "entertainer." Seamus, around five months old at the time, was propped up between my legs blowing strawberries. And Patrick and I were looking into each other's eyes. Those eyes aren't full of the same youthful excitement they were in Declan's baby pictures, but they twinkle in shared amusement at the insanity of attempting a professional portrait session with a preschooler and an infant. That's when the reality of my situation hits me. There will be no more family photo shoots. I will no longer have a partner to share a knowing look with during the chaos. Hell, I'm not even sure I'll be the one who gets this house. A crushing weight lands squarely on my shoulders and my legs buckle. I lunge the couple of steps to the couch, curl up in a ball and cover myself with the green plaid blanket that resides on the back for just such an occasion. A present from Mary a few Christmases ago. She said she wanted to give me something warm to snuggle up with on the nights Patrick was away. I wonder if she foresaw the demise of our marriage as well. I feel a stabbing pain in my thigh and I reach into the pocket of my leggings to extricate my phone. I switch it to silent and let sleep overtake me.

I'm startled awake by a loud banging at my front door. It's completely dark in the house and I have no clue what time it is. Given my state of exhaustion I would guess the middle of the night. I spot my phone on the reclaimed wood coffee table next to the couch. The clock says five past seven. I guess that makes sense given my plane landed at Midway around three-thirty. My phone shows four missed calls and three texts from Patrick. I turn the phone off with the messages unread. All the while the loud knocking continues at the door. I start to stand up to answer it when I hear the all too familiar tone of my former best friend:

"Maeve, I know you're in there. Answer the door, please."

I sit right back down. Zara must be out of her goddamn mind to think I'd let her in.

A few more seconds go by and the knocking resumes in earnest.

"Maeve, you know I'm not leaving. You can either answer the door or have this conversation within earshot of all your neighbors."

Shit! I don't need the whole block privy to my humiliation. Especially the cookie cutter family next door. Husband is a successful investment banker (which he reminds me of every time we meet), wife is an adorable blonde spin instructor (her ass is a thing of beauty I'll admit), and baby Charlotte is a pudgy cherub.

I quickly scamper over to the front door and say loud enough for Zara to hear, but hopefully no one else, "Zara, I don't want to talk to you right now. Or ever, actually. Please leave. You owe me that much."

Another pause. Zara responds, but quieter this time. I actually have to press my ear against the door to catch it all.

"Maeve, I know why you're mad. Patrick called me. He told me everything. Including what Ethan said about me. It wasn't true."

I don't believe her. She feels guilty and is about to engage in some revisionist history.

"So, let me get this straight. Ethan invented entire conversations where you two placed bets on how long it would take for me to figure out my husband's sexual orientation? Just pulled that nugget out of thin air?"

Zara sighs. "Okay, it happened, but it wasn't like that."

I punch the door in response. My knuckles scream in protest.

"It's just Patrick is always so well dressed and well groomed and well behaved, that Ethan and I would sometimes say we couldn't believe he was straight. Or even that I thought Ethan was more Patrick's type."

Oof! That went straight to the heart.

Zara realizes she's stumbled and tries to regain her footing. "But listen, it was in jest. I never actually believed Patrick would cheat on you. With any gender. I swear. Believe me, if I got even the slightest cheater vibe, I would have told you. I've always been straight with you. You know that."

My heart unclenches. Zara is telling the truth. She's been my best friend for over twenty years and in that time she's always had my back. She was the first person I told about my parents during a midnight talkathon fueled by a good amount of pot, and she never breathed a word of it to any of the other girls in our dorm. She would take my secret to the grave if I asked, which I did. I unlock the deadbolt and open the door. Zara is standing on my stoop with a bottle of wine in one hand and a box of Lou Malnati's pizza in the other. My stomach suddenly remembers that it's been empty for over twenty-four hours and comes to life with a roar. I relieve Zara of her peace offering, place them on the first stair, and rush into her open arms.

Chapter 23

Zara follows me into the living room where I immediately sit down cross-legged on the hardwood floor and house a good three quarters of the pizza straight from the box in less than five minutes. I then wash it down with a glass or two of a fine California cabernet, chugging straight from the bottle. After I'm satiated and slightly intoxicated, I have the nerve to ask the question that's been eating me since Zara arrived.

"Have you talked to Ethan?"

Zara squeezes her eyes closed before admitting, "Yes, briefly."

"Are you serious?" I bellow. "How could you?"

Zara grabs my arms to stop me from standing and storming upstairs. "I know. I know. He's a total shit. But I had to let him have it. I mean, working with you in the office everyday while he's shagging your husband on the side. That's pretty awful shit to do to a friend. But telling Patrick about your parents? That's what put me over the edge."

"I know!" I yell in agreement, nearly knocking over the bottle of wine with my wild gesticulations. "That was the nail in the coffin for me too. I keep thinking back to that night. It was the tenth anniversary of their deaths. Ethan and I were third years at the time. We were both working late on a doc review project for a pharmaceutical company. Ironically, we were reviewing documents to determine the sufficiency of a parent company's oversight of local pharmacies who were caught filling thousands of phony opioid prescriptions. He came by my office for a break. He barged in without knocking, as usual, and found me crouched between my desk and the wall in the midst of a full-scale panic attack. He helped me calm down and then took me out for a drink at Rivers. After a couple of vodka and Sprites, I spilled my guts. The next morning, after I had recovered sufficiently from my hangover, I went straight to his office and made him swear to secrecy. So much for that. That man would sell his grandmother's soul to the devil for a good screw."

Zara guffaws briefly before turning serious again. "He really is sorry, Maeve. For everything. He started crying a bit over the phone. He said that he was always jealous of your and Patrick's relationship and he wanted that for himself. I think he's been really lonely these last few years."

"He can join the club," I snap. "Patrick and I may have looked like the perfect couple on our few nights out, but appearances can be deceiving, you know."

Zara nods her head thoughtfully. "You're right." A minute or two passes before she adds, "I guess I just thought if you knew where he was coming from, however flawed his reasoning might be, it would help you hate him a bit less."

A wave of exhaustion hits me with Zara's words, and I lie down on the hardwood and stare up at the recessed LED lights Patrick researched obsessively before purchasing. Apparently, there are a lot of options in the eco friendly lighting market. Zara scoots her little legging-clad booty over and lies down next to me. She rests her head on my shoulder.

"I don't think I have any more hate left in me. It's too exhausting. And I wasn't blameless here. I told Patrick my mom died of cancer and my father of a broken heart soon after. That's way more than stretching the truth. I turned my *Breaking Bad* family into *Where the Red Fern Grows*."

We laugh and then lie quietly for a bit longer.

"When do you have to pick up the munchkins from their grandparents' house?"

The question whips me back to reality. "I asked Mary to take them to daycare in the morning. I'll pick them up after work. Ethan and I are scheduled to visit Tammy for trial prep. Should be an interesting meeting."

Zara giggles. "Oh, how I wish I could be a fly on the wall during that meeting. You two are going to make the killer mommy feel uncomfortable."

I smile before chiding, "Hey now. My client is innocent until proven guilty. And I for one think she'll be acquitted."

I find myself musing about the pros and cons of the case. Pro: the prosecution's case rests on this ridiculous blanket strangulation theory, which our expert should be able to debunk. Con: the adoption papers which may still be in Simon Harr's garbage waiting to be discovered. It seems wrong to just sit on this information. And what if there is something else the police overlooked in there that is helpful to Tammy's case? A jolt of adrenaline courses through my veins. I sit up so quickly my vision goes black and I have to brace myself to allow my blood pressure to normalize.

"Are you okay?" Zara asks, sitting up as well.

"Yeah, I'm fine. I just got a crazy idea. You want to let ourselves into a drug dealer's old apartment and do some digging?"

"Wouldn't that be a felony?" Zara asks incredulously.

"Oh, don't be so dramatic. The apartment has been abandoned." *I think.* "Who's going to complain?" *Except maybe neighbors.* "We'll just let ourselves in, see what we can see, and let ourselves back out. No one will be the wiser." *Let's pray.*

"Isn't it an active crime scene?"

"Oh, the police finished processing the scene ages ago. It's just an abandoned apartment at this point." Again, I should add, *I think.*

"What are you even hoping to find?"

I answer honestly. "I don't know. But ever since I talked to Simon, I've had the feeling that there might be something else there. Something that helps Tammy."

"Are you actually serious about this?" Zara is looking at me as if I've gone completely mental.

"Yes, I am," I say adamantly. "I'm sick of being the person things are done to. I'm ready to be the hero of my own narrative." After a quizzical look from Zara, I add sheepishly, "I may have read that on a T-shirt."

Chapter 24

The Lyft drops us off on the corner of Central and Marsh Avenues after ten-thirty p.m. As we start to open the door, the Lyft driver, a nice young woman named Charlene, stops us.

"How do you two expect to get back home?"

Silence. The plan up until this point consisted entirely of grabbing flashlights, gloves, throwing on jackets and calling a Lyft. I can feel Zara's eyes boring into the side of my head.

I stumble, "I guess we just thought we'd call for another Lyft?"

Charlene shakes her head. "This isn't the type of neighborhood Lyfts or cabs will respond to. It's a bit shady as you can see."

Yes, I guess neighborhoods where drug dealers live might not be entirely safe. Looking across at the townhome block where Simon resided, I see several boarded-up windows and graffiti-tagged bricks.

"Look, here's my card. When you two finish up with whatever it is you are doing here, why don't you give me a call. I'll come back around and get you. You can wait for me at the 7-Eleven up the block."

After many thank yous have been said, we get out of the blue Toyota Prius and exchange nervous glances. The street is dark and empty, but I can hear music coming from inside one of the houses down Marsh. We cross over to the townhouse complex. All the units on Central look abandoned and boarded up. I was counting on this. That means no neighbors to call the cops on intruders.

The front door of Simon's unit is locked and still has the yellow crime scene tape across it. I start to look at the windows to see if any are ajar when Zara pushes past me. She pulls a Target gift card from her wallet and slides it between the door and the frame. After a minute or two of adjusting it, Zara's able to use the card to push back the bolt and the door swings open. Zara then quietly removes some of the yellow tape and we step inside.

The smell of rotting food and bodily waste is oppressive, but I'm still too curious not to ask. "Ummm, did you forget to tell me you were a jewel thief back in Springfield, Maryland?"

Zara shakes her head. "Nothing like that. But as a preteen, I had dreams of working for the CIA. I was all into spy gear. I must have watched *La Femme Nikita* twenty times. Anyway, I begged my parents to buy me some spy books, and one of the tricks I learned was how to pick a lock."

"Unfortunately, not a very useful skill for a legal recruiting director," I note.

"Oh, you'd be surprised. During a holiday party I was tipped off that one of our highest earning partners had taken one of our new associates back to his office and locked the door. I had that door open in seconds and was able to put a stop to the situation before any clothes were removed."

"Are you serious!" I say, completely shocked.

"Yes, I'm serious," Zara responds with a satisfied smirk. "And I had all the locks removed from the office doors the very next day. The only people who can have locks on their doors now are those that are pumping, and the locks are removed when they are finished nursing."

"Go you, ya badass." And we fist bump.

Then our attention returns to the task at hand. We get out the flashlights I was able to find in our kitchen junk drawer. I remember needing them about a year ago when a snowstorm knocked out the electricity on our block overnight. Declan and I enjoyed PB&Js over flashlight. Seamus was still too young for solid foods. Then we all slept in my bed to keep warm. I smile thinking of their snuggles.

Shining the weak light around the living room, I can see little has been moved since the police photographed the place. Now there is just a thick layer of dust over everything. And some stray excrement. I silently pray it is rat and not human. And then find myself asking, is that actually better?

Zara turns to me with a serious expression. "Okay, Maeve. You have five minutes to play Nancy Drew and then we're out of here. What are we looking for?"

That is more than fair. "Okay, let's divide and conquer. Put on the kitchen gloves that I gave you and look in the trashcans. Simon said that Kyleigh tore up the adoption papers and threw them in the garbage. I'm just going to have a look in the other rooms to see if the police missed anything else important."

"Gee, thanks," Zara grumbles. "I love a good dumpster dive."

I ignore her and walk off into the kitchen. I shine my light and disturb a family of rats who have made a home inside a decaying pizza box. After a cursory glance around the rest of the room I have to turn off the light and back away to stop from retching. There are still old takeout containers strewn around the kitchen, and I think I saw maggots feasting on something on the "dining room table." The same table where Garrett had slept in his car seat while his mom lay dying in the bedroom.

"I found them," Zara calls.

I make my way back to the living room and find Zara trying to read from scraps of torn papers. A look over her shoulder confirms she has found what looks like legal documents. Zara holds up a quarter sheet entitled, "Adopt-200 Adoption Request." Next to the line labeled: "Your name (adopting parent)" is written in blue ink "Tammy Lynne Sanford." Looks like Simon was telling the truth. I snap a few photos with my iPhone.

"Okay, I found it. Can we go now?" Zara asks.

Not quite ready to give up, I plead, "Just give me a couple of minutes to check in the other rooms and then we're on our way to the 7-Eleven. I promise."

Zara holds up three fingers. "Three minutes. I'm serious."

I nod and hurry back toward the bedrooms. I briefly glance into the room where Kyleigh was found. It seems that someone has gone over this room with a fine-tooth comb. The bed is stripped. The closet is empty. Even the floor has been cleared of all the drug paraphernalia. I see some brown stains on the dresser and carpet that appear to be blood, but whether it is from Kyleigh on the night she died or from some random night when Simon was high is anyone's guess. I remember cleaning up blood from various parts of our house from Mom's drunken/drugged falls. Dishwashing detergent and water is really the best stain remover, I've found.

Knowing Zara's clock is ticking, I venture farther into the back of the house. Maybe the police wouldn't have searched the other bedrooms as thoroughly. The next room I come to doesn't have a bed per se. Just a thin mattress tossed against the back wall. The mattress is covered in stains, which appear to have been caused by bodily fluids. I struggle to control my gag reflex as I use a gloved hand to lift the mattress high enough to shine my light under. Nothing except the expected dust and grime. My optimism begins to waver.

The next room on the right of the hallway is small enough to have been intended for a nursery, but Simon appears to have used it as his man cave. Some wooden crates have been stacked into what appears to be a makeshift desk. There is also a beanbag chair in front of a fifty-two inch flat screen TV attached to some gaming system. The floor is littered with empty Coke bottles and crumpled bags of Doritos and Lays. I walk over to the crates. The only items on top are a black pen and a highlighter. Giving the desk a last once over with my light, I notice a two-inch gap between the crates and the wall. On a whim, I pull the left crate back and look behind it. Nothing. I then pull the right crate. Duct taped to the back is a black College Rule spiral notebook.

Having detached the notebook from the crate, I start flipping through it. Turns out Simon is quite the conscientious businessman. Each page details what sales he made and to whom. Most of the customers are listed just by first name followed by the amount paid. Under January 12, 2015 is written "Tony - $130. Brittney - $540. Wayne - $100. Brandy- $300." Next to a few entries there is an asterisk and a note to collect tomorrow. Each day's entries end with a grand total usually of around two thousand dollars. Seems that Simon was a fairly small-time dealer. I flip through to the back of the notebook and notice the sales entries stop on August 3, 2015. The same day Kyleigh died. But scrawled across the top of the next page is the word "LadderLife" with a toll free number written underneath. Is LadderLife a rehab facility or a drug abuse hotline? Beneath the phone number, Simon has written the letter K followed by eight digits.

"Maeve, your three minutes is up and I just watched two rats make love on an AC/DC T-shirt. We're leaving."

I pull out my phone and call the toll free number. A prerecorded voice thanks me for calling LadderLife Insurance and asks me for my policy number. My heart is thumping in my chest as I read out K54930573.

"Thank you for your policy number. Our records show that your life insurance claim of fifty thousand dollars for Kyleigh Sanford was deposited into a Chase bank account on August 9, 2015."

I drop my phone onto Simon's notebook, blood rushing in my ears. Simon had taken out life insurance on Kyleigh. He's the one with the motive.

Chapter 25

Tom and Ethan are waiting for me at the entrance of the Cook County jail when I pull into the visitor's lot on Thursday morning. I'm dressed in black suit pants and a lilac tank barely visible under my black blazer. The look is completed by my most expensive (and only) pair of black Louboutin pumps and a full face of makeup. No way was I going to show up looking sad and haggard in front of my husband's new boyfriend. Ethan, I notice, looks unusually unkempt, his basic black suit and white oxford are a bit wrinkled. He's not wearing a tie and he looks like he could've used a few hours more sleep. My insides do a silent victory dance as I walk the concrete pathway from the parking lot to the front door to meet them.

I forcibly steel my emotions and downshift to professional gear. "Good morning, Tom. Morning, Ethan."

Ethan is suddenly engrossed in inspecting his shoes as he mutters his greeting. Tom gives each of us a discerning look in turn before grumbling, "Morning, Shaw," and walking up the stairs to the front door. Ethan scampers after him and I take my time pulling up the rear reveling in the fact that I've made Ethan uncomfortable.

After waiting for what seemed like an hour in the security line, we wait another interminably long period before our client is finally escorted into the visitors' room. With each visit, Tammy looks a bit more hardened and life-weary. I feel bad for her. Even if she has made some mistakes, maybe even some big ones, her life has certainly not been an easy one.

Tom clears his throat and takes control of the meeting. "Tammy, we're here because we've been assigned a new judge and a new trial date. Your trial is now scheduled to begin two weeks from Monday."

Instead of the anticipated gasp of shock, Tammy emits a sigh of relief and smiles. "Oh, thank Christ. I can't take another three months in this place."

Tom is momentarily startled by Tammy's response, but quickly returns to his outline of topics and plunges forward. "Yes, while your feeling is understandable, this new date doesn't give us a lot of time to prepare. We have confirmed our expert is available to testify that week. We've also begun drafting our opening and closing statements." Tom pauses before nervously conceding, "Unfortunately, we haven't been able to identify many positive witnesses to call in your defense."

Tammy shrugs before offering, "There are no witnesses because no one else was there. Just put me on the stand and I'll tell the jury what happened."

Tom, Ethan and I all begin smoothing down our suits and shifting in our chairs uncomfortably. Has Tammy completely lost it? There's no way in hell we're putting her on the stand.

Tom is the first to recover and proceeds delicately. "Tammy, I understand why you would want the opportunity to tell your side of the story, but we advise against it."

Tammy interrupts. "Wait, you weren't planning on letting me testify? Do you *want* me to spend the rest of my life behind bars? Everyone knows that the only defendants who don't testify are the guilty ones."

"Fake news!" Tom says adamantly. "Defendants rarely testify at trial. It can improperly shift the burden of proof. While the burden of proving guilt is always on the prosecution, when defendants take the stand, juries will unconsciously expect their testimony to prove their innocence."

"That's nonsense," Tammy interjects.

"It's not nonsense," Tom retorts raising his voice, "it's jury psychology 101. Moreover, in your case, given the emotional circumstances surrounding your daughter's death, it would be too much for you to withstand on cross examination."

"What the hell does that mean?" Tammy shouts.

Unable to bear anymore of Tom's failing attempt at delicacy, I interrupt, saying, "It means Tom's worried you won't be able to control your temper on the stand. Which you won't."

Tammy guffaws. "Well, you might have a point. But who else are you going to call?"

All eyes return to Tom, who taps his pen against his notepad nervously. Pens really do seem to be his emotional support item. "Well…obviously we'll call our expert. And we're preparing strong cross examinations of the medical examiner and police officers at the crime scene."

The three of us wait for more, but after a minute or two passes, we realize Tom has no other names to add to the list of defense witnesses.

Tammy is the first to process the implication. "That's it? That's all you have?" Tammy shouts rising from her chair. A stern look from the guard by the door brings Tammy back to her seat. She shakes her head and asks Ethan for a cigarette. While we watch Ethan locate the pack he holds for these visits, I throw caution to the wind.

"What about Simon Harr?" My suggestion is met with shocked silence.

"What about Simon Harr?" is Tom's confused response.

"What if we call him as a witness?" I offer.

Now Tom fixes me with a cold stare before over-articulating, "And why on earth would we do that?"

I pounce. "To offer him up as an alternative suspect."

More stunned silence. Never one to pass up a chance to argue, Ethan counters, "But there's the security film from the 7-Eleven showing him leaving before Tammy enters the house and returning the next morning. He couldn't have killed Kyleigh."

"The 7-Eleven is down the street by at least a block." *I know because I walked it.* "And it isn't the only street leading to Simon's house. This is Chicago for fuck's sake, not Danville, Ohio."

Tom cautiously enters the fray asking, "And why would Simon kill Kyleigh?"

I know I'm on thin ice, so I tread lightly. "Oh, I don't know. A lover's quarrel. Maybe something to do with money." Innocently I throw out, "Tammy, do you know if Kyleigh had a life insurance policy?"

Tammy is thoroughly confused. She stutters, "Life insurance? Why would Kyleigh have life insurance? She was twenty-three and didn't have a job."

Tom knows something is up and does what any good lawyer would do, he shuts down the line of questioning. "I think that's enough speculation for today. Tammy, we just wanted to let you know about the change in trial date and where we are in terms of prep. We will be back next week to conduct a more thorough strategy session."

Tom rises and we all follow his lead. Once we're in the hallway though, Tom rounds on us. "You two drive straight back and meet me in my office." Catching my eye, he adds, "Shaw, I think you have some explaining to do."

Chapter 26

Stunned silence pervades the office after my breaking and entering confession. Tom is standing looking out of his floor-to-ceiling windows toward Lake Michigan. Ethan and I are sitting at the round glass table tucked away in the far corner of the office clearly intended for partner/associate meetings such as this. Both of us have our arms folded across our chests with our gaze firmly rooted on the floor. Finally, Ethan breaks the tension.

"We have to turn this information over to the prosecution."

Tom turns to face us and bellows, "Absolutely not," at the same time I voice my agreement with Ethan.

"What do you mean absolutely not? It would be unethical to hide this," Ethan vehemently responds.

"Look who is suddenly so interested in ethics," I mutter. I feel Ethan's eyes glaring at me from across the table.

"It's not unethical," Tom counters, shaking his head. "We are under no obligation to make the prosecution's case for them. The police searched Simon's apartment and failed to discover what Maeve was apparently able to locate in less than a half hour. The prosecution also had the same opportunity we had to question Simon and chose not to. That's on them. You two are citing discovery procedures in civil cases where both sides produce everything relevant. That's not how criminal law works."

"But we have material exculpatory and inculpatory evidence here," I remind him. "On one hand, the torn-up adoption papers certainly give Tammy a motive. On the other hand, the life insurance policy makes Simon a reasonable alternative suspect."

"Oh, and look who is suddenly so interested in disclosing material information," Ethan snarks.

I gasp and Tom clears his throat loudly before explaining, "Only the prosecution has a duty to produce material exculpatory evidence under the Brady doctrine. There is no corresponding duty on the defense. Now, if we were going to introduce the adoption papers or life insurance policy as exhibits during the trial, we would have a duty to turn them over to the prosecution in advance. But we aren't going to do that."

"How are we going to get it in then?" I question.

"We're going to follow your advice, Maeve," Tom says, walking over to the glass table and leaning on the back of the third chair. "We're going to call Simon Harr as a witness for the defense. And *you* are going to conduct the direct examination," he concludes, pointing his index finger in my direction.

Ethan is outraged. "So, we're going to let the *felon* conduct the direct?"

"Better than the cheat!" I snipe before asking Tom, "You think he'll just admit he cashed in on Kyleigh's life insurance policy without any incriminating evidence?"

Tom sighs before admitting, "It's going to be a tricky examination, but I think you can lead him to admit it. The harder task is drafting your opening statement to suggest to the jury there is another suspect while leaving us an out if he doesn't admit to it. We can't overpromise and then not deliver."

I can feel my stress level rising exponentially with each passing moment. It must be obvious to Tom as well because he adds, "Maeve, you got us into this little predicament. It's up to you to see it through."

A wrinkle in this strategy occurs to me and I raise it. "We will have to turn over our witness list to the prosecution prior to trial. They'll see Simon Harr's name on there and might go question him in advance."

Tom nods in agreement. "It's a possibility. But with this tight schedule, I think it's more likely than not that they won't consider Simon's testimony important enough to justify a trip up to Stateville. It's a risk we'll have to take."

Tom returns his gaze to Lake Michigan and Ethan and I take this to mean the meeting is over. Just as we are about to cross the office threshold, Tom adds, "And one more thing, whatever is going on between the two of you, resolve it. A woman has placed her freedom in our hands. This is bigger than whatever spat you two are currently having."

Ethan and I exchange a glance before turning in opposite directions toward our offices.

Back in front of my computer, I take a sip of Diet Coke and stare at the draft of my opening statement. How do I suggest the police didn't consider all suspects without explicitly promising to produce this mystery suspect at trial? As I ponder this conundrum, my phone dings. A text from Patrick.

Hey, I know you're avoiding my calls and texts. And I completely understand why. But I bumped up my flight. I can grab the boys from daycare and make dinner. Will you join us?

A few seconds later Patrick adds:

Please.

In the last twenty-four hours, Patrick has sent twenty-seven texts and left five voicemails. I've read and listened to them all. They mostly consisted of Patrick saying he was sorry in a variety of different ways. He also added in a few that he hadn't meant to hurt me. And they all ended with him begging me to let him explain. I hadn't responded to any. But this involved the boys. No matter how angry I am at Patrick, it wouldn't be fair to use the boys as punishment. It wouldn't be fair to Declan and Seamus either. Hadn't Declan told Ms. Feelings that he missed his daddy?

I have a lot of work to do. Why don't you enjoy the evening with the boys.

A minute or two goes by with no response, and I start to return to my opening when I hear another ping.

Okay, but will you come home when you're done so we can talk? We can't avoid each other forever.

Ugh! I am so not ready to have the breakup conversation. The one where we both assign fault before discussing next steps. But then again, when is anyone ever ready to have this conversation?

Okay. I'll be home around 9.

Patrick responds instantaneously.

Thanks, Maeve. I'll have a glass of wine poured.

I laugh in spite of myself. Patrick knows me well. My laugh dies as an IM from Ethan appears on my screen.

Do you want to talk about what happened?

I close the Jabber window and change my status to offline. I'm not feeling that forgiving.

Chapter 27

I take a deep breath in through my nose and exhale out through my mouth before sliding the key in the slot and turning the knob. It's a quarter past nine. The house is quiet so the boys must be asleep. I take off my Eddie Bauer black trench coat and hang it on my designated hook on the wall opposite the door. I climb the stairs to the living room and sit my bag down on the top step. Patrick is sitting quietly at the dining room table. He's drinking a Lagunitas IPA and has a glass of red wine next to him. There's a cheese and bread platter on the table as well. He looks up at me nervously.

"Hey, Maeve. Are you hungry?" He gestures at the platter.

"Famished. Thank you," I respond, making my way over to the table and taking a seat next to him. I take a long sip of the cabernet before snagging a piece of gruyere to munch on. I decide to begin with small talk. "How was dinner with the boys?"

Patrick's face brightens as he regales me with funny anecdotes from his night. Apparently Seamus took a number two during their shared bath. Declan spotted the floating turd first and screamed. This sent both boys jumping out of the bath and drenching the bathroom floor with water. Patrick had to mop the floor and bleach the bathtub before he could put them back in for a soap off. Seamus found the whole debacle hilarious.

A moment or two passes after we stop laughing and Patrick turns serious. "Thank you for letting me spend time with them tonight, Maeve. I haven't been with them enough lately and I miss them."

"Well, actually, that's why I flew to Boston yesterday," I say hesitantly. "I went to the boys' parent teacher conference the night before and Declan has been seeking out the resident counselor most days. He told her he misses us and we work too much."

Patrick drops his head into his hands while I nervously fiddle with the stem of my glass. When Patrick looks up again, his eyes are red.

"I'm so sorry. This is all my fault. I've been so consumed with figuring out who I am that I ignored those I love the most."

"And have you figured out who you are, Patrick?" I dare to ask though I'm confident I won't like the response.

Patrick looks at the table again for a minute or two seemingly pondering the question. He then looks up at me with a steady gaze. "I'm a lot of things, Maeve. I'm a man who was lucky enough to have married his best friend. I'm the father to two amazing boys who I love more than life itself. And I'm gay." He pauses for a moment before adding, "I'm sorry that in the process of figuring all this out, I hurt you so badly. I'll never forgive myself for that."

My throat tightens and I choke back tears. I take a small sip of wine to buy time before I ask, "Were you ever in love with me?"

Patrick grabs my free hand and looks me straight in the eye. "Of course, Maeve. I've always loved you. And I still love you. You truly are my best friend and there is no one else I would want to raise our boys with."

Patrick then hesitates so I prod him on. "But you aren't attracted to me?"

Patrick shakes his head sadly, and adds, "I'm sorry, Maeve. It has nothing to do with you."

"I know," I concede. Wishing I would've come to that realization on my own. Embarrassed that I'd ever tried a diet and exercise program to win back a man. I'll need to address my rampant insecurities another day. I then ask, "Have you always known?"

Patrick takes a swig from his IPA with his right hand while still covering my hand with his left. "I kind of figured it out in high school. But you know Mary and Cormac. Devout Irish Catholics. I didn't want to disappoint them. And then I met you and you were so wonderful. I thought if I could make this work with anyone, it would be with you."

"I think you underestimate your parents," I argue. "We kids of dysfunctional families can spot the real deal a mile away. Mary and Cormac will always love you."

Both of us take another sip of our respective beverages during the awkward pause that follows. Patrick sighs. "I'm sorry about that too, Maeve. Ethan shouldn't have told me. He broke your trust."

"Oh, I don't think it was only Ethan who broke my trust," I snap.

Patrick cringes and concedes, "Of course. I know that. I just meant…it wasn't his news to share."

"Uhh…ya think?" I snap again. But then I take a deep breath and admit, "But I shouldn't have lied to you about my past. A marriage can't be built on lies."

Patrick laughs sadly before acknowledging, "Well, we're both guilty of that."

We smile and I go for another piece of cheese. As I'm chewing, a question occurs to me. "Why did Ethan's texts come up as Macy?"

Patrick cringes again. "Remember how we used to tease Ethan about how he looks like a model?"

A memory floods back of the four of us at a bar watching the World Cup: Patrick, me, Ethan and Zara. Ethan looked especially dashing that day and we teased that we had a model in our midst. But then I added, "Don't get too full of yourself now. You're no runway model, Ethan. You're more the department store catalogue version: Macy's at best."

Patrick sees the recollection dawning on my face and explains, "Once we started flirting, I changed his name on my phone so if you ever saw it you wouldn't know it was him. Macy was the first name that popped into my mind."

We drink and snack quietly for a bit. Then Patrick draws a deep breath and asks, "Well, Maeve, where do we go from here?"

"Aren't you going to sleep at Ethan's pad?" I ask, confused.

"No, that ran its course," he says, shaking his head. "I needed someone familiar to come out to and Ethan was more than willing to be that person. But that's all it was."

I feel a tinge of sympathy for Ethan. I'm not sure that's all it was for him.

Maybe Ethan and I have something else in common: in the process of Patrick finding himself, we both got hurt. I decide to table that thought for now and get practical. "Patrick, you can sleep here on the couch for as long as it takes you to find a place, but I'd like to keep the house."

Patrick immediately agrees. "Of course, Maeve. The house is yours. And can we share custody of the boys? Maybe even spend holidays together?"

"Sure," I agree without conviction. "We'll be a real life *Modern Family*." If only life were that easy.

Chapter 28

The loud metal screech of the gate opening to allow another inmate into the visitors' room rouses me back to consciousness and I embarrassingly realize I've fallen asleep waiting for Tammy to arrive. I sit up straight, smooth down my hair, wipe a small amount of drool from the corner of my mouth and chance a glance at Tom and Ethan. Tom is staring straight at me with an amused smile. No way my nap went unnoticed by him. Ethan's focus, on the other hand, is on his legal pad. He's drawn a fair amount of spirals, stars, and boxes across the page and doesn't appear to be paying me or Tom any attention. I glance at my Fitbit and note we've been waiting for Tammy for over thirty minutes, meaning I probably had been sleeping for twenty-five of those. While cringe worthy, the rest was much needed. I've been trying to leave work no later than five o'clock to give myself an extra hour with the boys each night. The tradeoff being that I have to pick back up on trial prep from nine until two or three in the morning in order to keep up with the workload. Averaging four hours of sleep each night this week has apparently caught up with me. It's been over a decade since I regularly pulled all-nighters to study for law school exams, and Seamus started sleeping through the night almost twelve months ago.

Another glance across the table at Ethan shows he's not suffering from quite the same level of sleep deprivation that I am. Of course, he doesn't have kids to contend with. However, I'm again struck by the fact that Ethan doesn't seem to have recovered from Boston. His gorgeous blue eyes have lost their twinkle in the last week. My musing is broken by the arrival of our client escorted by a large guard bearing a striking resemblance to WWE star John Cena. The guard pulls out the empty chair and roughly "helps" Tammy into it.

"Good morning, Tammy," Tom begins immediately. "As you know, your trial begins on Monday and so we have a lot to cover today." Tom then pauses and seems to take stock of Tammy's appearance, finding it wanting. "Tammy, we'll have a black pantsuit for you to wear during your trial, rather than your prison uniform. You have the constitutional right to wear street clothes and not be shackled at trial. You'll want to take a shower before Monday and brush your hair thoroughly." Tom takes another pause before continuing awkwardly, "Do you maybe think you could try to lose a few pounds as well over the weekend? Nothing drastic, but we want you to look your best. Appearances do matter to a jury, unfortunately."

I laugh before I can stop myself and add sarcastically, "Tammy, if you could request the low carb gruel for dinner that would be great. Do the prison chefs offer a Paleo option?"

Tammy appreciates the levity and laughs along with me. "Oh yeah, and I'll make sure to book a facial at the prison spa while I'm at it."

Tom kills all merriment by growling, "Shaw, seeing as you've tried exactly zero murder cases, maybe let me take the lead here."

My face flashes hot and I avert my gaze to the floor as Tom launches into an explanation of jury selection. I struggle to overcome my mortification as Tom drones on about voir dire.

"We have seven preemptory challenges, meaning we can dismiss up to seven jurors for any reason at all. We have an unlimited amount of challenges for cause. Our goal is to strategically use these challenges so in the end we are left with an impartial twelve-person jury who will be able to weigh the evidence fairly. Of course, after the jury is selected, we'll take a break and the trial will officially begin with each side delivering its opening arguments. Shaw will be delivering ours."

As I was only half listening, I didn't catch Tom's unspoken cue that I should begin speaking. A kick under the table from Ethan, however, did the trick.

Grimacing and rubbing my sore right shin, I fumble, "Tammy, our opening statement will set the tone for our defense. We will describe how Kyleigh was an accomplished cheerleader and pageant winner who became addicted to the opioids she was prescribed to manage her back pain. How she battled back from her addiction in order to regain custody of little Garrett, but ultimately relapsed. How through all of this you supported Kyleigh financially and emotionally, even after she moved herself and Garrett in with her drug dealer. We will introduce Simon Harr as a low-level dealer who has been arrested on several occasions for possession of narcotics and assault and battery, including domestic assault. We will describe how, on the night of Kyleigh's death, you went over to Simon Harr's house to check on baby Garrett who you'd been told may have an ear infection. You and Kyleigh quarreled over money, which was not unusual, and then you left. Kyleigh was still very much alive at that time, but appeared to have been using prior to your arrival. We will then introduce our expert, Dr. Smart, and his theory that Kyleigh's cause of death is attributable to positional asphyxiation." I pause, feeling like a middle school teacher, and add, "Any questions?"

Tammy actually raises her hand and I suppress a laugh. "Go ahead, Tammy."

"Why are you talking so much about Simon? Did y'all decide to call him as a witness?"

I glance at Tom to see if he wants to address the elephant in the room, but he just looks back at me expectantly. I buy a bit of time to collect my thoughts by fumbling, "Well, Tammy, that's an interesting question.... In fact...we have...after much thought and deliberation... decided to add Simon Harr's name to our list of witnesses."

"Why?" Tammy demands. "What good will he do? He *hated* me. And he'll make Kyleigh look bad. What will the jury think of my baby after they see the creep she was hooking up with?" Tammy's eyes moisten and she looks away.

The enormity of the task I've been handed causes my chest to tighten, but I try to offer reassurance. "Tammy, it's precisely that Simon is such a creep that we have to call him. The jury will take one look at Simon and wonder why he's not the one on trial instead of the grieving mother."

Tammy looks back, confused. "So wait, are we now saying Simon killed Kyleigh? I thought we were saying no one killed Kyleigh. Kyleigh died from positional whatever-you-call-it."

Ethan bails me out. He leans across the table, puts his hand on Tammy's and explains, "We're giving the jury reasonable doubt, Tammy. In order to convict you, the prosecution has to prove *beyond a reasonable doubt* that you strangled Kyleigh. That means if the jury can find an alternative explanation to what happened that seems plausible, they must acquit. Our job is to give them that alternative or alternatives. The autopsy doesn't seem to indicate that Kyleigh was strangled by anyone. There are no marks. Instead, it is more likely that she died from positional asphyxiation. She died from a lack of oxygen because of how she was wrapped in the blanket and because she was too intoxicated to save herself. Then we say to the jury, even if you don't believe that, even if you think Kyleigh *was* murdered, it wasn't our client who did it. It is far more likely that her drug-dealing boyfriend, who she was living with and who found the body, is guilty. There is more than enough reasonable doubt here to merit an acquittal." Ethan pats Tammy's hand lightly before letting go and leaning back in his seat. He's done his job.

"Okay." Tammy seems to be mulling over Ethan's explanation. "That sounds okay, I guess." Then a light goes on and she excitedly inquires, "And once I'm acquitted, how soon can I pick up Rapscallion?"

My face flushes red, with anger this time. "Don't you mean Garrett?" I snap. I have yet to hear Tammy inquire as to her grandson's wellbeing.

Tammy shoots me a death glare and Ethan rushes to diffuse the situation. "Maeve, Garrett has been adopted by one of Tammy's cousins." A beat goes by before Ethan adds, "It's a closed adoption."

Shame rushes over me, but before I can apologize Tom plows forward. "Let's move on to discussing our witness strategy, shall we?"

Chapter 29

As we walk silently out of the front doors of the Cook County jail, Ethan picks up his pace, presumably to catch up with Tom and ask for a ride back to the office.

Impulsively, I call out, "Ethan, wait!" He stops and turns back to me. So does Tom. "I'll give you a ride back," I offer.

Ethan hesitates, but Tom responds approvingly, "Good idea, Shaw. I'll see you back there."

As Tom walks to his BMW, Ethan and I linger awkwardly until I regain composure and begin my own walk toward my decade-old Honda. We set off with just "Shallow" on the local pop station to break the silence. After a minute, I take a risk. I sing Lady Gaga's section at top volume. I'm mildly impressed I can hold the refrain without my voice cracking. Maybe I have a future as a karaoke star. Ethan doesn't react at first, but when Bradley Cooper chimes back in at the end, he belts it out. I join him for the last line.

For the first time in a week, we look at each other and smile. I use this momentum to begin, "Look, Ethan…"

But he cuts me off. "Maeve, let me start. I know it sounds heartless now, but I really never took you into consideration when I started things with Patrick."

The stabbing pain in my heart must also be visible on my face because Ethan rushes to explain, "The truth is, I've been crushing on Patrick ever since you brought him to the firm's first summer associate event. Remember, the architectural boat tour we took as 2L's?"

A memory of Patrick and me boarding the boat *Wendella* from the Wrigley stop on the Chicago River rushes back. Me wearing a floral sundress that went far enough past my knees to be professional but had spaghetti straps to highlight my youth. Patrick in khakis and a light blue polo. I remember being a nervous wreck that night. Firm summer events are notoriously drunken and raucous. It was paramount as a second-year law student that you proved you had the ability to drink and entertain clients at similar events in the future without going beyond the bounds of decorum. It was a razor thin line that not every summer associate could balance. Stories of law students who vomited or hooked up at such events and consequently didn't receive a permanent offer were bandied around as cautionary tales. I nod at Ethan and he continues.

"Well, that was the first time you introduced me to Patrick. You went off to charm some high-powered partner and left Patrick and me alone for almost an hour. We drank craft beer and joked about the extravagant boondoggles these summer associate events were. Even then, I felt sparks." Ethan's face grows somber. He pauses and looks out the window. I wait until he's ready to continue. What seems like five minutes pass before he turns in my direction and resumes. "Over the years, I've gotten butterflies every time we've hung out. But then something changed last year. I felt Patrick return the sparks. And I jumped at the opportunity."

"More like *jumped on* the opportunity," I snipe.

"Fair enough," Ethan concedes. "Look, Maeve, I know it was completely selfish. I went after what I wanted with no regard for you or our friendship." His voice cracks as he admits, "I guess I just thought he was the one." His eyes glisten and he goes back to looking out the window. After he composes himself, he adds, "I'm so sorry, Maeve. I'm sorry I ruined your marriage and broke up your family. I don't expect you to forgive me."

Having received the apology I was waiting for, I cut Ethan some slack. "You didn't ruin my marriage, Ethan. It was clearly unworkable. But you did betray my trust. And if I'm being honest, that will take quite a long time to rebuild, if ever."

Ethan nods and says softly, "I know." After a bit he adds, "I'd like to try though."

I can feel him looking at me with his panty-dropping beautiful eyes. When we come to a stop light, I return his gaze. "Okay, then. Why don't you start by telling me what happened with Garrett, so I don't mortify myself in front of our client again?"

Ethan smiles and I notice a trace of his former twinkle has returned. "There's not much to tell. Kyleigh never said who Garrett's father was. It's unclear if she even knew. He was never involved in Garrett's life. When Tammy was arrested, Garrett was taken by DCFS and placed with a foster family. Tammy didn't know how much longer she'd be in jail. I mean, Jesus, when she was first arrested, the State was talking about pursuing the death penalty. So, Tammy wrote a letter to one of her cousins who lives downstate and asked her to take Garrett. The cousin agreed, but only if she could adopt him outright and Tammy would sign away all of her custody rights. The cousin didn't want Garrett knowing the circumstances around his biological mom's death. I think it was hard on her, but Tammy agreed. She said she just wanted Garrett to have the chance at a good life."

I ponder this for a moment. "That was very mature of Tammy. I guess she learned a few things from the mistakes she made as a pageant mom. Still, it must be very hard for her to know that even if she's acquitted, she'll never see her grandson again."

"Yeah, I think that's why she's so obsessed with Rapscallion. That dog is the only thing she has left to love."

Chapter 30

The courtroom is packed on Monday morning. Tammy isn't expecting any support from family or friends, as she doesn't seem to have many, but the media has come out in force. It's not every day, after all, that a mother is on trial for killing her daughter. It may even make the evening news. I see Tom and Ethan already seated at the defense table and hurry to join them. I sit my caramel tote down and lay my black trench across the arms of an empty chair. I then smooth the wrinkles out of my chocolate brown skirt suit and take a seat to the left of Ethan. I take just a second to admire my jacket's sheen. Within the first month of my starting at Mulvaney Stewart, I was visited by a suit maker. He made office visits and confided that all of the important trial attorneys at the firm, including a couple I was dying to work with, had custom-made suits. Following the advice of "dress for the job you want," I ordered two: one brown and one navy. The order came to thirty-three hundred dollars and drained my checking account. In the last ten years, I've worn each suit approximately three times. Each time when I'd been given the opportunity to make the oral argument on a summary judgment motion. Civil cases rarely go to trial. Summary judgment hearings are as close as you get.

Tom looks down the table at Ethan and me. "Let's go back and visit Tammy in the holding cell. It's important for her to not look too nervous when she comes out. Potential jurors confuse nerves for guilt."

We stand on cue and head past the courtroom bailiff, a squat woman working on a crossword puzzle. When we enter the hallway of cells behind the judge's bench, we turn to our right.

"On trial days, Tammy will wait in a single cell away from the other prisoners," Tom explains. I breathe a sigh of relief that we won't have to parade past a group of inmates and be subjected to catcalls multiple times a day. A female guard stands at attention outside a cell at the far end of the hall. She's tall, brunette and built. She acknowledges us by stepping aside as we approach. Tammy sits on a bunk with a thin mattress. She took Tom's advice to heart and, while her roots could certainly use a touch-up, her hair is clean and well-brushed. The black pants suit that Tom picked out fits well and minimizes the extra prison weight she's gained. The lavender blouse makes Tammy's hazel eyes pop. Tom has impeccable taste. While Tammy's no movie star, she looks like a respectable, mild-mannered, middle-aged woman. One you would have a hard time believing could strangle anyone.

When she hears us approach, Tammy looks up and flashes a genuine smile. "What do you think? How do I look?"

It's evident that Tammy is relishing this upgrade from her prison jumpsuit. Seems that Yves Saint Laurent was right when he said that fashion wasn't meant to just make women more beautiful, but also to give them confidence.

Ethan steps forward and purrs, "You look fabulous. The suit fits perfectly." This is exactly what Tammy wanted to hear and who she wanted to hear it from. She's putty in his hands. Tom steps forward and puts an end to the lovefest.

"Tammy, Ethan is right. You look perfect. Hang on to that confidence today. You want to convey to the jury that you fully expect an acquittal after they hear all the evidence."

Tammy seems to deflate a little at the reminder of today's importance. I swoop in with some encouragement. "Tammy, we've got this. Tom is one of the best litigators in the city. We have mountains of reasonable doubt on our side. You just need to trust us."

Tammy's smile returns and she really looks at me for what seems like the first time. "Thanks, Maeve. I have total confidence in all of you. Especially you, since you're a mom and know how much I loved Kyleigh. Make sure the jury knows that too, will ya?"

My eyes begin to mist, but I blink it away and adamantly agree to do just that. Tom checks his watch before explaining, "Tammy, we need to get back out there and go over a few pretrial matters with Judge Tyler. We'll see you soon for jury selection."

Returning to the courtroom, we see Al Porter has taken his place at the prosecution's table. He is flanked by a breathtakingly beautiful African American woman, who must be his associate. She wears a fitted black dress suit, black heels, and a string of white pearls, her hair pulled back into a tight bun. She looks every bit the formidable opponent she most certainly is.

Before we reach their table to introduce ourselves, the bailiff announces, "All rise. The Court of Cook County is now in session. The Honorable Clarence Tyler presiding." Judge Tyler quickly enters the courtroom and takes his seat on the bench. He is a surprisingly attractive man with dark hair just speckled on the sides with gray and dark brown eyes. The rapidity with which he entered the courtroom makes me think he's a runner. I've always had a thing for slender, athletic men. Blood rushes to my face, and lower extremities, as I find myself mentally disrobing him.

Thankfully, I'm brought back to my senses by the bailiff calling our case. "Your Honor, this is *State of Illinois v. Sanford.*"

I shake my head to clear away the naughty thoughts. What the hell was that about? I guess it has been a while since I've gotten laid, but still, I'm not prone to flights of fantasy. Certainly not when I'm at work.

We barely make it to the bench before Judge Tyler warns, "I trust both sides are ready to proceed. I believe my clerk made it clear I would not be allowing any more continuances."

"Yes, Your Honor," we assure him in unison.

"We did file two pretrial motions," Tom begins before being summarily dismissed.

"They're both denied," Judge Tyler declares with a bang of his gavel. "The media has a right to be here and evidence about the defendant and her daughter's turbulent relationship goes to motive."

"But Your Honor," Tom respectfully continues, "the benefit of both are vastly outweighed by their prejudicial effect on our client."

"I said denied," Judge Tyler decrees emphatically. After leveling Tom with a warning glare, he turns to his bailiff. "Judy, bring in the jury pool."

Crestfallen, we return to our table. Judge Tyler certainly won't be doing us any favors. Moments later, bailiff Judy opens a door off the left side of the bench and ushers in what looks to be about fifty potential jury members ranging in age, shape, and ethnicity. All, however, appear to be firmly middle to lower class. Wealthy professionals always seem to be able to wrangle out of jury duty just by placing a simple phone call to a well-connected friend.

Once the potential jurors are seated in and around the jury box, Judge Tyler addresses them, "Thank you all for doing your duty and showing up here today. You are to be commended. By way of background, this is a criminal case, specifically a first degree murder case. The defendant who will be on trial is Tammy Sanford. If any of you have seen or heard anything about this case on the news or through other media sources, please stand."

Four people stand and are immediately dismissed with Judge Tyler's thanks. He then proceeds, saying, "The defendant, Tammy Sanford, has been charged with first degree murder in connection with the death of her daughter, Kyleigh Sanford. Is there anything about this case that would cause you to believe that you could not consider the evidence fairly and impartially according to the law?" Two middle-aged women stand and are again dismissed with thanks. Judge Tyler then nods at Al, who rises and stands in front of the jury box.

"My name is Al Porter," he explains, "and I represent the State of Illinois along with my co-counsel Lexi Banks." The gorgeous Ms. Banks gives a faint smile and nod to the jury before resuming her impassive stare. "Please stand if you know either myself or Ms. Banks in any professional or social capacity." Tom stands, identifies us, and asks anyone to stand who knows us.

Done with the familiarity questions, Tom and Al move on to impartiality. "Have you or a loved one been the victim of a violent crime?" "Have you or a member of your family been convicted of a felony?" "Are you or any of your family or friends currently serving or have served as a law enforcement officer?" "This is a criminal case in which the government must prove guilt beyond a reasonable doubt. That means you must be firmly convinced that the defendant is guilty. Would any of you have any difficulty in holding the government to its burden?"

With thirty-seven potential jurors left, we move to the general questions including marital status, children, education, employment, and hobbies. Jury selection isn't an exact science. You're trying to weed out prejudice and retain open-minded people that will listen to all of the evidence before making a decision. You are also trying to assemble a group of twelve people who can work together and agree on a verdict. Tom is very good at eliciting information, getting the potential jurors talking so he can get a sense of their personality before making a call on their selection. After about an hour, he and Al Porter are able to assemble a diverse group of twelve jurors and two alternates, in case one or two of the chosen jurors gets sick or is found to be biased. As Tom had hoped, the woman-to-man ratio tilts in our favor, eight to six. We all three agreed that women would be more likely to be understanding given the circumstances. With the jury set and the initial instructions given, it is time to begin opening statements. Since the prosecution bears the burden of proof, they have the privilege of going first.

Lexi takes a moment to review her notes and then steps up to the railing separating the jury from the courtroom floor. "Ladies and gentlemen of the jury, who here has watched the show *Toddlers & Tiaras*?" About half of the jurors smile and raise their hands. Lexi continues, "Well, for those that haven't, let me give you a taste of what you're missing. *Toddlers & Tiaras* is a show about middle-aged moms who are absolutely obsessed with having their daughters win pageants. So obsessed, in fact, they do things like pad their five-year-old daughter's dress to give the appearance of cleavage. One contestant even had her six-year-old pretend to smoke on stage." Lexi has the jury in the palm of her hands. Several women are covering their mouths in shock while multiple men are tsking and shaking their heads. "Well, what *Toddlers & Tiaras* doesn't show is what happens to those moms once their little golden tickets stop performing. But that is precisely what you will see in this trial. Kyleigh Sanford was the twinkle in her mama's eye until she hurt her back at a cheerleading competition and wasn't able to perform anymore. Once she was damaged goods, Tammy kicked her out of her home and Kyleigh fell into addiction and poverty. You will hear testimony from the officers present at the scene that night about the drug-filled and dirty conditions in which Kyleigh had been living with her infant son, Garrett. You will also hear testimony about a previous incident between Kyleigh and Tammy. Kyleigh asked Tammy for money to care for Garrett and Tammy responded by physically pushing Kyleigh into the street. The night Kyleigh died, she was worried that Garrett had an ear infection. Being a new mom, she wasn't sure what to do. So, who did she call? Her own mother, of course. But instead of receiving reassurance and support, she was met with contempt and rage. Rage so intense that it ultimately led to Kyleigh having the life choked out of her by the very person who had given it to her a mere twenty-three years prior. And after Tammy ended the life of her only daughter, she left her only grandson to sit alone in a filthy drug den."

I instinctively put my hand on Tammy's arm for reassurance. She's rigid and stone-faced, but I can tell she's fighting back tears. Lexi is holding no punches and one look at the absolutely horrified jury shows she's done her job.

Lexi finishes her statement with a plea, "Once you have had the opportunity to listen to all of the evidence, we will ask you to give justice to Kyleigh Sanford by returning a verdict of guilty. Thank you."

Once Lexi retakes her seat beside Al, I give the jury a moment to collect themselves while I review my notes. I'd practiced this opening at least fifty times in front of my bathroom mirror this past week, pausing for emphasis at the right moments and making sure I made eye contact with all twelve jurors. I could recite it in my sleep. But after Lexi's performance, I realize I'm going to need to improvise a bit. I take a deep breath and walk the few steps to the center of the courtroom.

Facing the jury, I begin theatrically, "Wow! A tip of my hat to Ms. Banks for one gripping tale." I can feel Lexi boring a hole in the side of my head, but I continue, "I mean who doesn't love *Mommie Dearest*? Faye Dunaway plays the perfect mother you love to hate." The jury's faces seem a bit confused, but I sense they are following, so I continue, saying, "But unfortunately, real life doesn't usually resemble the movies. This isn't the tale of a fame-obsessed pageant mom. This is a story that is unfortunately all too common these days. The story of a hard-working single mom who did her best to raise her beloved daughter, only to watch her life unravel from addiction." I've made a connection. I see several knowing nods and shaking of heads.

"To address the elephant in the room—did Tammy sign Kyleigh up for pageants? Yes, she did. And dance lessons, gymnastics lessons, and voice lessons? Yes. Judge all you want, but you know what? Kyleigh was thriving. As a junior in high school, Kyleigh was in the top ten percent of her class. She was smart, popular and the head cheerleader. But that is when Kyleigh's life took a dramatic left turn she couldn't recover from. After suffering a fall from the top of the cheer pyramid, Kyleigh went to see her doctor for back pain. The same general practitioner who had treated Kyleigh since she was born. And what did this doctor prescribe this healthy, vivacious girl? Rest? No. Ice? No. He prescribed her Vicodin. Not once. Not twice. No, this general practitioner refilled Kyleigh's prescription twelve times in two months. He gave a sixteen-year-old two hundred and forty pills over the course of about sixty days." Audible gasps escape from several members of the jury.

"And that's all it took. She was hooked. Tammy tried to help her. She even got Kyleigh into treatment after Garrett was born, but Kyleigh always went back to using. There was nothing Tammy could do."

I shake my head and give the jury a moment to digest this before continuing. "I'm sure some of you know a person who has struggled with addiction. Maybe even a child, niece, or cousin? If so, then you know that until they are ready to get help, there is nothing you can do except love them." A couple of jurors give knowing nods making me feel better about our chances.

"Unfortunately, sometimes the best love is tough love. And that is what Tammy had to do. She didn't want to kick Kyleigh and Garrett out of her house, but she was forced to after discovering Kyleigh had sold her grandmother's wedding rings to buy drugs. As for Garret, Tammy helped the only way she could: by giving Kyleigh baby food and diapers. Things that couldn't be sold for drugs." More head shaking and tsking from the jury.

"On the night of Kyleigh's death, Kyleigh didn't want baby food or diapers. She wanted money. Money that she was going to immediately hand over to her drug dealer boyfriend, Simon Harr, in exchange for heroin. Knowing this, Tammy did what she had to do. She refused and went home. Even though it broke her heart. Even though she desperately wanted to pick up that precious little boy and take him with her. But she couldn't do that. You will hear testimony that Kyleigh had called the police on previous occasions when Tammy had taken Garrett home, claiming interference with her parental rights. So, Tammy left Kyleigh and Garrett and went home bearing the anguish that no mother should have to bear. The anguish of seeing your daughter at her lowest and being unable to help." I know I'm pulling on some heartstrings with that one.

"Well, what happened to Kyleigh after Tammy left? You will hear testimony from a leading expert in asphyxiation that Kyleigh was not strangled. For one, there are no strangulation marks. It's pretty hard to strangle someone with your bare hands and not leave any marks. For another, there is a bone in your neck, called the hyoid bone." I point in the general area on my own neck before continuing. "This bone often breaks during strangulations. Well, Kyleigh's hyoid bone was found intact during the autopsy. So how did Kyleigh die? Our expert, Dr. Smart, will testify that sometime after Tammy left Simon's apartment, Kyleigh went to bed. Being distraught, she wrapped herself up tightly in her comforter before dozing off. Unfortunately, she wrapped herself so tightly that she wasn't getting sufficient oxygen. Now, if this happened to you or me, our brain would send a signal to our body to loosen the blanket. But Kyleigh's brain was deadened by the opioids she had taken, and so it couldn't send a signal. Kyleigh was not murdered, ladies and gentleman, she died of positional asphyxiation or, as you might be more familiar with the term, SIDS." Every juror is looking straight at me, hanging on my every word. I could end my statement here, but I have to introduce the other suspect.

"You will hear testimony from Simon Harr about how Kyleigh was wrapped up so tight when he found her, he had trouble getting to her. You should note that it is the defense who is calling Simon as a witness. Simon didn't make the prosecution's list. Even though Kyleigh was found by Simon in his apartment. Maybe the State didn't want you to hear about how Simon was the only person besides Kyleigh who had keys to the apartment. Or maybe the State didn't want you to hear about Simon's criminal history, including previous arrests for domestic violence." I see Al and Lexi exchanging troubled glances out of the corner of my eye and I decide I've said enough for now.

"In closing, ladies and gentlemen, we ask that you keep an open mind until you hear all of the evidence. And then we trust you will return the verdict of not guilty for Tammy Sanford. Thank you."

As I return to my seat, Tom whispers, "Well done, Shaw," while Ethan and Tammy greet me with beaming smiles. I chance a look at Judge Tyler and my heart jumps as I catch him watching me. Am I imagining it or is there interest in those eyes?

Chapter 31

I arrive at the courthouse on Tuesday morning wearing my second and last tailor-made suit and clutching my coffee like it's my lifesource. Which, at this point, it pretty much is. Thank God Patrick offered to work remotely from home this week. Yesterday, I left the house at seven and didn't return until after our witness prep session for today ended a little after one a.m. No amount of coverup will mask the deep purple circles under my eyes. As I open the doors to Judge Tyler's courtroom and glance toward the defense table, I see Ethan hunched over Tom's shoulder. There's an air of tension surrounding them that makes me uneasy. Today was supposed to be a cakewalk. The State is expected to call the officers who processed the scene and the medical examiner. We're fully prepared for cross.

Before I'm even able to hang my trench coat over the extra chair, Ethan spins toward me with panic in his eyes. "Al added a surprise witness to his list this morning."

"What!" I exclaim. "Who?"

"Brandy Lynn Nelson. Tammy's cousin who adopted the baby." Ethan is speaking so rapidly, I'm assuming the twenty-ounce Starbucks in his hand is not his first of the day.

"Why would Al call Brandy Lynn to the stand? The fact that she adopted Garrett after Kyleigh's death is irrelevant. And even if it was relevant," I add, "he should have included her in the witness list he produced to us weeks ago."

"Well, according to Al, Brandy Lynn has been dodging his calls and visits. He claims she only returned his call after seeing Tammy on the news last night."

Trying to process this information, I reason, "Well, if Brandy Lynn really only contacted Al last night, there's a chance Judge Tyler will allow her to testify. But can she add anything substantial to his case?"

Without looking up from his legal pad of notes, Tom joins the conversation. "Apparently, Brandy Lynn and Tammy were close when Kyleigh was younger. She's going to testify about their relationship over the years."

There's a sinking feeling in my stomach as I ask rhetorically, "I assume she's not being called to portray Tammy as June Cleaver."

Both Ethan and Tom shake their heads in disappointment. Then Tom stands and says, "Let's go fill our client in on this development."

After Tom breaks the news of the surprise witness to Tammy, she stands in her cell silently covering her open mouth. Her reaction confirms the worst of our fears. Brandy Lynn is going to be a terrible witness for us.

The eternal optimist, I try, "Well, Brandy Lynn can't be all that bad of a witness. I mean, she did adopt Garrett when you asked."

Tammy drops her hand and cracks a rueful grin. "Shit, Brandy Lynn adopted Garrett because she couldn't have babies. Her and her husband had been trying for years with no luck. Doesn't mean she doesn't think I was a shit mom."

Undeterred, I retort, "Not that any of this matters. Whether or not you were mother of the year is irrelevant to whether you killed Kyleigh."

Never one to let a point go unchallenged, Tom morosely points out, "It matters to the jury, though. If they think Tammy was mean or abusive to Kyleigh when she was a child, they are more likely to believe she was capable of murder."

All four of us stand in silence for a moment contemplating the tiled floor. Ethan finally looks up at Tammy and provides some hope. "That being said, we'll establish during cross that you and Brandy Lynn haven't been close for years and she has no idea what happened the night Kyleigh died."

Tammy gives Ethan a weak smile in appreciation. "I'm sure you will. Thanks, Ethan." She then turns her back on us, walks over to her thin cot, and takes a seat. Her head between her hands. Eyes on the floor. Not one ounce of yesterday's confidence is present.

As we walk back to the defense table, dejected, my mind begins to race. Our case could use its own surprise witness right about now. One that could lend credence to my alternate suspect theory. Sure, the life insurance was a great find, but it doesn't mean much if Simon wasn't there the night Kyleigh died. As I take my seat, I pull out my cell phone.

Me: Any chance you have a few free hours today?

Zara: My schedule is a bit light. What's up?

Me: I want you to canvass Simon's neighbors and see if anyone saw him come home after Tammy left that night.

Zara: Are you insane? I'm not an investigator. Besides, don't you think the police already did that?

Me: Actually, they didn't. They knocked on a few doors, but once they got the 7-Eleven video showing Simon leaving before Tammy, they were convinced she did it. They arrested her the very next day.

Zara: Okay, even so, this is still crazy. No one is going to remember where Simon was two years ago. And, if they did remember, they would have called the police right after the murder.

Me: I know it's a long shot. But we're desperate. Please!!!!!!

Three dots appear. Then disappear. Thirty more seconds pass.

Me: Think of ten-year-old Zara. Just pretend you're a CIA agent.

More dots.

Zara: I'll give you an hour. That's it.

Me: You're the best!

I am just putting my phone away when the bailiff announces Judge Tyler's entrance. He doesn't look happy.

"Counsel, approach," he barks. Al, Lexi, Ethan, Tom and I all scurry up to the bench like children about to receive a tongue lashing. Which, I guess, we are.

Judge Tyler turns to Al and demands, "What is this I hear about a last-minute witness? You know better than to pull this crap in my courtroom."

Al looks chastened, but resolutely declares, "Your Honor, believe me, there is no gamesmanship going on here. We have records showing we have left over twenty-five voicemails with the witness over the last several months. We even made the five-hour round-trip drive on two occasions hoping to catch her at home. All to no avail. Then, out of nowhere, we had a voicemail when we got back from court yesterday."

Judge Tyler grows tired of the long-winded explanation and cuts to the chase, "Why is she suddenly so keen to testify?"

"Well…it seems…" Mr. Porter stutters, "There was a misunderstanding."

"What kind of misunderstanding?" Judge Tyler demands.

"She was avoiding us because she thought Tammy was trying to contest custody of her grandson. You see, the witness adopted Kyleigh's son."

Judge Tyler appears incredulous. "Did you identify yourself as a prosecutor for the State of Illinois on these voicemails?"

"Yes, of course, Your Honor. But Brandy Lynn was afraid Tammy was claiming she took Garrett without permission and that was why the State of Illinois was involved."

Tom senses an opening and pounces. "Your Honor, Mr. Porter's story is dubious, at best. And we haven't had a chance to interview the witness or prepare for our cross examination. The witness should be barred from testifying."

Judge Tyler leans back in his seat and forms a steeple with his hands. After considering the issue for a moment or two, he asks Mr. Porter, "On what issue is the witness going to testify?"

Thrilled to be gifted a softball question, Mr. Porter quickly reassures the judge, "Ms. Nelson was very close to the defendant and the deceased up until a few years ago. She will testify as to the nature of their relationship."

"Which is irrelevant," Tom interjects.

Judge Tyler takes a few more moments to consider the issue before sitting up to deliver his ruling. "I'll allow it."

Although Ethan, Tom and I all assumed this would be his ruling, it still feels like yet another gut punch. We turn to retake our seats when Judge Tyler adds, "On the condition, that after Ms. Nelson testifies, the defense team will be granted an hour's recess to prepare their cross."

Surprised, I turn to thank Judge Tyler for the courtesy. "You're welcome,

Ms. Shaw." He then gives me a small smile before adding, "Nice opening yesterday, by the way." As a startled Ethan and Tom turn back toward the bench, Judge Tyler stands up and quickly walks into chambers to allow the jury to enter the courtroom.

When we retake our seats, Ethan scribbles something on his legal pad and pushes it in front of me. "Does someone have a crush?" it reads.

I elbow him hard in his defined bicep, tear out the sheet, crumple it into a ball and deposit it into my purse. He's such a juvenile. Yet, I have to admit, Judge Tyler has a cute smile.

The prosecution calls Brandy Lynn as its first witness. She nervously takes her seat in the witness box, fidgeting with the sunglasses she's placed on top of her head. Brandy Lynn has long brown hair and is wearing strategically torn jeans with a green floral shirt and a white cardigan. While Brandy Lynn dresses like she's late twenties, the wrinkles at the corners of her eyes and mouth coupled with her stomach pouch say she's pushing mid-forties.

Al approaches the witness box and thanks Brandy Lynn for appearing today. "Now, Ms. Nelson, how do you know the defendant, Tammy Sanford?"

Brandy Lynn mumbles inarticulately while gazing at her lap, "She's my cousin."

Judge Tyler instructs, "You'll need to speak louder, Ms. Nelson."

Brandy Lynn nods and Mr. Porter continues, "Did you know the deceased, Kyleigh Sanford?"

Brandy Lynn raises her head and deliberately speaks into the microphone this time, "Yes, I was over at their house a lot when Kyleigh was growing up. I babysat all the time."

Brandy Lynn may have only called Al yesterday, but they've clearly had time to go over her direct in detail because Mr. Porter nods as if she's following a script. "And how would you describe Kyleigh as a child?"

On cue, Brandy Lynn eagerly offers, "She was a beautiful child. So happy. And talented too. She used to put on little song and dance shows for us. Tammy loved to show her off. She'd go on and on about how little Kyleigh was going to have her own star in Hollywood someday."

"And how would you describe the defendant as a mother?"

Brandy Lynn shoots Tammy a nervous glance. "Well…she doted on Kyleigh when she was little. Drove her all over the state to those pageants. Spent all her money on lessons for Kyleigh: voice lessons, tap lessons, gymnastics classes, you name it."

Al was clearly expecting something more, so he prods, "What about when Kyleigh was older. How was Tammy then?"

Brandy Lynn exchanges a long look with Tammy now. I put my hand on Tammy's arm for reassurance. Then Brandy Lynn reluctantly continues, "That's when things turned bad. Kyleigh fell when she was cheerleading. Messed her back up something awful. But Tammy kept pushing Kyleigh to get back to cheerleading and dance. Kyleigh told Tammy she couldn't. That her back hurt too much. But Tammy wouldn't take no for an answer. She would make Kyleigh keep practicing even when she was crying in pain."

Tom jumps out of his seat. "Objection. Hearsay."

Judge Tyler throws us a bone. "Sustained." Then to Mr. Porter, he cautions, "Make sure the witness has personal knowledge before you continue down this road."

Al nods and continues, "Ms. Nelson, were you ever at these cheerleading practices with Tammy and Kyleigh?"

Brandy Lynn looks down and nods.

"We need an audible answer, Ms. Nelson."

Brandy Lynn looks nervously back up at Mr. Porter. "Yes, I was. Tammy was upset with Kyleigh. Thought she was faking. She asked me to come with her to cheerleading practice to see for myself." Brandy Lynn shakes her head regretfully before continuing, "I told Tammy to back off and let Kyleigh rest. The girl was clearly in pain. After every jump or kick she'd grab her back. But Tammy wouldn't listen. A few weeks later, Tammy called and told me she thought Kyleigh was taking too many pain pills. Things went downhill from there and I stopped taking Tammy's calls. It was just too sad. I got married a year or so later and moved downstate anyway."

Brandy Lynn wipes away a tear and I chance a glance at the jury. A few of them seem to be on the verge of tears themselves. This isn't a good look for Tammy.

"Thank you for your time, Ms. Nelson. I have no further questions." As Al walks over to the prosecution's table, Judge Tyler leans toward his microphone to announce our recess.

Tom interrupts, "Judge Tyler, if it pleases the court, we only have a few questions for Ms. Nelson."

Judge Tyler looks surprised, but after a brief pause, acquiesces. "You may proceed."

Tom leans over Ethan and Tammy saying, "Shaw, you take the cross. Just get Brandy Lynn to admit she hasn't had any contact with Tammy in years. Doesn't know anything about how Kyleigh died. We're not going to get anything else out of her."

Butterflies in my stomach tell me this isn't a good plan. "Don't you think we should take the recess and prepare? This feels rushed."

Tom is frustrated. "Shaw, just ask her when she last talked to Tammy and be done with it. If you aren't up to it, Ethan can step in."

"No, no. I've got this," I assure him halfheartedly. Tammy looks at me with trepidation, but whether she's nervous about this line of questioning or just generally being on trial for murder, I can't tell.

I take my time making my way to the witness box, mulling over how best to proceed.

"Ms. Nelson, thank you for coming today," I say to buy time.

Brandy Lynn gives a slight nod as I can feel the eyes of twelve jurors on me. I take a deep breath and plunge ahead. "You admitted that after Kyleigh's fall, you and Tammy grew apart, correct?"

"Yes," Brandy Lynn acknowledges.

One for one, I tell myself before launching question two. "And after you moved downstate, you didn't come over to their home as often, correct?"

Again, Brandy Lynn nods. "That's correct."

With each admission, my confidence rises. I can do this. "And so you don't have any personal knowledge about Tammy and Kyleigh's relationship in the months preceding Kyleigh's death, do you?"

"No, I don't," Brandy Lynn admits.

I breathe a sigh of relief. I've done my job. I start to say no further questions when Tom's instructions come back to me. I turn back to Brandy Lynn for my final question, "Oh, and Ms. Nelson, you and Tammy hadn't spoken in years prior to Kyleigh's death, correct?"

"No, that's not correct," Brandy Lynn says adamantly.

She must have misunderstood. I rush to clarify, "But Ms. Nelson, you previously testified that you stopped speaking with Tammy after she told you about Kyleigh's drug use, correct?"

Brandy Lynn looks at her hands folded in her lap and quietly continues, "I stopped picking up her calls after that and we didn't speak for years. But then, Tammy called me right after Kyleigh's twenty-third birthday. She told me that Kyleigh was doing drugs and living with a dealer. She told me about her son, Garrett, and the conditions he was living in." Brandy Lynn takes a deep breath, looks Tammy directly in the eyes, and adds, "And then she made me promise that I'd look after Garrett if anything ever happened to her and Kyleigh."

Chapter 32

I'm barely cognizant of the remaining proceedings that day. The police officer's description of Simon's drug den washes over me as does Ethan's cross. I note that he scores an admission from the officer that there was no physical evidence in the apartment connecting Tammy to the crime, but on redirect Lexi has the officer confirm the only person caught on the 7-Eleven camera going into Simon's house that night was Tammy. Tom gets the medical examiner to admit Kyleigh's hyoid bone was intact during the autopsy and there was no visible bruising around her neck. At one point, she also seemed to claim that Kyleigh could have been strangled or suffocated as those terms are used interchangeably. While that gaffe put the medical examiner on shaky ground, on redirect, Mr. Porter was able to repair some of the damage by confirming the hyoid bone and bruising are not the only indicia of strangulation. As I do my best to retain the facade of engagement in the proceedings for the jury's benefit, my internal voice is screaming at me for breaking the cardinal rule of cross examination. That being you never, under any circumstances, ask a question you don't already know the answer to. That one question too many can blow up in your face: as it just did with me.

As the medical examiner exits the witness box, Mr. Porter stands in front of the prosecution table and announces, "Your Honor, the State rests its case."

"Thank you, Mr. Porter," Judge Tyler responds. "This concludes the proceedings for today. The jury is excused and we will see you back here tomorrow at eight for the commencement of the defense's case."

We pack up our things in silence as the bailiff escorts Tammy to her holding cell. As soon as Tom zips up his Tumi briefcase, he makes a beeline for the back of the courtroom. Ethan and I grab our things in a heap under our arms and rush to catch up.

Immediately upon reaching Tammy's cell, Tom barks, "What the hell was that?" Ethan and I come to an abrupt stop behind him, almost dropping all of our belongings in the process.

Tammy, confused, asks, "What was what?"

"Come off it," Tom responds. "I had to lean across you to discuss my strategy with Shaw. You heard me tell her to ask Brandy Lynn about the last time she talked to you. Why the hell didn't you give us a heads up that we were walking into a trap?" Tom kicks the cell bars in emphasis.

"I thought you'd be mad," Tammy admits sheepishly.

Tom has reached the end of his rope. "Mad? You thought we'd be mad! This is a murder trial, Tammy, not fucking high school!"

"Mr. Gaines," a timid voice interjects.

Without even turning to determine the voice's identity, Tom bellows, "What?"

"Can I have a word with you and your team?" All three of us turn to see none other than Al Porter and Lexi Banks waiting at the other end of the hallway.

"This is a privileged conversation, Al," Tom responds in a hostile tone. "I would appreciate it if you and Ms. Banks would wait for us in the courtroom."

"Of course," Al politely responds. And with a nod of his head, he heads back into the courtroom with Lexi at his side.

"What do you think that is about?" Tammy asks anxiously. She had grabbed onto the bars to give herself a better view of the hall. Her knuckles are now white.

Tom regains his composure. "They want to offer us a deal," he states matter-of-factly.

"What? Why?" Tammy questions.

"Because we're losing," I utter quietly as the realization dawns on me.

"Look, Tammy, we're going to go out and hear what they have to say and we'll be back shortly." Turning to the guard on duty, Tom commands,

"Officer Bridges, make sure Tammy isn't moved before we return." The female guard from yesterday nods in agreement and we head back to the courtroom.

As Tom and Ethan approach the prosecution's table, I lay my trench coat down and dig into my purse for my phone. No update from Zara.

Me: Find out anything helpful? Literally anything?

The seconds pass as I hear Lexi summarizing where things stand to Tom and Ethan. The jury has seen the 7-Eleven video showing Tammy arrive at Simon's apartment on the night of the murder. That same video shows Simon leave forty minutes later. Only after Simon leaves does the camera show Tammy turn right off their street. They've heard the medical examiner describe that Kyleigh presented with enough of the indicia of strangulation for that to be ruled the cause of death.

Mercifully three dots appear on my screen.

Zara: Sorry Maeve. I got nothing. Most people weren't home and the few that were told me to get off their lawn. Literally.

I tune back into the beautiful Ms. Banks. "But the most important thing the jury heard today was Tammy's own cousin testify that Tammy was planning this murder months in advance. That's premeditation a.k.a. first degree murder. Tammy will spend the rest of her life in prison."

Me: I wouldn't ask this if it wasn't important. But could you do one more canvass of the neighborhood tomorrow before work? I would do it, but I have a feeling I'll be spending all night in the office prepping Dr. Smart.

"Thanks for the recap, Ms. Banks, but I was there too," Tom responds confidently. "And I heard a medical examiner who seemed a bit shaky on the exact cause of death. Strangulation and suffocation are the same thing? Our expert will have a field day with that tomorrow. No one denies that Tammy visited Kyleigh the night she died. So that leaves you with Brandy Lynn's testimony painting Tammy as a concerned grandma. No harm no foul."

Lexi smiles smugly. "Nice try, hot shot. But we wouldn't have caught you screaming at your client just now if our case wasn't solid."

Tom's face flushes red with rage. "That was a privileged conversation. I could file a complaint with the ethics committee."

Lexi steps closer to Tom, a finger pointed in his chest. "There's no expectation of privacy in a hallway in front of a prison guard, counselor."

Ever the pacifist, Ethan steps between them. "Hey, now. Let's all calm down. Lexi, you clearly have an offer you'd like to give us. Let's hear it."

Lexi steps back and lets Al break the news. "Second degree. We'll recommend ten to twenty."

Ethan and Tom exchange meaningful glances. Ten to twenty means that after she gets credit for the time she's already been in jail waiting for trial and credit for good behavior, Tammy will most likely only serve another five years behind bars. She'd still have a life ahead of her. If the jury finds her guilty of first degree, on the other hand, she will most likely die in her cell.

In that instant, I'm certain Tom will urge Tammy to take the deal. I have to do something. "Will you give us until the start of trial tomorrow to answer?"

Four heads whip toward me questioningly.

Trying to mask the urgency in my voice, I explain, "This is a big decision for our client. She deserves the chance to sleep on it."

Al ponders my request momentarily, before ultimately agreeing. "You have until nine a.m. tomorrow to give us your client's decision. After that the offer is off the table."

I turn back to my phone and plead.

Me: Please, Zara. I need something by 8:00 a.m. or Tammy takes a plea.

Chapter 33

The four hours I lay in bed last night did not give me any needed rest. Those hours were mainly spent tossing and turning while words like positional asphyxiation, adequate pulmonary ventilation, indicia of strangulation, and partial airway obstruction skated across my mind. While I had every confidence that Dr. Smart would make a great witness, I couldn't convince myself his theory of death would sway the jury. It felt too ivory tower when compared to the State's more relatable version of the facts. Disappointed pageant mom strangles drugged-up daughter begging for more money. A jury can wrap its head around that story. As I enter Judge Tyler's courtroom for most likely the last time, I've done a pretty good job of convincing myself the plea deal is Tammy's best option.

I take my time making my way to the defense table. The heaviness I feel in my chest is not only disappointment at our inability to secure Tammy's acquittal, but also dread. During the last few weeks of feverish trial prep, I'd managed to push aside the memory of my last meeting with Jabba the Hutt. But the minute Tammy enters her plea, I'll be forced to face reality for what it is. My career at Mulvaney Stewart is over. I'll need to polish up my resume and see what other firms, if any, are desperate for a twelfth-year associate with no defined niche. The knot in my stomach tells me my options will be slim to nil.

With that uncomfortable dose of reality fresh in my mind, I mutter an unconvincing "Good morning" to Tom and Ethan. They both appear to be in similarly sullen moods. Though, while they may feel disappointment over the results of the trial for a few days, they both have successful careers to jump back into to distract them.

Tom turns to me and Ethan. He appears to be struggling to find the proper words to memorialize the moment of our defeat.

"Shaw, Ethan, you should be proud of all the work you put into this case. The only reason Tammy is getting this generous plea deal is because the prosecution is scared. They are scared the jury will believe Dr. Smart and conclude Kyleigh's death was accidental. And they still might get that chance, but we need to be supportive of whatever decision Tammy makes now. A day in prison is a day too many for most people. And Tammy's already served more than two years. Presented with the possibility of dying behind bars, being released in five looks very attractive."

Ethan and I both nod somberly. We know what Tammy will choose. Hell, it's probably what Ethan and I would choose if put in her position. We take a deep breath and prepare to take our final walk to the holding cell when my phone chimes.

Tom is instantly irritated. "Shaw, put your device on silent."

I reach into my purse to do just that when I see a text from Zara.

I'm in a cab with Simon's landlord. She saw him go into his apartment after Tammy left that night.

Tom has almost reached the door leading back to the holding cell with Ethan close behind. I jog after them as fast as my three-inch navy and plum heels will allow. I reach Ethan first and grab his arm.

"Stop. We need to talk. Let's find a conference room." I say breathlessly.

Tom spins around and demands, "What are you talking about? We have less than an hour until the prosecution's offer expires. We need to meet with Tammy and see if she's taking our advice to accept."

"I've found another witness. Let's hear her out before we speak with Tammy."

Tom shakes his head, "I don't..."

"Please," I beg, my hands in a prayer position.

Tom sighs heavily. "You have five minutes, Shaw."

I ask the bailiff to point us to an available conference room, and she indicates a door next to where the jury is congregating. Once we're all inside, I start explaining. Quickly.

"Don't judge until you've heard me out, okay?"

Tom and Ethan share a beleaguered eye roll before nodding their agreement.

"Okay, I really think the best way to secure an acquittal is by casting suspicion on Simon. The life insurance policy was a huge find, but it isn't enough if he didn't have the opportunity to commit the crime. So yesterday when Brandy Lynn appeared, I threw a Hail Mary and asked my friend Zara to canvass the neighborhood for anyone who might have seen Simon coming home the night of the murder."

"You what?" Ethan exclaims.

"Who's Zara?" asks Tom confusedly.

"No interruptions," I remind them before continuing. "Well, yesterday she struck out."

"You're mixing up your sports metaphors," Ethan mumbles cattily.

"Shut up," I warn him. "As I was saying, Zara didn't have any luck yesterday. But I asked her to go back and conduct one more canvass this morning. It's why I asked the prosecution to hold their offer open. Anyway, Zara found Simon's landlord. She says she remembers Simon coming home that night. They're on their way here."

"Are you serious?" Ethan asks. "This is huge." The amazement evident in his eyes fills me with a rush of pride.

Tom checks his watch. "It's eight-twenty. We have until nine to talk with Tammy and advise the prosecution on how we will proceed. How quickly can they get here?"

Me: Are you close?

Zara: Stuck in traffic. Still 15 minutes away.

That's cutting it too close. Okay, I need to improvise. "Let's call them and hear what the landlord has to say. Then we can advise Tammy accordingly."

"Good thinking, Shaw." Tom nods. "Dial her up."

Zara picks up on the second ring. I put her on speaker.

"Zara, I'm here with Tom and Ethan. Can you have your witness tell us what she saw that night? We need to make a strategy decision before nine o'clock.

"Okay. Her name is Fern Mott. I'll hand you over."

After a few seconds of ruffled static while the phone is exchanged, an elderly woman's voice says, "Hello?"

"Hi, Fern," I say and take a deep breath. I need to slow down so she can understand me. My natural speech pattern is a mile a minute. "We understand you have information about the night Kyleigh Sanford passed away."

"Oh, yes," she replies. "I remember that night well. I only live five houses down the street and I like to keep an eye on my rentals. The neighborhood isn't what it used to be, you know. Back when my husband and I bought our place in nineteen sixty-six, the neighborhood was a quiet Polish community. Everyone took such good care of their homes and mowed their lawns. But I just don't know about these young people these days. They're all on drugs, if you ask me."

Tom gives me a move this along signal.

I interrupt. "Fern, I'd love to hear more about the history of the neighborhood another time, but could you tell us about the night Kyleigh died. We don't have much time."

Fern makes a tsking noise to let me know she doesn't care for being rushed, but continues. "Well, on the night that poor girl died, I heard yelling in their unit. It was around eleven, so I decided to take my dog, Mickey, for his last walk of the night and check it out. When I passed by Simon's house, I heard loud voices and knew it was Kyleigh and her mom. I'd heard them go at it before. So, I took my time going around the block. By the time I got back home, Tammy came storming out of the house and peeled off in her car."

Ethan gives me a "so what" shrug.

Prodding I ask, "Any chance you were still watching the house when Simon came home?"

"Why, yes, I was. Now I don't sleep well, you know. I spend most of my nights dozing in my living room recliner watching TV. Well, around one. I hear the backfire of a car engine. I knew it was Simon's car. My husband was a mechanic for fifty years and I told Simon to have it checked out. My guess was a cracked distributor cap, but he wouldn't listen to me. Damn fool!"

"Wait, Ms. Mott," I interrupt, "are you sure you heard Simon's car outside his house around one on the night Kyleigh died?"

Irritably, Fern admonishes me, "That's what I just told you, didn't I?"

"How can you be sure though?" I press. "Couldn't it have been a different car that backfired that night?"

"No, it couldn't," Fern snipes. "After the car woke me up, I got up to go to the bathroom. I'd had a urinary tract infection for the past three months. Antibiotics didn't do anything. Anyway, I passed by my front window and saw Simon's car parked outside his house."

Jackpot. I look at Tom for confirmation, but he still looks unconvinced.

"But how can you be sure that was the same night that Kyleigh died?" Tom pushes.

"And who are you, Mister? I was talking to the nice lady."

I hide my laugh with an unconvincing cough. "Fern, that is my boss, Tom Gaines. Would you mind answering his question?"

Fern grumbles before acquiescing, "Well, I guess. Your boss could use a lesson in manners though. Wasn't he ever taught not to interrupt?"

I don't even bother to hide my chuckle this time. "No, I don't think he was. He interrupts me regularly. But his question is important." Tom rolls his eyes dramatically.

"Well, I know it was the night Kyleigh died, because I woke up hearing ambulance sirens the next morning and I watched that poor girl being carried out on a stretcher."

Tom can't help himself. "I'm sorry to interrupt, Ms. Mott..."

"Again," Fern points out.

This makes even Tom smile. "Yes, again. But why didn't you tell the police all of this before now?"

Fern jumps on this one. "They never asked me, that's why. I'm old, you see. And nobody respects their elders anymore. They think we're daffy. Well, I might not be able to get around like I used to, but there's nothing wrong with my brain."

I cover the speaker to address Tom and Ethan. "The police reports show they only questioned a few neighbors. One of them told them they had heard shouting between Kyleigh and her mom that night. Between that and the 7-Eleven video, the police narrowed their focus to Tammy."

Tom and Ethan nod and I uncover the speaker. "Thank you so much for talking to us, Fern. I look forward to meeting you in person very soon. Goodbye."

I hang up and breathlessly ask, "So what do we do?"

Tom stands up straight and declares, "We tell Tammy to turn down the deal. We're going to win this son-of-a-bitch."

Chapter 34

Simon, wearing his orange prison garb, slouches in the witness chair picking his nails and looking disinterested. I take a deep breath to collect myself. This is the make it or break it moment, and it's all on my shoulders. No pressure though, I think sarcastically. I push back my chair and walk over to the jury box ensuring I'll have their attention. For better or worse.

"Good morning, Simon," I say cheerfully. "I'd like to begin by asking you a few questions about your relationship with Kyleigh Sanford. Would that be okay?"

Simon shrugs and continues to pick at the thick black gunk lining his nails.

"You'll have to answer audibly," I remind him.

"Yeah, okay," he grunts.

"Thank you. Now can you tell us how long Kyleigh and her son, Garrett, were living at your apartment?"

"I don't know. Maybe a year?" Simon guesses. "I'm not the type to really keep track of stupid things like anniversaries," he says, smirking.

The jury's distaste for Simon is palpable and it's exactly what I'm counting on. I push forward. "And Kyleigh's son, Garret. Was he your son as well?"

"Ummmm, no." He chuckles. "I've made it twenty-nine years without supporting any baby momma. Knock on wood," he says while rapping his knuckles against the side of the witness box.

"Congratulations," I say. "But speaking about potential 'baby mommas,'" I say using air quotes for the jury's benefit, "as you so nicely put it, you've had quite a few girlfriends over the years, right?"

This gets Simon's attention. He smirks at me lustily. "Why? You want a turn?"

I give the jury an exaggerated eye roll before responding, "No, I think I'll pass. See, I've had a chance to review your criminal history and noticed you've had quite a few arrests for domestic disputes."

Simon's feathers are ruffled. "That was one time and it was the other way around. *She* hit me. But of course when the police arrived, she started sobbing and guess who got arrested? Fucking bitch."

Judge Tyler sits up at attention and scoots his roller chair as close to the witness box as he can. "I'll only say this once, sir, so listen up. That language will not be tolerated in my courtroom. Understand?"

Simon slouches in his seat but nods at the judge all the same.

Judge Tyler is not satisfied. "I need you to answer orally so I can make sure we're on the same page."

"Yeah, okay, Jesus," Simon agrees.

Judge Tyler still isn't pleased, but apparently decides to not push it further. He leans back, but keeps his eyes fixed on the witness.

I walk over to the defense table and pick up a copy of Simon's criminal history from Tom. He gives me an encouraging smile as he hands it over. "Come now, Simon. I think you're being modest. By my count there are, one, two, three, no four separate arrests for domestic assault here. Do you really expect us to believe you were always the victim? A big strong man like you?"

Simon mutters incoherently, but the point has been made. "Let's move on," I concede. "What can you tell us about the day Kyleigh died?"

Simon lets out a long sigh as if the subject of his former girlfriend's death has grown tiresome. "There's not much to tell. It was a normal day. I do remember the baby wouldn't shut up. Cried all...damn...day. I finally told Ky she needed to do something about him. I couldn't get any sleep. She said she would call her ma for money to take him to the doctor. She thought he had some kind of infection. Her mom was supposed to show up around eleven, so I took off just before that. I couldn't stand that bitch. Still can't for that matter," he says as he gives Tammy a leering smile.

"This is your second warning, Mr. Harr," Judge Tyler cautions. Simon's leer turns into a scowl.

"So you left your apartment a bit before eleven that night, correct?" I confirm.

"Yeah, that sounds about right," he agrees as he smooths down his greasy ginger ponytail.

"And what time did you return home that night?" I ask, trying to mask my anxiety. Simon's answers to the next few questions are crucial.

Simon raises his gaze from his nails and looks me dead in the eye. "I didn't," he says resolutely. "I came home around nine the next morning and found Ky dead in my bed."

I can feel the jury behind me holding its collective breath. "Are you sure about that?"

"Yes. Very sure."

I make my way slowly from the jury box to stand right in front of the witness. Simon's nerves start to show as he begins quickly bouncing his left leg.

"The thing is, Simon," I say maintaining eye contact, "that's hard to believe. See, we all just heard from a credible witness who saw you come back to your apartment around one o'clock that same night." I gesture to the jury who sit in rapt attention.

"What witness?" Simon demands. "They're lying!" But his denial lacks real conviction.

I shake my head and make my way to stand in front of the defense table. I want Tammy in Simon's line of sight. I'm counting on her to unnerve him even more. "I don't think so, Simon. The witness was able to describe your car very specifically. Even down to its tendency to backfire due to a broken distributor cap."

"That old bitch," Simon shouts causing audible gasps from the jury box. Judge Tyler sits at attention, but doesn't interrupt.

I try to suppress a smile as I ask, "So I take it you know who saw you that night?"

Simon is too enraged to control himself. "My fucking busybody landlord.

She was always spying on us from her living room. And she was always talking shit about my car. Like that old prune was ever a mechanic."

I flip through Simon's criminal history for a minute or two to let his admission sink in before continuing. "So, where was Kyleigh when you came home at one that night?"

"What?" Realization that he just blew his alibi dawns on Simon. He stammers as he tries to figure out his next move. "Uhhh...yeah...so I came home that night. Who cares?" he says defensively. "The house was finally quiet, so I assumed Ky and the baby were asleep. I lay down to watch some TV and fell asleep too. I didn't check on Kyleigh until the kid started crying the next morning. I'd already been out making deliveries before that."

"I see," I say to buy time. I have opportunity sealed up, but still need motive. "And that's when you called nine-one-one, right?"

Simon has regained his footing. "Yeah, I went in to tell Ky to feed the baby and she wouldn't wake up. I shook her a couple more times before I realized she was dead. Then I called the ambulance. Not much good they could do at that point though."

I take a breath and a leap of faith. "And how many days later did you cash in Kyleigh's life insurance policy?"

The courtroom comes alive. Al leans over to confer with Lexi. The jurors start gossiping amongst themselves. The media wakes up and begins frantically taking notes. Judge Tyler puts a quick kibosh on the ruckus. "Order in the court," he demands. "Order, I said." He punctuates his words with a loud gavel bang. The courtroom goes silent. All eyes on Simon.

Simon puts both hands under his legs and leans forward nervously. He bares his yellowed teeth and asks, "What are you talking about? What life insurance policy?"

"Oh you know," I say without a hint of doubt in my voice. "The one you took out from LadderLife. How much was it for again?"

Simon attempts to call my bluff. He smiles and says matter-of-factly, "I don't know what you're talking about."

"Oh really," I counter. "So, if I were to show your bank account records to the jury right now, you're telling me they wouldn't see a deposit from

LadderLife a mere week after Kyleigh's death."

Simon looks ready to issue another denial, before I point out, "Let me remind you, Simon, you are under oath. Perjury is a crime that could add additional time to your sentence."

There's a pause. Simon and I are playing chicken. If he calls my bluff and denies the insurance payout again, I'll have to move on. I can't admit I broke into his apartment. I have no admissible proof. We're looking straight in each other's eyes. Sizing each other up. But Simon breaks eye contact first. "Fine," he barks. "So what? Kyleigh had life insurance. There's no law against that."

Jackpot. My heart is pounding so hard it feels like it's going to burst through my chest. I prod a bit further, "You're right. There isn't a law against taking out life insurance. In fact, it's good financial planning. Especially for a person with a child. And what was the amount of the life insurance policy, Simon?"

Simon's bravado fades as he nervously mutters, "Fifty thousand."

"Wow!" I say in amazement while turning to the jury to confirm they're getting this. "That's a sizable amount of cash."

Simon is back on the defensive. "What of it? Ky hadn't paid for food or rent for a year. She owed me that much and more."

"And you were the sole beneficiary?" I continue.

"Duh," he says sarcastically. "You think Ky would put her mom down? After all the shit she put her through?"

"And what gave Kyleigh the idea she needed life insurance?" I ask. "She doesn't strike me as a planner."

"Well, I did, of course." Simon admits unabashedly. "She was sitting on my couch with no money getting high off my stash every day. As I said before, she owed me."

"Let's recap," I say, turning to the jury. "You have a history of assaulting your girlfriends. You were home during the window of Kyleigh's death. You lied to the police about your whereabouts. And you were the sole beneficiary of a fifty-thousand-dollar life insurance policy that you insisted Kyleigh take out. Which sort of begs the question, doesn't it?"

"What question is that?" Simon asks belligerently.

"Why you aren't the one on trial for Kyleigh's murder?" I say, never taking my eyes off the twelve men and women who hold Tammy's fate in their hands.

Al, seeing his case crumble before his eyes, has had enough. He stands abruptly and shouts, "Objection, Your Honor, is Ms. Shaw questioning the witness or testifying?"

I turn and give him a big shit eating smile before conceding, "I'll withdraw that last one, Your Honor. No further questions."

Chapter 35

I'm riding a wave of pride as Dr. Smart takes the stand. As I assumed, he's a great witness. He makes the most out of the medical examiner's slip that strangulation and suffocation are one and the same. He highlights the lack of physical evidence of strangulation, made even more remarkable by the prosecution's theory that this was a crime of passion. And lastly offers his more reasonable theory that Kyleigh, after fighting with her mother, got high. She then curled herself up in a comforter to sleep, never to waken. Her body unable to rescue itself from asphyxiation due to the mind-numbing effects of the opioids. His testimony was well reasoned and logical. And the prosecution was unable to poke many holes in the theory during cross.

As Dr. Smart makes his way out of the witness stand, Tom stands and addresses the court.

"Your Honor, the defense rests."

As Judge Tyler turns to the jury to announce the commencement of closing statements, Tom interrupts.

"Your Honor, the defense doesn't feel there is a need for closing statements. We are moving for a directed verdict under section 5/115 of the code of criminal procedure."

Audible mutterings from the jury, as Al Porter jumps to his feet. "Your Honor, this is ludicrous. The prosecution has produced more than sufficient evidence of Ms. Sanford's guilt and now it is up to her peers to deliver a verdict. It wouldn't be right to take the decision out of their hands."

Tom calmly rebuts, "Your Honor, the code of criminal procedure is clear.

If, after the close of evidence, the prosecution's case is insufficient to support a verdict of guilty, the court may enter a judgment of acquittal. That is all we are asking the court to do here."

Judge Tyler nods gravely before turning to the jury. "Ladies and gentlemen, I'm going to take this motion under advisement during the lunch hour. Please be back here in exactly one hour for my decision. At that time, I will either grant the motion and you will be excused or we will proceed with closing arguments." With a quick tap of his gavel, Judge Tyler is out of his chair and heading briskly for chambers.

Tammy turns to Ethan, confused. "What's happening? I thought we were going to have closing arguments before lunch."

Ethan pats Tammy's hand. "This is good news, Tammy. Tom has asked the judge to find you not guilty. To find the State didn't prove its case. In an hour, you could walk out of here a free woman."

Tammy closes her eyes and tilts her head toward the ceiling in what looks like silent prayer. The bailiff then appears to take her back to her holding cell for lunch. As she's led away, I recall the odd thing that happened the first time I was in court with Tammy. When she appeared to smile self-satisfied at the judge, but then her expression hardened once she saw me watching. As Tom and Ethan are gathering up their things and discussing the best place to grab a quick bite, I put the scene and the troubling feeling that accompanies it out of my mind.

Lunch turns out to be a coffee and banana from the Starbucks in the basement of the courthouse, though I've barely managed to consume half of the fruit due to nerves. Each of us is scrolling through emails and social media posts while silently begging the time to go by faster. Finally, Ethan breaks the silence by announcing he needs to take a leak. I go back to skimming an article about which items Jennifer Aniston took from the *Friends* set on her last day of filming. Spoiler alert, it was the Central Perk neon sign.

"So, Shaw, what cases will you turn to after this trial is over?" I guess this is Tom's idea of small talk. He couldn't have picked a worse topic. The nervous butterflies in my stomach are immediately replaced by a hard rock of dread.

"Well...I had been working on some RESPA cases for Elizabeth Townley."

"Had?" Tom picks up on my hesitancy.

Might as well lay it all on the table. The gossip of my imminent departure will be swirling through the firm soon enough. "The truth is, Tom, the only thing I'll be working on after this trial's over is my resume."

"What?" Tom seems genuinely shocked.

I emit a long sigh, not wanting to recount the painful memory. "I spoke to Chris Bines a week or so ago." So much has happened in the last couple of weeks, I honestly can't remember how long it has been. "He's been unhappy with my billable hours for the last few years and told me in no uncertain terms that my career at Mulvaney Stewart is over."

"No, that can't be right." Tom shakes his head in disbelief. "Just wait until he hears about the amazing work you've done on this trial."

"It won't matter, Tom." Another steadying breath before delving into yet another painful topic. "Chris only cares about billables. I have two kids at home and am about to be going through a divorce. I just can't put in the kind of hours that are required to make partner here." I feel my eyes start to tear and my throat tighten. I do everything in my power to shore up my emotional levee before the tears burst through.

Tom is clearly out of his comfort zone. "Shaw...I'm so sorry...I had no idea."

I'm saved any further embarrassment by Ethan's return from the bathroom. Unsurprisingly, he doesn't seem to pick up on the tension. "Judge Tyler should be back in fifteen minutes. You two ready to head back upstairs?"

"Absolutely," I say as I take a last long sip of my skinny vanilla latte and rise from my seat.

Tom rises as well and places both of his large hands on the back of his now abandoned chair. He then takes a moment to compose himself before giving Ethan and me his full attention. When he speaks, it's in a somber tone. "I'm reminded of a quote by another incredibly dashing man named Tom, this time Tom Hanks in the film *Philadelphia*. In essence, he said that occasionally lawyers get to take part in justice being done." Tom then gives us an encouraging smile before finishing with, "Let's go take part in justice being done for Tammy Sanford, shall we?"

We walk back into a much different courtroom than we first encountered on Monday. Far from the atmosphere of a group of people trapped in a shared irksome requirement, there is a feeling of anxious excitement about to boil over. I walk over to the defense table, but find myself unable to sit, preferring instead to stand and flip through Ethan's prepared closing statement while silently praying it won't be necessary.

Judge Tyler roughly opens the door leading up to the bench and is in his chair within seconds. "Bring in the defendant," he orders the bailiff. He then turns to his clerk. "Have the jury wait in their meeting room while I announce my ruling."

Tammy is led from the back of the courtroom by Officer Bridges. She's doing her best to conceal it, but anxiety is written all over her face. As she takes her seat next to me, I remind her to breathe. I then take one of her hands as Ethan holds the other.

"Will the parties please rise," Judge Tyler directs. Al and Lexi stand first, looking stoic.

Tom leans over to Ethan, Tammy and me and tries to diffuse the tension. "Remember, Judge Tyler is only ruling on our motion here. Even if he denies it, we will proceed to closing statements. I have every faith in the jury to grant your acquittal." With that, we stand as a team and face Judge Tyler.

Judge Tyler fiddles with his papers before stating, "The right to be judged by a jury of your peers is an essential component of our criminal justice system. For a judge to take that decision away from the jury and himself deliver a verdict of innocent is a judicial prerogative that should only be employed in the starkest of situations. Situations in which the evidence suggesting guilt is so thin as to be gossamer." Judge Tyler reaches for his glass of water and takes a sip while the courtroom holds its collective breath.

After quenching his thirst, Judge Tyler continues with a nod toward the prosecution. "Mr. Porter and Ms. Banks are accomplished attorneys representing the State of Illinois. They have appeared before me on numerous occasions and have always conducted themselves with the utmost integrity. They have done so in this case as well."

Judge Tyler smiles at Al and Lexi before turning to the defense's table. "Ms. Sanford, you were appointed a team of pro bono counsel of the highest caliber. They have gone above and beyond their ethical obligation in their investigation and preparation for this trial. You are very lucky to have them representing you here as not all defendants are given this type of representation. I would go so far as to say, most defendants receive representation of much lower quality, unfortunately," he says, giving a disappointed shake of his head.

"With that, I will turn to the merits of the defense's motion. The defense has asked me to find the prosecution's case insufficient to support a verdict of guilty. In reviewing the evidence before me, I find the prosecution has shown video of the defendant Tammy Sanford entering the victim's home within the time frame of the victim's death. I have further heard evidence that a neighbor overheard a fight between the defendant and the victim soon after Ms. Sanford's arrival. Ms. Sanford was then seen leaving the victim's apartment a short time later. The next morning, a call was placed by Simon Harr to emergency services indicating the victim was unresponsive. While there is circumstantial evidence of the defendant's guilt, that is all it is. Circumstantial."

A flicker of hope rises in my chest as Judge Tyler takes a pause before continuing. "On the other hand, the defense has presented evidence that the victim's boyfriend was also present in their apartment during the window of the victim's death. The victim's boyfriend also has a history of domestic violence and received a financial benefit from the victim's death. Further, the defense has offered the testimony of a renowned forensic pathologist who, having reviewed the medical examiner's report and police investigation, has reached the conclusion the deceased was not a victim of a violent crime but instead succumbed as a byproduct of her opioid addiction."

Judge Tyler takes a moment to review his notes before delivering his ultimate verdict. "On the basis of the evidence before me, I find no conscientious jury could find Ms. Tammy Sanford guilty of the first-degree murder of her daughter Ms. Kyleigh Sanford beyond a reasonable doubt." At these words, Tammy crumbles into her seat in sobs of relief.

Judge Tyler finishes with, "The defendant will be released after processing and the jury can be excused with our thanks." He then nods to counsel and makes his way back to chambers.

I put my arms around Tammy as she continues sobbing. The exhilaration I feel in this moment is one I've never experienced before in my professional career. I look up at Ethan who smiles back at me with tears in his eyes. Tom beams at us both, pride emanating from his accomplished face.

A soft, "Congratulations," from the railing dividing the "well of the court" from the public benches jolts me back to reality. It's Zara looking happier than I've seen her in a long time. Ethan takes my place comforting Tammy so I can embrace my bestie.

As we hug, Zara whispers in my ear, "You should be so proud. You just saved Tammy from a lifetime behind bars."

I release her so I can look into her beautiful brown eyes. "You mean *we* saved Tammy. I could have never done this without you. Thank you." I then add with a smile, "You would've made a helluva CIA agent, you know."

Zara wipes a tear from her eye, before regaining her composure. "I took the rest of the day off. I'll wait here while you finish up. This calls for champagne at the Peninsula."

"It most certainly does." I resolve to spend the remainder of my afternoon and evening enjoying a glass (or four) of ridiculously expensive bubbly at a five-star hotel bar. Resumes and divorce lawyers can wait until tomorrow.

.

Chapter 36

I arrive at the Breakfast House in Lakeview with a pounding headache, not being able to recall the last time I split two bottles of champagne over the course of an evening. I'm quickly seated at a two-top by the windows, and I immediately put in an order for water and coffee. A few moments later, I spy Tom walking in the front door of the local diner with the same assurance that he exhibits entering a courtroom. Seeing as he's dressed in jeans and a wool pullover, I'm guessing he's also "working from home" today. He slides onto the stool across from me and gives me a charming smile.

"Thanks for meeting me this morning, Shaw." After giving me a once over, he adds, "I take it you did some celebrating last night?"

"You could say that," I admit, wincing. "I may never drink champagne again."

Tom pushes my water glass across the table and advises, "You need to rehydrate."

"Thanks." I take a long sip, wipe my mouth with my napkin and cut to the chase. "What is this about, Tom?"

"Relax, Maeve. Order some eggs and we'll talk." He effectively shuts down communication for the present by picking up his overly large menu and perusing the options.

While I resolve to stop pestering Tom until after our orders have been taken, once I request huevos rancheros and Tom orders oatmeal with bananas from the kind elderly waitress with blue hair, I pick up where I'd left off.

"I appreciate the breakfast invite, Tom, but I'm confused as to why we are meeting outside the office. If this has to do with my impending divorce, I'd really rather not go into the sordid details with you either at work or over coffee."

Tom puts up his hands to stop my oversharing. "I'm not trying to delve into your personal life, Shaw. I'm here because I think you're a talented lawyer. And those talents have been wasted on routine RESPA motions."

"Ouch!" I cringe, before going on the defensive. "Representing student loan companies may not be glamorous, but it pays the bills."

"Fair enough," Tom admits. "I've taken on my fair share of 'routine matters.' Particularly as a young associate. But you aren't that young anymore, are you, Shaw?"

"Jesus!" I choke, spluttering on my last sip of coffee. "I get it. I'm a shitty attorney. I already got this speech from Jabba. I don't need it from you too. Thanks for the coffee," I say while grabbing my purse and slipping off my stool.

Tom grabs my arm. "Shaw, sit down." When I don't budge, he adds, "Please."

I scowl at him but deign to retake my stool.

"I'm doing a piss-poor job at this, I admit. Let me just cut to the chase. Shaw, I think you are a gifted criminal attorney, whose talents are being wasted by the likes of Chris Bines and Elizabeth Townley. I would like you to consider accepting the newly created position of Director of Pro Bono at Mulvaney Stewart."

"What exactly would that entail?" I ask dubiously.

"Indulge me for a moment. For the last few years, the only pro bono cases that Mulvaney Stewart has taken on are those that have been sought out and supervised by individual partners. As you may imagine, what with the workload of most litigation partners, those partners willing to take on and supervise additional non billable work are a small group of suckers like myself. Yet, pro bono work is so important, both to the clients who desperately need quality representation and to the Mulvaney Stewart associates who desperately need the experience. I mean, how can we expect associates who have done nothing but draft routine motions for years, to be ready to argue dispositive motions and lead trials once they're promoted to partner? So, for the last year, I've waged a campaign with the executive committee to create the Director of Pro Bono position. And after I told the committee about our impressive trial win yesterday, they finally relented."

"Congratulations," I say half-heartedly. "But, again, what does the job entail?"

Tom is clearly disappointed in my lack of enthusiasm for his Herculean efforts but deigns to continue. "My vision is the Director of Pro Bono will be the liaison between the various courts and organizations looking for pro bono representation and the firm. The director will decide which cases to accept and will staff them accordingly. When the circumstances warrant, such as in the case of a murder trial, the director will supervise and try those cases with her selected team."

"Hmmm," I say, unconvinced.

Tom goes into pure salesmanship mode. "Don't you see, Shaw. This is a job you can shape around your life. It's a nine-to-five position most days. Sure, there will be long days leading up to trial, but you determine how many trials to take on. And you'd be doing good work and giving back to the community. The same can't be said for tanking class actions against student loan giants."

I finish my last scrumptious bite of egg, black beans, salsa and tortilla and put my fork down. A position that offers work/life balance along with the opportunity to be lead attorney in criminal cases of my choosing doesn't come along every day. Although I had previously sworn off ever doing criminal work, the Tammy Sanford case changed that for me. I was engaged in my work in a way I'd never been in my previous twelve years at Mulvaney Stewart. And I was good at it too. I need to give this some serious consideration.

"Okay, let's say I was interested," I begin.

Tom breaks into a self-satisfied smile. "I knew you'd come around."

I shake off his enthusiasm and caution, "Don't go popping the champagne just yet, I need some more information. For example, I need to work from home at least one day a week so I can pick up the boys a bit earlier from daycare. Or stay home with them when they're sick. I'm not just going to foist them on their grandparents anymore. Would that be a problem?"

Tom brushes off the question. "Of course not. It's a director position, Shaw. You make the schedule work for you."

Okay, that's one concern addressed. Now comes the biggie. "I notice the title is director, not partner. Will this position come with a salary commensurate with a first-year partner at Mulvaney Stewart?"

Tom leans back, smiles, and considers me a bit before responding. "I'm proud of you, Shaw. It wasn't only Tammy who got something out of this trial. It has brought out a spark in you that was noticeably lacking just a month or so ago. While we hadn't contemplated paying quite that much, I think your request is fair and I'll take it back to the committee with my recommendation that we agree. Any other concerns you would like to raise?"

"I truly can't think of any right now." Beaming, I add, "Thank you, Tom. Not only for this exciting opportunity, but for the faith you put in me throughout the trial. It has meant more than you know."

Tom gives me a meaningful look. "You earned every bit and more."

I feel the telltale lump in my throat forming and decide to cut this lovefest short before I embarrass myself with tears. "Well, thank you again for the delicious breakfast and exciting opportunity, but I need to run. Ethan and I are going downstate today to pick up Rapscallion."

Tom chuckles. "Tammy will be thrilled to get her baby back."

We both rise from our stools and shake hands. "I'll let you know when I hear back from the committee, but you can plan on starting your new position on Monday."

I thank Tom again before grabbing my handbag and heading for the exit.

"Hey, Shaw."

I look back and Tom asks, "Who's Jabba?"

My cheeks flush hot. I only use that disparaging nickname with Ethan or Patrick. "Umm...I'm embarrassed to say it's something I came up with to refer to a certain head of our practice group who shares some of the same attributes as the *Star Wars* villain. Please don't tell him," I add urgently.

Tom chuckles and waves me off. "Your secret is safe with me."

After buckling into my mom-mobile, I pull out my phone to text Zara the good news.

Tom offered me the position of Director of Pro Bono at the firm. I'll get to choose which cases the firm will take on and staff them with associates. And I'll be the lead trial attorney for any criminal cases. I'm so excited!

Three dots immediately form in response.

That's amazing, Maeve. I'm so happy for you. And it is totally deserved.

I smile with pride before adding,

Better brush up on your investigator skills. I may need you again.

Chapter 37

The drive to K-9 Kennels is two and a half hours *each way*! I can't believe Ethan rented a car and made this godawful drive every couple of months just to bring back cute dog pictures. Underneath all the self-centeredness, Ethan can be a sweetheart at times. He even does his best to make the time go quicker by playing his new "Girl Power" Spotify mix. We pass the first hour car dancing along to "Waka Waka" by Shakira, "Jenny from the Block" by who else, and "Applause" by Lady Gaga. But soon after, Ethan leans his seat back for a nap and I do my best to keep my speed within ten miles of the limit. When we finally pull up to the kennel, which occupies a whole five acres of what is otherwise farmland, I wake Ethan with a firm slap on the thigh and a question that has been plaguing me the last ninety miles.

"Why in the hell did Tammy board her dog all the way in Springfield?"

Ethan emits a long and loud yawn while stretching his arms over his head. His boyish movements remind me a bit of Declan.

"Fuck if I know. I assumed her cousin boarded the dog. She lives around here, I think."

We exit the maroon Odyssey and head up the lane to the yellow-and-white-trimmed house out of which the kennel operates. We are greeted at the front desk by a middle-aged woman with frizzy brown hair pulled back into a high ponytail. A thick set of bangs covers her forehead. She's wearing a grey shirt with the K-9 kennel logo and her name emblazoned above her right breast.

Ethan elbows past me and approaches her with arms outstretched. "Karen!

So good to see you again. How are the kids?"

Instantly overcome with happiness, Karen comes around the desk and into his arms stuttering, "The boys are great! What brings you here?"

Releasing Karen from his embrace, he responds, "We're here to pick up Rapscallion. Didn't Tammy call you?"

"Oh, that's why his things are packed. I just got here about five minutes ago and haven't had a chance to read the notes."

The implications of our visit set in and Karen sticks out her lower lip like a pouting middle schooler who has just been told her favorite boy band broke up. "Wait, that means we're losing Scallywag *and* the pleasure of your visits."

Ethan nods. "Afraid so, but maybe I'll find an excuse to come back and visit my favorite kennel someday soon." With that, Ethan puts his arm around Karen's shoulders and together they head toward the back door.

I try to keep my gag reflex under control as I follow them from the yellow house into the fenced-in backyard carpeted by turf and adorned with a doggy play area. Six or so dogs of various breeds run happily around the yard.

Karen calls out, "Scallywag," and a set of big brown ears on an otherwise diminutive doggy rise to attention. I have to admit, Rapscallion is a cutie. He trots over to Karen, who bends down and picks him up affectionately.

"Oh, we're going to miss this little guy so much," she says, putting her face close to his and giving him air kisses. "He's been here so long, we consider him one of our own. Heck, we even came up with our own nickname!"

The questions that plagued me during the last hour or so of the drive rear their ugly heads again and before I can help myself I'm back in lawyer mode. "Is it customary for a kennel to keep an animal this long? I always assumed boarding was a temporary arrangement."

Karen, still loving on Rapscallion, brushes off my concerns. "Well, our typical arrangement is for a week or two, but we've had dogs stay with us for longer. One time a new State Farm employee had to live in corporate housing for over a year because he couldn't sell his house back in Texas. We kept his two golden retrievers that whole time." She laughs and adds, "I mean, as long as the person keeps paying, we're happy to keep their pooch."

Karen and Rapscallion head back into the house with Ethan and me following. Once inside, Karen hands Rapscallion to Ethan and walks over to a bench holding what appears to be the dog's bed, toys, and leash. While Karen seems untroubled by Rapscallion's long stay, I can't seem to let it go.

"You mentioned that the owner has to keep paying in order for their dog to stay here?"

Karen turns to me, puts her hands on her ample hips, and laughs. "Well, of course, sweetheart. We're a kennel, not a shelter. The owners have to pay upfront for their dog's care."

Feeling as if I'm closing in on something, I push, "Well, how did Tammy pay for Rapscallion's care if she didn't know how long he'd be here?"

Karen furrows her brow before admitting, "Hmmm, I'm not quite sure. Let me take a look at the ledger." She drops Rapscallion's bed and belongings back down on the bench and heads over to the front desk. Pulling a large notebook out from under the counter, she flips through it until she reaches what must be Rapscallion's page.

"Well, see this makes sense. Given that Scallywags was going to be boarding with us for an indefinite period, Tammy set up a monthly auto pay. We deducted the boarding fee from her account each month. See, all the transactions are listed here." She points, indicating a page full of dates and fees.

Ethan, growing tired of Rapscallion's enthusiastic kisses, seeks to put an end to my inquiry. "Thanks for all your help, Karen, but we better hit the road if we want to be back in Chicago before dark."

"Oh, we'll miss you both," Karen coos.

Ethan enacts an exaggerated sad face, saying, "We'll try to come back for a visit soon. Won't we Scallywags," he says, giving the dog nuzzles for effect.

I concede and go fetch Rapscallion's things from the bench where Karen left them.

"Thank you again for taking such good care of our boy." Ethan beams at Karen before opening the front door. "And good luck keeping Hunter and Gavin under control."

Karen laughs. "Oh, I'll need it. They're a handful." They share a laugh at what I assume to be Karen's boys' expense. Ethan then proceeds down the front steps with Rapscallion under his arm. I'm about to follow when one last question brings me to a halt.

"When was Rapscallion dropped off?"

Karen, still leering at Ethan's departing buttocks, is caught unaware. "Excuse me?"

"The date. What date was Rapscallion dropped off with you?"

Perturbed by my relentless questioning, Karen says dismissively, "How would I know? I wasn't here."

With a feeling of anticipation growing in my stomach, I persist. "Wouldn't it be written in the ledger?"

Karen lets out an exasperated sigh. "Oh, I guess it would. Let me take a look here." Karen runs her fingers up the payment column. Having reached the top of that page, she loudly flips back to the previous page and does the same. "Finally. Here it is. Scallywags was given to us on August 2, 2015." She then mutters, "Not that I can see what difference it makes."

My heart skips a beat, but I need a second confirmation. "You're sure about that, Karen. This is important. Please double-check."

Karen rolls her eyes so far back in her head that for a second I only see the whites. She then looks back at the column and says slowly, "Yes, that's what it says right here. Date: 8/2/15. Note: Rapscallion registered. Payment to be made by monthly autopay."

My chest constricts and I almost drop Rapscallion's things. Tammy sent her beloved dog to a long-term kennel two and a half hours away from where she lives the day *before* Kyleigh was killed. What have we done?

Chapter 38

The distant sound of sirens snaps me back to reality. I try to rise from my tight hiding spot only to find my legs have gone to sleep, the numbness interrupted by the pain of what feels like a thousand tiny needles stabbing me from ankles to hips. I clumsily squeeze out from behind the china cabinet and stumble toward the front door. With each step the dread of what I'm about to see rises. I reach the screen door and give it a push, but it doesn't open. Looking down, I see Mom lying face-down on the porch in a pool of red, her feet blocking the door. Her immaculate cream pants now riddled with blood stains emanating from a hole in the back of her navy blouse. My stomach turns, and I retch onto the floor by the door. I begin to back away when I see my father crouched against the porch railing, clutching his knees and handgun to his chest. I guess both bullets had been for mom.

"Dad?" I whisper hoarsely, my face pressed up against the screen.

He looks up and our eyes meet, his wet with tears. The sounds of the sirens getting louder with each passing second.

"Maeve," he utters with more tenderness than I'd heard it spoken in a long time, a sad smile forming on his lips.

Tears flow freely down my face now. "Why, Dad?

He shakes his head. "I'm sorry."

Panic takes hold in earnest and I ask, "What are we going to do?"

Another sad shake of his head. "Nothing to be done, Maevey."

The screech of the sirens hurts my ears as two police cruisers make the same turn onto Spruce Drive that I'd run only minutes earlier. But that seems like a lifetime ago now. Dad tightens his grip on the handgun.

"It would've never stopped, Maeve. You need to understand that," he says firmly. "Even if I'd let her go, she'd have kept finding new ways to destroy us. That's just what addicts do."

The cruisers pull up in front. I see Sheriff Quaker opening the driver's side door of his patrol car, every fiber of my body alive with fear.

"Dad," I say slowly. "Please put down the gun. It's over."

Looking me right in the eye, he slowly raises the gun to his temple. "I did this for you, Maeve. Remember that. I did this so you could be free."

And then his head explodes.

Chapter 39

I don't disclose Karen's revelation to Ethan, but the speed by which I haul ass back to Chicago makes him suspicious. This suspicion reaches its apex when I pull up in front of his condo with Rapscallion still in tow. With his eyebrows arched as far as they can go on his forehead, he asks, "Aren't I coming to Tammy's with you?"

Not wanting to play any more games, I answer bluntly, "No." Seeing his swift disappointment, I try to soften the blow. "I'm sorry, but I need to talk to her alone. I can't tell you more than that."

Ethan nods and exits the van. I merge back into traffic and speed west toward Tammy's house. Tammy lives in a run-down three-bedroom brick ranch house in Humboldt Park. The humble abode is surrounded by a rusty wire fence bearing a sign that reads, "Beware of the Dog." Assuming the sign is referring to the dainty, spoiled Rapscallion, that I'm currently clutching easily under one arm, it's quite a stretch. With the guard dog in tow, I pull up on the latch and make my way to the front door. Tammy answers on the second knock as if she's been waiting all day for that sound.

"Rapscallion! My baby!" she cries, snatching the dog from my arms and proceeding to cover him in kisses. A minute or so passes before the lovefest subsides and she notices I'm alone. She looks behind me to my parked car to see if Ethan is just lagging before inquiring as to his absence.

"Ethan has plans tonight and needed to get home. So, I offered to drop off Rapscallion. May I come in?"

Tammy appears taken aback by my impudence but knows she doesn't have much of a choice given the hours of driving I put in today all to retrieve her beloved pooch.

"Sure," she responds dejectedly. "Come on in."

There's a small living room off the entrance furnished with two matching grey couches arranged in an L-shape. Between which stands a floor lamp with a dingy white shade. On the wall hangs a flat screen television with the wires visibly hanging down. Tammy gestures to one of the grey couches and sits with Rapscallion on the other. I take a seat and then quickly readjust myself so the spring no longer pokes me directly in the rear.

After a moment's silence, Tammy offers awkwardly, "Would you like some tea? Or maybe something stronger?"

"No, thank you," I decline. Silence falls between us again as I fumble with how best to proceed. I decide to lead with my ace and take the legal route. "Tammy, do you know what double jeopardy means?"

Tammy answers slowly and cautiously, "It means me, or anyone else for that matter, can't be tried twice for the same crime."

"That's right," I confirm. "The prosecution can't try you again for Kyleigh's murder. You know, that's true even if the police discover new evidence incriminating you. For example, you could walk up to them tomorrow with the murder weapon and there'd be nothing they could do."

Tammy furrows her brow in suspicion. "Maeve, would you mind telling me what this is about?"

"You should have picked up your own dog," I answer bluntly.

Tammy's eyes go wide and she puts a hand to her chest in offense. "Excuse me. I'll have you know, missy, that Ethan *offered* to pick up Rapscallion. I didn't ask him to."

"I know," I say, "but you'd have gotten away with it if you'd just picked up your own dog."

Offense turns to nervousness. "Away with what? What are you talking about?"

With Tammy off balance, I enact the reveal. "I checked with Karen. You kenneled Rapscallion the day *before* Kyleigh died. Why? Why would you have done that unless you were worried you'd be going away for some time? Like for a crime you'd been planning for months, maybe even years."

Tammy shakes her head, but not in earnest. "I don't know what you're talking about. Karen probably wrote down the wrong date."

I shake my head firmly. "Impossible. That's what was bugging me on the long drive to Springfield: the timeline. Kyleigh was found early in the morning on August third. The police picked you up for questioning later that same evening and then booked you. When would you have had the time to drive five hours to lodge your beloved papillon? You wouldn't have."

I see Tammy fumbling for a plausible explanation. "Well, maybe I dropped him off on the second. It was three years ago! I can't remember every detail. I probably couldn't handle him anymore and deal with all of Kyleigh's drama. So, I took him someplace that could."

"That's bullshit. You know it and I know it." I lean toward Tammy, arms resting on my thighs, bringing our faces closer together. I want to rekindle some of the intimacy we had gained over the course of the trial. "I've already explained you can't be tried again for Kyleigh's murder. So why don't you just tell me why you did it?"

Tammy gives a small head shake. She's on the ledge. I just need to give her a shove. "This is just between you and me," I assure her, "but I need to know."

I can see Tammy struggling internally with what to do, but after a while her face hardens, and I can see she's made up her mind. "I did it for Garrett," she says matter-of-factly. "Kyleigh was never going to stop using. Yeah, she went to rehab after he was born," she says, "but she started up again just a few months later. She didn't want to stay sober." Tammy looks me directly in the eye and adds, "If it had just been her, I would've washed my hands of it. But I couldn't watch that poor baby suffer anymore."

I'd assumed this would be Tammy's go-to excuse, but it didn't sit right. "Couldn't you have called children's services? Gotten Garrett taken away for good this time?"

"You think I hadn't already tried that?" Tammy spits at me. "I called children's services at least fifteen separate times. They finally stopped logging my complaints. And it wasn't just me. Garrett's pediatrician even called them for 'unexplained bruising' and 'signs of neglect.' They sent a case worker out to visit and Kyleigh charmed the pants off of him. Bought her story hook, line and sinker. You know, 'she's a struggling single mom trying to straighten her life out.' Oh, she sure put all those years of pageant training to good use. She could manipulate her way out of anything." Tammy reaches for a pack of cigarettes and lighter. I note this must be her usual smoking spot because there are small burn holes covering this arm of the couch. After she lights up and takes a drag, she points the cigarette at me and says, "You don't know what it's like living with an addict. All they care about is getting high."

Her words touch a nerve and I retort more forcefully than I had intended to, "Actually, I've had my fair share of experience with addicts."

Tammy seems shocked. "Well then what are you pestering me for? If you'd lived with an addict, you'd know I had no other choice. I did what I had to do."

"So, you strangled her?" I ask bluntly.

Tammy's jaw drops. "I didn't strangle my own daughter. What kind of a monster do you think I am?" Tammy visibly fights to maintain control before explaining, "The medical examiner screwed that up in her report. She tried to fix it at trial, but it was too late. Your expert made her look like a fool." Tammy's expression saddens as she shakes her head. "Truth is your expert was mostly right. Tammy had gotten high before I got there. After she tore up the adoption papers, she ran into the bedroom and threw a fit. Crying and carrying on something awful. I sat and waited in the living room for her to settle down and go to sleep. She was already wrapped up tight in her blanket, so I gently put a pillow over her face and waited until she went to sleep for good. She was so out of it, she didn't even put up a fight." Tears stream silently down Tammy's face as she adds, "She went peacefully."

With the truth finally out in the open, Tammy and I sit frozen for what feels like an hour but is probably only a matter of minutes. Finally, I regain enough composure to rise. "Thank you," I say turning toward the front door.

Tammy remains silent until she hears the doorknob turn. "I never thought I'd get away with it, you know. I was sure I'd spend the rest of my life in jail. But I was willing to risk it. So Garrett could have the chance of a good life. So he could be free of her."

And with that I leave. Resolving to take this conversation to my grave.

Chapter 40

We pull into Crown Hill Cemetery on an unseasonably sunny and warm day in May. Patrick puts the car in park and turns to see how I'm holding up.

"Are you sure you're ready to do this?" he asks.

"As ready as I'll ever be," I answer.

He puts his hand on my arm and flashes a supportive smile, before calling to the back, "All right, boys. We're here."

Patrick's voice startles both of them awake. We proceed to slowly coax them out of the car. Patrick finally relents and carries Seamus while I hold Dec's hand. Together our broken little family bravely makes our way up the hill to confront my past. At the top stands a plain, grey gravestone with JOHNSON inscribed across the center. Underneath it to the right reads:

Michael Johnson

June 4, 1948 - April 16, 1996

To the left reads:

Joanna Johnson

November 19, 1952 - April 16, 1996

We stand in silence. Me overcome with too many emotions to process. Patrick, most likely, unsure of what to say. Finally, Declan asks, "I thought we were going to see my grandparents."

Declan's innocent question instantly grounds me. I kneel down beside him still holding his hand. "We are, sweetie. Remember, how I told you that my parents died when I was young?"

Declan gives a slight nod.

"Well, sometimes, when people die, they are buried in a cemetery. That is what this place is: a cemetery." I gesture around us to the acres of gravestones. "We bury our loved ones here so we can come and visit them after they're gone. I brought you here so my parents could meet you."

I look at the gravestone and awkwardly announce, "Mom and Dad, these are my wonderful boys, Seamus and Declan." Dec gives my hand a little squeeze. Seamus is resting his tired head on Patrick's shoulder. Looking at Patrick, I hesitate for a moment deciding how best to introduce him. I decide on, "And this is my best friend, Patrick."

Patrick meets my gaze and gives me an approving smile. He then pulls a bouquet of flowers from a bag he'd been discreetly carrying in his free hand. It's a gorgeous arrangement of white calla lilies. I briefly recall that calla lilies are meant to represent purity and faithfulness. Two qualities I'd never use to describe my parents. But the gesture is touching, nonetheless.

Patrick hands the bouquet to Declan saying, "We brought these for your grandparents. Would you like to give it to them?"

Declan fidgets nervously before taking the arrangement from Patrick. He then gathers up his courage to drop my hand, walk up to the gravestone, and carefully lay the arrangement on top.

As my emotions threaten to overwhelm me, I hear a familiar dulcet voice behind me whisper, "Is this a bad time?"

I break into an appreciative smile and turn to greet my soul sister. I stop short when I realize she isn't alone. Beside her stand Cormac and Mary, the rest of my broken family. I let the tears fall.

Cormac smiles, embarrassed, but Mary pulls me into her warm embrace. After a bit she releases me, and grabs both of my hands in hers. "We wanted to meet your parents, dearie, and let them know they have nothing to worry about. We're going to keep taking good care of you for them."

Cormac bends down to pick up Declan and we all proceed to pay our respects to the flawed people who made possible this messy but beautiful life.

The End

Acknowledgments

Darkness Drops Again is a story I've been mulling over for a decade. Only recently, however, have I been able to dedicate time to putting pen to paper as it were. As this is my first novel, I experienced countless moments of uncertainty and despair. Thankfully, I'm blessed with a large support group to call upon at such times.

1. My husband, Joe, who supported this project from day one and who patiently listened as I talked through various plot points and word choices. I am forever grateful that I agreed to go see *Titanic* with you back in high school.

2. The wonderful writer Juliette Sobanet who acted as my mentor and editor throughout this long process. She was my sounding board and chief supporter and without her this novel would have never been published.

3. My friend Jason Caldeira, design director for Nerve Collective, for designing a cover far exceeding my vision/expectations and an amazing author page.

4. To the wonderful copy editor, Alicia Street, for her insightful comments and revisions. This is a much more polished novel because of you.

5. My sisters, Letitia, Mary, and Vicki who read along as I wrote and offered comments and feedback, but mostly praise and belief. Thank you for being my cheerleaders.

6. My sister, Monna (yes I have a lot of sisters), who was an excellent beta reader. You should seriously consider copy editing/proofreading on the side.

7. My mother. As grandma always said, I will never be able to repay you for all you've given me. But I can buy you Baileys Irish Cream. So there's that.

8. To my dear friend, Agnese. The night before we ran the Chicago marathon, she texted me "An ordinary life is boring and unchallenged. Let's go be extraordinary tomorrow." This is now my mantra.

9. To her daughter, Sophia. I hope this book does well enough to convince you becoming an author isn't a fool's errand.

For more about Melissa E. Manning please visit

www.melissaemanning.com
www.instagram.com/mmanning.writes/
www.facebook.com/mmanning.writes
https://twitter.com/mmanning_writes

Made in the USA
Monee, IL
23 March 2021